THE CRIPPLED STARSHIP
CAME ALIVE. . . .

On the monitor screen on *Deep Space Nine*, Commander Benjamin Sisko watched as a vibrant surge lit the cruiser from stem to stern. It raked the nearby Klingon vessel with an array of photon torpedoes, doing its best to protect the tanker it had been ordered to guard—a tanker filled with vital, deadly antimatter.

"Those idiots!" Sisko shouted. "If even one blast gets through to those storage pods, this whole system will be blown to atoms . . ."

Look for STAR TREK Fiction from Pocket Books

Star Trek: The Original Series

Star Trek: The Next Generation

Star Trek: Deep Space Nine

STAR TREK
DEEP SPACE NINE®

ANTIMATTER

John Vornholt

POCKET BOOKS
New York   London   Toronto   Sydney   Tokyo   Singapore

An *Original* Publication of POCKET BOOKS

POCKET BOOKS, a division of Simon & Schuster Inc.
1230 Avenue of the Americas, New York, NY 10020

This book is published by Pocket Books, a division of
Simon & Schuster Inc., under exclusive license from
Paramount Pictures.

ISBN: 0-671-88560-X

First Pocket Books printing November 1994

10 9 8 7 6 5 4 3 2 1

POCKET and colophon are registered trademarks of
Simon & Schuster Inc.

Printed in the U.S.A.

For hardworking sysops everywhere

CHAPTER
1

SUNK DEEP IN A GIANT PIT was an Ambassador-class starship, looking as if it was about to be swallowed whole. An intricate network of walkways and turbolifts spanned its gleaming hull, and workers swarmed over the helpless ship like hungry ants. The scene reminded Benjamin Sisko of the Lilliputians who tied down Gulliver and crawled all over him. But even if the shackles were removed, this sleeping giant was not about to rise, not for another few days. It was missing the most crucial element of its being, the thing that would give it life and send it streaking across the galaxy, the most dangerous substance ever discovered: antimatter.

"Isn't it magnificent?" said Kira Nerys beside him. "It's so thrilling to see the Okana Shipyards open again. You don't know it, Commander, but this ship-yard has seen centuries of history. Songs have been written about it, and plays. We're very proud of it."

1

"Impressive," answered Sisko. He didn't tell his Bajoran first officer what he was really thinking, that the shipyard was crude by Federation standards. It had been centuries since Terrans had built starships under normal planetary gravity—they much preferred moon-based or orbital shipyards with little or no gravity. Of course, the Bajorans had once had a state-of-the-art orbital shipyard, but it had been utterly destroyed by the Cardassian invaders. With its ravished economy, Bajor could hardly afford to build a new orbital shipyard, so they had reopened the surface shipyard. They were happy just to be building a ship, even if it was under a Federation contract.

Sisko also didn't mention that the design of the Ambassador, one of the workhorses of the fleet, was an old one. Its construction kinks had long been worked out. The saucer section was considerably smaller than that of a Galaxy-class vessel, such as the *Enterprise,* and its hull was cylindrical rather than squat. The twin nacelles were also directly behind the saucer section rather than under it. But the seven-hundred crew-member starship was an extremely economical vessel, and it could go farther and run longer than a Galaxy-class ship on the same amount of antimatter. It was a perfect choice for its mission—a long-range exploration of the Gamma Quadrant, on the other side of the wormhole.

Most important, Sisko knew that this was the first starship to be built on Bajor since the Cardassian invasion over fifty years ago, and he was determined to help them succeed. In one respect, he agreed with Major Kira. The Okana Shipyards were a magnificent sight—six monstrous pits spread across the vast Okana Desert, each one crisscrossed by six gigantic arches that curved to an apex almost a kilometer above the ground.

He was standing on one of those archways now, and the view it afforded was incredible, despite the intense heat that made his neck crawl with sweat. He knew that soon—after the antimatter arrived and was installed in the reactor—tractor beams along the arches would be activated, and the giant starship would rise out of the pit half a kilometer above the ground. The ship's inertial damping and structural integrity fields would have to be adjusted to compensate for Bajor's gravity, but they would be returned to normal once in space. The launch was an event he didn't want to miss. Until then, he could enjoy the endless horizon and a respite from the rigors of commanding *Deep Space Nine.*

"You're smiling," observed Kira. "May I ask what you find so humorous?"

"I'm just enjoying myself," Sisko admitted. "It's so peaceful out here—like being at the ends of the Earth. Or in this case, at the ends of Bajor."

"I knew you would enjoy it," said Kira with pleasure. "I came here once as a child, and I've never forgotten it."

"Best of all," said the commander, "I'm pleased that everything is going so well. Right on schedule. Maybe a little bit later we can go down and take a closer look at the *Hannibal.*"

Kira wrinkled the ridges on her nose and muttered something under her breath.

"Did you say something, Major?"

"It's that name. What does it mean?"

"Hannibal?" asked Sisko. "Why, he was a great African general. He did incredible things, like leading an army of elephants over the Alps to attack Rome. It's also a town in Missouri."

Kira nodded glumly. "Terran history."

The commander smiled. "So what would you name it?"

The Bajoran tightened her jaw. "I can think of several worthy names. *Okana* would be nice, in honor of the shipyards that built her. Or *Kai Opaka,* in honor of her memory and her sacrifice."

Sisko touched Kira's shoulder for a moment. "Don't worry, Major, the time is coming when Bajor will build her own ships again. First, you must build up your economy and feed your people. This is a big step in that direction."

"I know," said Kira, leaning on the railing. "Patience has never been one of my virtues." After a moment's reflection, she stood erect and managed a smile. "I'll contact Director Amkot and see if he can arrange a tour of the *Hannibal* for us."

But before she could tap her communicator badge, an explosion rent the desert air and rocked the walkway beneath their feet. Kira was thrown against the railing, and only her strength and quick reflexes kept her from plunging into the abyss a kilometer below them. Sisko staggered toward her and gripped her tunic, pulling her to the metal walkway just as another explosion jarred the structure. With an awful groan, the archway tilted, and they began to slide across the slick metal into the empty air beyond.

Kira rolled to her back and slapped her comm badge. "Emergency!" she yelled. "Two to beam off arch three! Immediately!"

Sisko's Starfleet comm badge wasn't patched into the Bajoran system, so he could do nothing but hang on to Kira and try to place his feet against the railing supports. He managed to brace one foot, but their precipitous slide continued. With the crook of her arm, Kira grabbed the handrail as her legs swung off, and she dangled in midair, groaning from the exertion required to hold on. Sisko let go of her but not soon enough, because her momentum pulled his foot off the support and started a headlong slide into oblivion. He grasped at the railing as it passed over his head, and his arms were still flailing as he sailed into the air . . .

And materialized in a crowded storage room, stretched out on a transporter pad. Kira stood beside him, her arms still twisted around a railing that was no longer there. She let out loud gasp and sank to the platform, and Sisko gripped his chest. He felt as if his heart would pound straight out through his rib cage.

A young Bajoran transporter operator stared at them from behind his console. "I . . . I got everybody, didn't I?"

"You did fine, son," breathed Sisko.

Kira scrambled to her feet and bounded off the platform. "What by the holy orbs happened?"

"I don't know," the Bajoran answered. "We don't keep any explosives near the arches. One of the pylons just blew up!"

Kira slapped her comm badge again while Sisko rose slowly to his feet. Maybe he wouldn't come back here to witness the *Hannibal* being launched, he decided. He could monitor it just fine from the space station.

"Major Kira to Director Amkot," she barked. "Director, I need to speak with you. Now."

"Major Kira!" came an excited male voice. "Are you all right?"

"We should be dead, but your transporter is at least working. What happened to that arch?"

There was a pause before Amkot responded, "We won't know until we conduct an investigation."

"You can't even make a guess?" asked Kira incredulously.

"If I had to make a guess," said the hoarse voice, "it would be sabotage. Our security around the ship has been tight, very tight, but perhaps it wasn't tight enough aboveground. Offhand, the only thing I could imagine that would cause those explosions would be timed charges planted inside the pylon. We are reviewing maintenance records to see who had access to it."

Kira glanced at her commander to see if he wanted to interject anything, and he nodded. "This is Commander Benjamin Sisko of *Deep Space Nine*," his voice thundered. "I think we should meet to discuss this."

"Of course, Commander!" came the reply. "I want to assure you that this incident had nothing to do with your presence here, nothing! Arch number three is the center arch, so it was the most obvious target. The charges could have been set days ago, or weeks ago. You know, there is considerable opposition to us building a starship for the Federation, instead of Bajor."

"Will you be able to repair it in time for the launch?" asked Sisko.

"Yes, Commander. It will take some doing, but we can move a center arch from one of the other bays. They're not in use. If you would like to discuss this further, I am headed to my office now."

"We will meet you there," Sisko concluded. He nodded to his first officer.

"Kira out," she replied through clenched teeth.

Commander Sisko just looked away, deeply saddened by Director Amkot's explanation. The planet of Bajor could be a paradise, as it once was, but sabotage and terrorism had become a way of life for too many Bajorans. If only they could stop this insanity! Until they did, the Bajorans were every bit as dangerous and unpredictable as the antimatter that was headed their way.

In his spartan, windowless office on *Deep Space Nine*, Security Chief Odo continued to page through various Starfleet reports and documents concerning the shipment and handling of antimatter. For two days, he had been boning up on the subject in anticipation of the shipment that would arrive by convoy in about twenty-four hours. Having never served aboard a starship, the alien shapeshifter had little firsthand experience with matter/antimatter propulsion systems and antimatter storage pods. He knew only one thing for certain: the more he read about the stuff, the less he liked it.

In his analytical way, Odo summarized the most important points about antimatter on his computer screen. Thus far, everything he had learned was troubling. For the hundredth time, he turned to his screen and studied his notes:

1. Antimatter is the most dangerous substance ever discovered. When it comes into contact with matter, both are annihilated in a devastating explosion.
2. Under controlled circumstances, this power is used to drive a starship, but a warp-core meltdown can result in total destruction.
3. When not in use, antimatter must be stored in a special pod that contains the substance within magnetic fields. If the pod is breached or ruptured, the result is total destruction.

4. The danger to a starship is so great that the warp core and antimatter pods are designed to be ejected in an emergency.
5. Antimatter cannot be transported, except in minute quantities. Antimatter storage pods must be shipped and handled manually.
6. Antimatter cannot be replicated. It is generated in a handful of major Starfleet refueling facilities, all of them deep in Federation space.
7. The expected shipment, 2,000 cubic meters of antimatter in 20 storage pods, is enough to power a starship for two years.
8. Starfleet only ships antimatter in special tanker craft that are protected by a minimum of two Starfleet cruisers.
9. Antimatter is one of the rarest and most valuable commodities in the galaxy.

Odo couldn't bear to read any more. He shut off his screen, leaned back in his chair, and stared at the wall. Despite the lack of features in his oddly unformed face, no one could have mistaken the look of concern in his tightened jaw and pinpoint eyes. After the arrival of the tanker and her escorts, *Deep Space Nine* was to be the waystation for twenty antimatter storage pods, until the Bajorans sent enough shuttlecraft to take them to the shipyard on the planet. Between the arrival of the convoy and the departure of the last storage pod, he didn't want to think about all the terrible things that could happen.

His door chimed cheerfully, and he scowled. "Enter."

The door whooshed open, and the cherubic face of Miles O'Brien peered around the corner. "You wanted to see me, Constable?"

Odo's scowl deepened. He despised that obnoxious nickname pinned on him by Commander Sisko, but he would let it pass today. He had more important worries. "Yes, Chief. Thank you for coming."

O'Brien strode into the room and stood at easy attention. After a moment, he said with concern, "Are you all right?"

"I am most certainly *not* all right," snapped Odo. "How would you feel if you were in charge of the safekeeping of twenty containers of antimatter?"

"Oh, that," scoffed the chief. "We had thirty storage pods aboard the *Enterprise*. Never gave us a lick of trouble." He frowned in remembrance. "Well, maybe I shouldn't say 'never.' Antimatter is always tricky stuff."

"Just how volatile is it?"

O'Brien chuckled. "How volatile is it? Well, let's put it this way—a fistful of antimatter would be enough to destroy half this station."

When he saw that his answer didn't do much to lighten Odo's mood, O'Brien added, "But it's perfectly safe, if it's contained. We have ships docking here all the time that have antimatter on board."

"But we've never had any on board the station," Odo countered. He shifted in his seat, uncomfortable to be exhibiting so much fear. "I've been reading everything I can find about it, and I don't like what I'm finding out. Do you have any recommendations?"

The chief of operations considered the question for a moment before replying, "Only one thing. There's quite a black market in the stuff, because almost every ship with a warp drive needs it. And the storage pods are self-contained—you could take one and leave the rest alone. I'd be more concerned about thievery than an accident."

"Thievery," Odo repeated thoughtfully. He stood with determination. "Chief, may I buy you a drink down at Quark's establishment?"

Despite the fact that Director Amkot said he was headed straight for his office, Commander Sisko and Major Kira sat impatiently in uncomfortable chrome furniture for almost half an hour. For the dozenth time, Sisko surveyed the room. Like most things Bajoran, the furnishings were stylish, even if some of them had seen better days. A double-paned window looked out upon a pair of robotic arc welders, which now sat quietly, their job over. Behind them, one of the gleaming nacelles of the *Hannibal* was visible, looking like a sleek silver fish. Natural light from above filtered into the immense pit, adding to the underwater illusion.

Amkot's desk looked like a slab of black epoxy, although it was chipped and scratched in various places, as if it had spent several years in careless storage. His chair looked considerably more comfortable than the one Sisko was sitting in. At least it had padding. A huge diagram of the *Hannibal* covered one entire wall, and behind the desk were a number of diplomas and citations, all etched on brightly colored slabs. There were blank spaces on the walls, too, where citations had apparently been removed.

More for the sake of conversation than from overwhelming curiosity, Sisko asked, "What do you suppose went in those blank spaces on the wall?"

Kira stiffened in her seat. "Commendations, I suppose—from the Cardassians. It's well known that Amkot Groell was a collaborator. But he managed to keep this facility open, even if they didn't build any ships. He maintained the equipment, waiting for this day. We all had to do unpleasant things, Amkot more than most. He is still resented for it in some quarters."

"How does the provisional government feel about him?"

Kira smiled grimly. "That depends on how the Federation feels about their new starship. If it brings more business to the shipyards, he'll be a hero. If it's a failure—" She didn't have to finish the sentence.

The door opened abruptly, and both Kira and Sisko stood, relieved to finally see somebody. Amkot Groell was a small man, with disheveled white hair that made him look like a mad professor. He was followed into the room by a distinguished older woman wearing a finely tailored suit. The ridges on the bridge of her nose looked like manicured hedges, and she wore a jewel that dwarfed one entire ear.

"Please excuse me, please!" begged the director. "Just as I was coming here, I heard that Minister Roser was en route. Naturally, I had to meet her. Excuse me again—I am Director Amkot Groell, and this is Roser Issa, Minister of Public Works."

Sisko nodded. "Commander Benjamin Sisko of *Deep Space Nine*. This is my first officer, Major Kira Nerys."

"Of course, of course," stuttered the little man. "How are you, Major? It's a pleasure to see you again. The major was a student when she first came here on a field trip, but that was many years ago. How do you like seeing the yard in operation?"

"I thought it was wonderful," replied Kira, "until it nearly killed me."

"Most regrettable." Amkot shook his head with genuine sorrow. "We have doubled security, I can assure you. In some respects, it's amazing we haven't had more incidents."

"That's nonsense," claimed Minister Roser. "How could we possibly know that anyone would want to sabotage the shipyards? Frankly, I am stunned."

Director Amkot looked like he wanted to correct the minister, but he screwed his mouth shut. She must have control of the purse strings, thought Sisko. His first officer, however, felt no such restraint.

"Aren't you being a bit disingenuous, Minister?" asked Kira. "I can think of a dozen factions who oppose building this ship, from pacifists to nationalists, with every terrorist organization in between. And what about the Cardassians? They're hoping that if they bide their time, the Federation will get sick of supporting us and just go away."

Minister Roser gave her a tight smile. "Of course, Major, you would know about terrorist organizations."

From the way that Kira bounced on her feet and balled her hands into fists, Sisko could tell that she was about to explode, and he quickly interjected, "As a representative of the client, let me say that I'm very pleased with the progress you've made. Frankly, I didn't think you would finish the *Hannibal* on schedule, but you have. Now that we're so close to completion, let's not spoil it. We all want the same thing, don't we?"

"Yes! Yes, we do," agreed Amkot. "Thanks to the Federation, we have the raw materials we need, and the work. That's what we need the most—work."

Minister Roser added, "We could also use a fusion device and positron beam accelerator to generate our own antimatter."

"Let's not push things," answered Sisko. "That would be a very tempting target, and Starfleet is too far away to protect it. We'll get you all the antimatter you need—to power whatever you build."

Kira seized upon that small opening. "Commander, does that mean we could build our own starships?"

Sisko smiled. "We have a saying: 'All things come to those who wait.' Now, let's get to practical matters. What kind of explosive was it? Can we catch whoever did it?"

Amkot sighed and shook his head. "There isn't much left, but we found traces of sarium krellide, which is a common detonator and casing material."

"I'll send down a forensic team from the station," promised Sisko. "Perhaps they can help."

Amkot clapped his hands together and tried to appear cheerful. "Commander, may I take you on a tour of the *Hannibal?*"

"I'm afraid we don't have time now. We have our own preparations to make. In addition to the antimatter, the convoy is bringing the crew for the *Hannibal's* test flights. I may assign some of my own people to go along."

"Can I volunteer?" asked Kira.

"We'll see." Sisko managed a smile before he tapped his comm badge. "Sisko to Hage. We are ready to beam back to the runabout."

"Yes, sir," came the reply. "Locking on to you and Major Kira."

"Energize when ready."

They barely had time to nod their good-byes before the transporter beams scrambled their molecules and whisked them away in a blaze of colored lights.

By the time Sisko and Kira stepped from the small transporter platform into the cramped cockpit of the *Mekong,* the smile had vanished from the commander's face. It was replaced by a concerned frown, matched by that of Major Kira.

"They don't seem to realize the danger they're in," said the Bajoran.

"No," answered Sisko, "and I'm not sure we do either." He wondered if it was really a coincidence that the arch was sabotaged just as they were standing on it. He didn't like the fact that a relatively common-place operation—the transfer of antimatter to a new ship—should be a flashpoint for bitter hatreds. Most of all, he didn't like his lack of control over the Bajoran side of the operation.

"Shall I take us out of orbit?" asked Ensign Hage.

Sisko was stirred out of his troubled thoughts. "Let me take the controls," he answered, slipping into the conn seat. "I want to see if I can get us back in under two hours."

En route to Quark's Place on the bustling Promenade, Chief O'Brien heard his communicator beep, and he stopped midstride to answer it. Odo waited patiently beside him.

"Chief," said a concerned voice, "the level-three diagnostic you ordered on cargo bay one has picked up a few anomolies. They're probably just bad seals or worn sensor arrays, but I thought you might want to take a look."

"I'll be right there," muttered O'Brien. "Out." He turned to Odo and muttered, "Bloody Cardassians never replaced a seal in their lives. I'd better go check this, Odo. That's the cargo bay where we're storing the antimatter pods."

"Then by all means, don't let me detain you," said the morph. "I am quite capable of questioning Quark by myself."

O'Brien smiled. "Yeah, but I don't know when you'll offer to buy me a drink again."

"Probably never," Odo answered honestly.

"Maybe you could give me a rain check."

Odo tilted his head puzzledly. "Why would I check for rain in a space station?"

"Never mind," muttered O'Brien, starting off. "I'll make that cargo bay the safest place on the station."

Odo offered him a slight smile. "If you do, I will buy you that drink."

After O'Brien strode off in the opposite direction, Odo put his hands behind his back and continued his stroll down the Promenade. He passed a combination grooming/tattoo salon, a gift shop specializing in holographic wormhole ornaments, and a restaurant that featured live food. All of the establishments were crowded. Publicly, Odo often complained about the rowdy lot who passed through the station, but privately he preferred to see it bustling and busy than deserted and comatose. He liked the stimulus of so many visitors, even if each one presented a unique security risk.

He could spot the tourists—the ones who had come simply to see the only stable wormhole in existence. And he could spot the adventurers—the ones who were not content just to see it but had to pass through to the little-explored Gamma Quadrant on the other side. It was the others who concerned him—the ones who came to this far-flung corner of the galaxy for personal gain. Some were attracted by the lawless elements of Bajor, a chaotic planet struggling to rebuild itself while coping with the windfall generated by the wormhole. Some came for honest commerce, hoping to discover new products, services, and customers in the Gamma Quadrant. Others came to steal, pure and simple, to take what wasn't theirs and make it their own. He couldn't tell who those people were by sight, but he knew one thing about them:

Sooner or later, they would congregate at Quark's Place.

Odo rounded the doorway into the gaudy, neon-lit den of debauchery and heard the usual whoops and hollers from the gaming tables. He smelled the noxious intermingling of odors from a dozen alien foods, none of which were ever meant to be eaten in the same room together. He heard the clinking of glasses containing substances that were, to him, incomprehensible in their appeal. And he saw the Ferengi servers hurrying about—big-eared snaggletoothed scavengers—grubbing money from every possible source. Most incomprehensible of all was the steady flow of customers marching up and down the staircase, plunking down hard-earned cash to indulge sexual fantasies in the holosuites overhead.

Odo sighed, noticing that his presence did nothing to curb any of this obnoxious behavior. The security chief wouldn't care to admit it, but he probably spent more time in Quark's Place than anyone, except the employees and a chubby alien named Morn. His presence had long since failed to raise any eyebrow ridges.

He strolled over to the bar, where the proprietor, Quark, was going over inventory on a computer padd. Odo leaned on the bar and asked without enthusiasm, "How's business, Quark?"

The Ferengi frowned. "Pretty good, until you came in."

"Would that was so," muttered Odo. He glanced around the saloon and said matter-of-factly, "How many people here have private starships?"

Quark laughed and replied, "Almost all of them. We can't all be privileged enough to belong to the Federation or the Klingon Empire."

Odo nodded. "How many of those starships are powered by matter/antimatter reactors?"

Now Quark set down his padd, leaned across the bar, and lowered his voice to say, "What are you getting at, Odo?"

"How much is antimatter worth?"

Quark smiled. "Why, have you got some?"

The shapeshifter grimaced in disgust. "No, but the station is getting some. Twenty storage pods of antimatter. But of course, you knew that."

Quark picked up his padd. "Well, it's not a secret. At least, not much of one. If some of that shipment were to be, shall we say, diverted—I'm sure a considerable profit could be turned. We're in an excellent position to sell antimatter, because any ship would want to be well stocked before they enter the wormhole and begin a long journey in the Gamma Quadrant."

"How much profit? Give me an estimate."

Quark smiled with the pleasure of estimating the profit on an illegal deal. "It's a substance that cannot be replicated or easily manufactured. Of course, storage is a problem. I could probably get seven bars of gold-pressed latinum for an *empty* storage pod. A full one would net sixty, if the bidding were spirited."

Odo stood erect. That was more than he had estimated—considerably more. He looked around the room. "You would tell me, wouldn't you, if somebody were planning to steal any of that shipment?"

"Steal it?" scoffed Quark. "From a Starfleet convoy guarded by a couple of cruisers? Antimatter is valuable, but it's not worth getting killed over."

Odo lowered his voice. "What about stealing it from a cargo bay?"

"That would depend," said Quark. "What cargo bay is it going to be in?"

Odo gave the Ferengi a sly smile. "You didn't answer my question, so I'm not going to answer yours. I will just say one more thing: If I hear of any conspiracy to steal even a single pod of that antimatter, I will throw whoever is involved—and I mean whoever—off *Deep Space Nine* for good. Do I make myself understood?"

Quark laughed nervously. "Why tell me that? I'm a bartender, not an antimatter merchant. Now, you're wasting my time, and I've got business to attend to."

"By all means," said Odo snidely, "don't let me keep you from your business." The shapeshifter strode quickly toward the door.

Odo had learned from long practice that it was wise not to hurry away from Quark's establishment. To attract customers, there were several gaudy blinking signs in the windows of the place, and he had found that he could stop just outside one of them and peer in, with the bright lights affording him a bit of camouflage. From that vantage point, he often saw what Quark did immediately after one of his visits, and that knowledge was often very elucidatory.

He could see Quark summon his brother, Rom, to the bar and whisper something to him. Rom scurried off and returned a moment later with another Ferengi whom Odo didn't know. The discussion between Quark and the strange Ferengi quickly turned into an argument, and the customer waved his hands and stalked off. Quark shook his head glumly, as if he had just lost money.

Odo walked away from the window, content that he

had warned Quark off trying to pull anything with the antimatter shipment. But Quark was only one Ferengi, and there were scores of them infecting the station at the moment. For sixty bars of latinum, most of them would do almost anything, including selling their naked mothers into slavery. Plus, there were all those other unsavory characters around.

The security chief would not rest comfortably in his pail until the last storage pod of antimatter was safely off DS9 and on its way to Bajor.

CHAPTER
2

JADZIA DAX PULLED BACK her sleek dark hair and fastened the subdued ponytail with an ornate silver barrette. The style revealed the intricate pattern of small spots that ran along her hairline and down her slender neck and shoulders. She fastened her tunic, noticing her nicely formed breasts, which were impossible to hide in a Starfleet uniform. Dax did her best to look plain and unassuming, but it was a losing battle. Men's heads turned in her direction wherever she went on the station, and some did more than look. Quark usually licked his lips and proffered obscene proposals, and Julian Bashir—sweet childish Julian—kept asking her out on dates. Unfortunately, she found men's advances to be more amusing than seductive, and she attributed that to the fact that in several of her host lifetimes, including the most recent, she had been a man.

Dax seldom thought in terms of being two distinct

identities merged in one body—one a three-hundred-year-old androgynous scientist and the other a twenty-eight-year-old woman—but at times one or the other of her components would exert itself. In her last incarnation, as Curzon Dax, the humanoid part of her being had often taken the lead, especially in terms of the hell-raising and womanizing he was famous for across the galaxy. The current Trill was not at all like that character, much to the amazement of Benjamin Sisko. Benjamin kept expecting to see some of that old devil-may-care attitude, but Curzon Dax was dead, even if his memories and knowledge lived on. Jadzia, the young woman who had volunteered at an early age and trained all her life to be a host, was serious and levelheaded, which was how she thought a host ought to be.

She sighed as she considered her fair reflection in the mirror. The more she considered the exploits of Curzon Dax, the more she wondered if she was in some way failing as a Trill. Curzon Dax would have undoubtedly bedded a fair number of the female population of DS9 by now, but she couldn't even bring herself to bed a single man, when the candidates were both plentiful and eager. Curzon Dax had been able to party all night, but Jadzia Dax preferred to snuggle up in bed with a badly written Cardassian operations manual.

While training, she thought ruefully, she had heard all about the scientific and humanitarian exploits of Curzon Dax. When meeting people who knew him, all she heard about were his romantic escapades and death-defying adventures. Her merged memory was full of them. Perhaps that was why she felt little need to pursue the sensual side of life. She realized now that it was pure luck that Curzon Dax had lived to be an old man.

She remembered her training. They drilled her on Trill traditions, physical stamina, adaptation techniques—all the preparation necessary to make a smooth transition. But they didn't tell her that merging with the symbiont was the easy part. The hard part was living up to everyone's expectations, including her own. People expected a Trill to be some kind of superbeing, possessed of several lifetimes of knowledge and experience. But Jadzia Dax couldn't be all those people, even if they all combined to make her what she was. She could only be herself.

Sometimes she felt like an inexperienced person with overexperienced memories. It was an odd dichotomy, thought the Trill, and she wondered how much she could trust her secondhand memories.

Her comm badge beeped, and she blinked herself out of her reverie. "Dax here," she answered.

"It's Kira," came the reply. "I know you're off duty. I hope I'm not interrupting anything."

Dax smiled at the irony. "No, I'm just getting dressed." Kira was one of her best friends aboard DS9. Benjamin Sisko was an old friend, but he was a friend of Curzon Dax's. Kira was the only friend Jadzia Dax had made, if you didn't count Dr. Julian Bashir, who wanted other things than just friendship.

"I was wondering if we could get together for a drink, or an I'Danian spice, or something?" asked Kira.

"Certainly," answered Dax. "How was your trip to the shipyard?"

"Well, good and bad. Somebody tried to sabotage the bay where they're building the *Hannibal,* but it won't stop us. We're going to launch that ship."

"I'm sure you are," said Dax, sensing the worry in her friend's voice. "Where shall we meet?"

"Quark's Place?" answered Kira. "Or any place is okay."

"No," said Dax, "Quark's Place will be fine."

"Ten minutes then?"

"Ten minutes," Dax agreed.

Commander Sisko paced around Ops, the control center of the station, and Chief O'Brien could tell that he was worried. The commander hadn't gone into much detail when he had summoned the chief, so he couldn't tell how serious it was. But coming on top of Odo's concerns, all of this fuss over the antimatter shipment was getting to be a nuisance. Didn't any of them realize that handling antimatter was a piece of cake? A Starfleet tanker would certainly have storage pods of the latest design, as well as automated loading and unloading facilities. Cargo bay one was in good shape, at least as good as could be expected for anything built by Cardassians.

Of course, other things were going haywire all over the station, which meant that O'Brien didn't have the luxury of worrying about one shipment of antimatter.

"To make a long story short," said Sisko, "somebody sabotaged one of the arches that span the bay where they're building the *Hannibal*. I don't suppose, Chief, that you know anything about planetary-based shipyards?"

O'Brien scowled. "I've read about them in history books."

That brought a smile to Sisko's face. "I know the technology is outdated, but it's still fairly impressive. They use tractor beams to lift the ship out of the pit, and that's where the arches come in. Anyway, I want you to take a team down there and check out the site of the explosion. They couldn't find much, but I'm not sure how hard they looked. I would like to catch whoever did it before they try something else."

"Begging your pardon, sir, but the power is out in airlock six, and I have to rebuild one of the microwave links. Plus, I have a dozen complaints about the air quality on level nineteen in the habitat ring, and . . ."

Sisko held up his hand to silence the chief. "I know you've got more than you can handle already, but it will be a disaster for the Bajorans if that ship doesn't launch on schedule. And I simply don't have anybody else I can trust with this matter. Actually, I want you back in twenty hours, when the antimatter shipment is due to arrive, so you won't be gone forever. But you must leave as soon as you assemble your team."

O'Brien nodded with resignation. "Is nepotism allowed, sir?"

"Nepotism?"

"In other words, could I take my wife? Keiko has been dying to see something else besides these damned gray walls. She's an excellent chemist, and she always knows who in her classroom threw the spitball."

Sisko smiled. "Certainly, Chief, it's your team. If you find anything unusual, let me know first, before you tell Director Amkot."

"Yes, sir," agreed O'Brien. Heading toward the turbolift, he was already assembling his team in his head—himself, Keiko, a Bajoran for political considerations, and the best pilot he could find on short order.

After reaching the bar, Dax and Kira had barely alighted in their chairs when the obsequious Quark was headed in their direction. He was rubbing his hands in anticipation. In anticipation of what, Dax didn't want to imagine.

"Hello, ladies," he intoned, grinning like a feral rat. His eyes never left various parts of Dax's anatomy. "What will be your pleasure today?"

"Just a Tellarite fizz for me," said Kira.

Dax smiled pleasantly. "I'll have some water and a grilled cheese sandwich."

Quark blinked in amazement. "A grilled cheese sandwich? Isn't that some sort of terribly mundane Terran food?"

"Yes, it is," said Dax. "I've never had one before, but I remember that I used to like them."

Quark started off, then paused to do a double take. The Ferengi finally just shook his head and scurried to the food replicator.

Kira raised an eyebrow. "You never had one before, but you know you like them?"

Dax nodded. "It's something that Curzon Dax used to eat a lot. I've decided to try a few of the things he liked—if they're not too dangerous or disgusting."

Kira didn't pursue the matter, because she had more pressing concerns. "Let me tell you what happened on Bajor," she began. In concise detail, she related the near-fatal accident that resulted from explosive charges planted in the pylon of an archway. Dax listened with growing alarm, because she knew how important the shipyards were to the Bajoran recovery program. More disturbing was the possibility that the shipyards weren't the primary target.

"Nobody else was in danger?" asked Dax.

"No, not immediate danger," answered Kira. "We were the only ones up there. I know what you're thinking, but I don't think they were after us. Killing us wouldn't stop anything. I know these people and their methods, and they'll just try again, probably closer to the launch date."

"What can we do to stop them?"

Kira leaned forward and said, "That's what I wanted to talk to you about." But before she could continue, Quark appeared with a tray containing a tall bubbling drink, a glass of water, and something flat and oozing on a plate.

"Here are your orders, ladies," he smiled. He set down the drinks and looked suspiciously at the gooey sandwich. "Are you sure you want to eat this, Lieutenant? It looks like something a Denebian slime devil would drag into its nest."

Dax tried not to look dismayed. "Are you sure you cooked it long enough?"

Quark nodded eagerly. "Oh, I'm sure of that. It didn't look very good when I took it out the first time, so I ran it through again. I'm afraid it looks worse now."

"Leave it, and I'll just try a bite," said Dax.

"You'll still have to pay for it," Quark insisted.

"Understood."

The Ferengi grinned and rubbed his hands together. "Of course, Lieutenant, we could work out a sort of barter system. I can get you plenty of these, if you would just consent to—"

"Thank you," said Dax, cutting him off. "Bring me the bill."

Quark shrugged, as if there was no harm in asking, then scurried off.

Kira sighed impatiently. "I wonder if he has a holosuite program where I could bash his head in? Anyway, Dax, I can tell you what I think we ought to do. I don't think we should wait until the antimatter arrives and the *Hannibal* is officially launched. I think we should send a crew down to that starship, demand that they raise it from the bay, and take it into orbit right then and there. The impulse engines don't need antimatter to work."

Dax shook her head. "But the shakedown crew is coming with the antimatter. They're going to want to go over every centimeter of that ship, and check the launch procedures thoroughly. There are about six volumes of Starfleet regulations to govern the first flight of a new starship."

Kira slammed her fist on the table. "The hell with regulations! If we wait that long, they're sure to strike again. Believe me, these people are capable of anything, including a suicide mission. Do you think you could tell the commander to adopt this emergency plan?"

"Why don't you tell him?"

"He won't do it if I tell him. But he'll listen to you."

Dax shook her head. "I'm sorry, but the chances are nil of getting Benjamin Sisko to commandeer a Federation starship that hasn't even been checked out yet. Unless an admiral tells him to do it."

The Bajoran's shoulders slumped. "Then we're in serious trouble," she muttered. "I want to see that starship handed over to the Federation—intact."

"So do I," answered the Trill. "But if we can't do it safely, under the proper precautions and regulations, the Federation is not going to be impressed. Your people have to rise to the occasion. They have to protect the *Hannibal* until it's officially launched. This is a test for them, I know, but they're going to have to be responsible."

Kira gnawed her lip and lowered her head. Dax touched her friend's hand and added, "I will ask the commander if there's anything we can do to help with security. But we have our own responsibility— keeping the antimatter safe."

From the corner of her eye, Dax saw a figure lurking nearby. She turned to see Quark, standing within easy earshot. He smiled and hustled forward to set a small tray in front of her.

"Your bill."

Dax mimicked his obsequious smile. "How long have you been listening to us?"

"Listening to you?" asked Quark with alarm. "I only stopped to . . . to recheck the figures on your bill. I wasn't sure how much to charge for a grilled cheese sandwich."

Kira gazed up at him. "What have you heard about the launching of the *Hannibal?* Have you heard of anybody who's planning to disrupt it?"

The Ferengi looked aghast. "Odo was in here today asking very similar questions. Do I look like some sort of repository for rumors?"

"Yes," the women answered in unison.

"Well, I'm not!" he protested. "I mean, I hear a few rumors, but what do they really mean? I think that most people are excited about the Bajorans building ships again. More business for them means more business for all of us. Get you another fizz, Major?"

Kira opened her mouth to respond, but her comm badge beeped instead. She answered it with a curt "Major Kira."

"Commander Sisko," came the deep-voiced reply. "I understand that Lieutenant Dax is with you."

"Yes, she is, Commander."

"Could both of you report to Ops as soon as possible? I want to go over our preparations for the arrival of the convoy tomorrow."

"Certainly, Commander. Kira out." The Bajoran stood abruptly. "I am going to tell him what I think, even if he doesn't listen."

"That's your prerogative," said Dax. She stood and placed a few coins on the table, then looked pointedly at Quark. "You will tell us if you hear anything, won't you?"

"Of course," answered the Ferengi. After the officers walked away, he smiled, picked up the coins, and added under his breath, "If there's something in it for me."

A sudden wind kicked up bits of the crusty sand that covered twenty million square kilometers known as the Okana Desert, and Keiko O'Brien pulled the goggles over her eyes. When Miles had promised her a trip to the planet, she had envisioned green forests, perhaps a lake or a stream. Instead she got a barren desert with hot gritty winds. For this, she had canceled her afternoon class? Well, at least her reprieved students were enjoying themselves, even if she wasn't.

With her gloved hands, the petite woman of Asian descent continued scraping burn residue off a large chunk of mangled metal into a small plastic pouch. Miles and one of his Bajoran assistants were crouched about twenty meters away, scouring the sand for bits of the bomb casing that had scattered in the explosion. Keiko tried not to let her mind wander, but this was tedious, brain-numbing work. Still, it was a break from her routine. One thing you could say about Bajor, she decided, was that it was geologically diverse. Deserts, forests, seas, mountains—you could find it all without looking very far, much like Earth. She instantly regretted thinking about Earth, because that only made her homesick.

Suddenly, her knife struck something hard, much harder than burn residue. She peered closely at the area she had been scraping and saw tiny formations of crystal. That certainly wasn't supposed to be there, and it didn't jibe with what they had been told about the explosions. She looked up at the immense black arch that curved off into the distance. The explosions had damaged it and buckled it in places, but they hadn't come close to bringing it down.

Over a kilometer away, Keiko could see a Bajoran work crew gathered around a similar arch that spanned an unused bay. They were painstakingly dissassembling the pylon in preparation for moving the arch to the active bay, to replace the damaged one. Two Bajoran shuttlecraft sat grounded nearby, waiting to lift the arch. Directly in front of her, an immense open pit surrounded a gleaming starship that had never flown, nor moved so much as a centimeter. Behind it, the sun was beginning to slip beneath the pockmarked plain.

"Miles!" she called. She had to scream his name again in order to be heard above the wind.

He came jogging toward her, his Bajoran assistant close behind. "Only you!" she called. "Redac can keep working."

Miles nodded and instructed his assistant to keep scouring the sand for evidence. He ran the rest of the way and knelt down beside her.

"What have you found?"

"This," she said, pointing to the crystallized remains. "I think it's the fixative that held the charge in place. Or what's left of it."

O'Brien squinted at the deposits. "What is it?"

"Unless I miss my guess," said Keiko, "it's bad

news. I want to take a sample and go back to the runabout right away. I don't want to alarm anybody until I have the computer analyze it."

"Okay," said O'Brien. "I'll stay here and keep looking. If you find something really strange, contact the commander first."

"I will," she promised.

Benjamin Sisko had just lain down for what he hoped would be a brief but relaxing nap. His head hurt from all the conflicting theories and safeguards his officers had proposed at the briefing. Major Kira wanted to hijack the *Hannibal* to head off another attempt at sabotage on the ground. Odo was certain that Ferengi scoundrels would try to steal the storage pods from the cargo bay, and he wanted the Starfleet tanker to keep the antimatter, docking directly with the Bajoran shuttlecraft. Dax wanted to beef up the security at the shipyards, without any regard to the touchy political considerations. And he could well imagine O'Brien chiming in, telling everyone they were crazy.

The fact of the matter was that time was running out. The convoy was en route at warp speed, and would arrive in less than twelve hours. It was already night on Bajor, and there wasn't a damned thing anybody could do, except follow Starfleet procedures and hope for the best. Sisko would never admit it, but he was still shaken by almost losing his life on that swaying archway. He had instructed his officers to make no mention of the mishap, because he didn't want word of it to get back to his son, Jake. But that didn't stop Sisko from worrying about it.

Just as his eyelids fluttered shut and he had almost

surrendered himself to blessed sleep, his communicator sounded. The commander slapped the badge with considerable force.

"Sisko here. I thought I left word not to be disturbed?"

"I'm sorry, sir," responded Kira, "but it's Keiko O'Brien with the away team. She insists upon speaking to you immediately."

Sisko sat up, willing himself awake. "Patch her in. Private channel."

"Yes, sir."

The next voice was one that Sisko seldom heard over a communicator. "Commander Sisko?"

"Yes, O'Brien. What can I do for you?"

He could hear Keiko sigh. "I'm afraid I have disturbing news for you, sir. We were given to understand that the charges that blew up the pylon could have been set any time in the last several days."

"That is correct." Sisko felt his throat getting dry.

"That doesn't appear to be so. I found crystallized traces of the fixative that was used to hold the charges in place. It's an organic substance called deveride, which the Bajorans chew for pleasure, much as Terrans used to chew gum, betel nuts, and tobacco. I know about deveride, because we've been studying Bajoran customs in my class."

"So?" asked Sisko. "I can imagine that somebody chewed this stuff, took a wad out of their mouth, stuck it to the charge, and slapped it in place. It only means they were using what was at hand."

"That's true," agreed Keiko. "But after mixing with enzymes in the mouth, deveride completely dissolves in the air after two hours, which is why Bajoran mothers don't mind it so much. The only reason we found any of it was that the heat of the explosion crystallized it. That charge was planted only a short time before it exploded."

Now it was Sisko's turn to sigh. "Are you sure about that?"

"Positive. The computer aboard the runabout has made a positive identification. To be fair to the Bajorans, we had to look pretty hard to find it, so they may have made an honest mistake by telling you that they found nothing."

"Thank you," said Sisko. "I'm glad your husband insisted upon taking you along. Considering the danger, I'd like all of you to return to DS9 immediately."

"Understood, sir. Keiko O'Brien out."

Benjamin Sisko lay back in his bed, but sleep wasn't on his mind anymore. Instead he had to cope with the fact that somebody had tried to kill him and his first officer. Perhaps Kira was the primary target; she had her share of enemies. Or maybe the timing of the bomb was still just a coincidence! What had looked so promising—the building and launching of the first Bajoran-built starship in fifty years—had become a magnet for sabotage and attempted murder.

Maybe, he told himself, this was the end of it—the last gasp of some disgruntled fringe organization. They had failed to disrupt the launching, had failed to kill either him or Kira, and now they would just go away and accept the fact that Bajor was building a starship. What was so terrible about that? Why couldn't people accept peace and progress?

His troubled thoughts turned to his arrival on *Deep Space Nine,* when he had hated the assignment, had hated the station, and, most of all, had hated Captain Jean-Luc Picard. He had been one breath away from resigning from Starfleet over his combined hatreds, and now he couldn't imagine a more demanding and fulfilling post in all of Starfleet than DS9. He knew from firsthand experience that peace was hard to accept, because it meant giving up treasured hatreds. It meant accepting the past as gone and turning one's attention to the future.

He heard the outer door whoosh open and shut, and he knew his son, Jake, had returned for the evening. The adolescent certainly wouldn't expect his old man to be in bed before he was, but Sisko felt like staying in bed. What had started out as a nap now sounded more appealing as a good night's sleep—a sleep with dreams in which there were no terrorists, or bombs going off. He would wake up, and it would be a new day, a day in which the antimatter was transferred from the tanker to the *Hannibal* without incident. A day in which Bajor was at peace and full of pride over the starship she had built.

He was smiling when a knock sounded on his door. "Dad, are you in there?"

"Sure, son," said the weary commander, rising from his bed. "Let me kiss you good night."

Ops was crowded in the minutes leading up to the arrival of the convoy. On hand were the trio who usually ran the control center, Commander Sisko, Major Kira, and Lieutenant Dax, a full relief crew, plus Chief O'Brien, Odo, and Director Amkot Groell from the shipyards.

Sisko didn't mind having the director present, because it was up to the Bajorans and their shuttlecraft to get the storage pods off-loaded as quickly as possible. The director was in charge of dispatching the shuttlecraft, and he had to get a feel for the pace of the station's cargo movements. Sisko hadn't mentioned anything to the little man about Keiko's discovery. If at all possible, he still wanted to treat the attempted murder as an aberration.

"Bearing sixteen-mark-two-one-oh," said Dax. "It looks like they're coming out of warp at a considerable distance from the station. Considerable distance from the planet and the wormhole, too. I estimate their reentry coordinates will put them about twenty thousand kilometers from us."

Kira made a wry smile. "I guess they don't want to take any chances. Probably nobody on these ships has ever been here before."

"They've come a long way with your antimatter," Sisko reminded the Bajoran. "All the way from Alpha Centauri. So forgive them if they don't know the territory and are a little cautious."

"They may not have been here before," said Chief O'Brien, "but there will be a veteran crew on that tanker, I can tell ya. And the shakedown crew will all be senior officers."

"Expect to see somebody you know, Chief?" asked Kira.

O'Brien shrugged. "You never know."

Sisko queried, "What's their ETA?"

"Two minutes and thirty seconds," answered Dax.

Sisko looked around at faces that were intent but calm, and he wondered what he had been worried about. The *Hannibal* was nearing completion right on schedule, and the antimatter was likewise arriving on schedule. Two Starfleet cruisers would take up residence around DS9 until the transfer was complete, and security had been doubled at every level. It would take more than a couple of little bombs to upset this applecart.

Sisko was growing more confident by the moment, until he caught sight of Odo's seamless face. The veins on the morph's neck were taut, like cables, as his head swiveled from one console to another, double-checking everyone's readouts.

The commander cleared his throat. "Constable, I presume you are happy with your security preparations?"

"'Happy' is not the word I would use," snapped Odo. "I am satisfied that I have taken every precaution available, but there are too many inherent dangers with this antimatter. I'll be 'happy' when it's gone."

"Neutrino level increasing," announced Dax.

"Neutrino level?" echoed the commander. "We weren't expecting any traffic out of the wormhole."

Dax squinted at her readouts and shook her head. "It's not coming from the wormhole, Commander. The source is unknown, just a general increase."

"That wouldn't have anything to do with the tanker, would it?" asked Amkot Groell.

"It shouldn't," said the commander. Without appearing unduly concerned, he strode slowly behind Dax's console. "Lieutenant, check for other readings, like plasma trails or unusual heat sources."

Dax looked up at him with her expressive eyes, and he knew she understood what he was thinking. She said nothing, and if anybody else suspected what was on their minds, they said nothing. Chief O'Brien, however, began to pace at the edge of the circular room.

"ETA in one minute and fourteen seconds," proclaimed Dax. Then she bolted upright in her chair. "Sudden influx in both heat and plasma readings!"

Sisko leaned over her shoulder. "Where! Can you pinpoint them?"

"Bearing five-mark-two-nine." She stared at him. "Nineteen thousand kilometers away. That's out of our phaser range, but we might be within theirs."

"Red alert!" shouted Sisko. "Shields up! Kira, hail the tanker."

Kira punched a few buttons on her panel; then her eyes widened with horror. "We're being jammed! Every subspace frequency. Massive interference!"

"What is going on?" asked Odo.

O'Brien stepped toward the viewscreen, staring at what looked like thousands of harmless kilometers of empty space. "Bloody hell," he muttered. "Who's out there?"

"Somebody who's jamming us like crazy!" shouted Kira. She slapped her board with frustration. "We can't hail the convoy unless we boost our signal. And we can't do that with our shields up."

O'Brien muttered, "We can't do that, anyway, unless we switch a lot of relays manually. Idiot Cardassians."

"Keep trying to hail them," ordered Sisko. His face became an ebony mask of calm control that belied the turmoil in the pit of his stomach. He leaned over Dax's shoulder. "How many are there? Can you tell?"

"At least two," she said. "They've stopped, so their heat trails are becoming undetectable."

"Two what?" Odo demanded.

"Cloaked ships," answered Sisko. He stood at attention and announced in his sternest voice, "Attention, all hands! This is Commander Sisko. The station is on red alert. There are at least two cloaked vessels in immediate proximity, and their intentions are unknown. If you are in an airlock or the docking ring, make an orderly withdrawal. Avoid those areas until further notice. Sisko out."

"The convoy is coming out of warp," said Dax.

Sisko's jaw tightened, and he had the unpleasant feeling that he knew why somebody had tried to kill him yesterday.

CHAPTER
3

"I'M STILL TRYING to hail the convoy!" Kira said with frustration. "But they're still jamming us!"

Sisko prowled behind the consoles, his fists clenched. "Is there any way we could divert more power to communications?"

"There's not enough time," replied the Trill. "They're coming out of warp in ten seconds—with shields down."

O'Brien gripped the handrails. "Good God, they're sitting ducks!"

Sisko slammed his fist on the back of Dax's chair. "Can we do anything, Dax? What are the options?"

She shook her head glumly. "None, Benjamin. We're out of transporter and weapon range, and we can't move the station fast enough to do any good. We can put it on the screen and watch—that's about all."

"We can protect the wormhole," Sisko vowed. He

slapped his comm badge. "Sisko to runabout pad A. Which runabout is fueled?"

"The *Mekong* is ready, sir."

"Prepare it for launch. Sisko out." His jaw tightened as he ordered, "On screen."

Panning the coordinates twenty thousand kilometers away, Dax picked up three blinding streaks, which abruptly turned into three midsize starships and came to a complete stop. The two Starfleet cruisers looked like silver wedges, built for speed and the ability to escape if they were outgunned. The tanker was a boxy construct, like a large shuttlecraft, with a complex docking nose that could match up with just about anything that flew or orbited. Each ship had a crew of about twenty, Sisko knew, plus passengers, who in this case were the test crew for the *Hannibal*. He racked his brain, trying to think of something to do, while he waited for an innocuous patch of space to turn into something deadly.

He didn't have to wait long, as two rapacious-looking Klingon Birds-of-Prey shimmered into view, a microsecond before their phaser banks opened fire. Beside him, O'Brien cringed at the onslaught and lowered his head. The first volley raked the two cruisers and crackled along their hulls like lightning, and the ships teetered back and forth. But they held together. At least, thought Sisko, the Klingons weren't fool enough to shoot at the tanker itself; the resulting explosion would probably obliterate all of them.

"I'm getting through!" announced Kira. "I told them to put their shields up. They're trying to do so."

"Get me an ID on those Klingons," ordered Sisko. "I don't see any official markings."

"Running scanners," answered Dax.

The next volley was even more devastating. One of the cruisers was completely disabled and went as dark as the deadest asteroid. The other one took a blast, then blipped away into warp drive. Sisko couldn't blame them—in a massacre, it all came down to survival. He hoped the tanker would be lucky enough to escape into warp drive.

"They're locking on to the tanker with a tractor beam," announced Dax.

"Of course!" said Sisko, pounding his fist into his palm. "That's how they're going to take the antimatter. They can't beam over because the tanker has her shields up. They have to take the whole ship." He grew somber. "Any word from the cruiser that's out of commission?"

"None," answered Kira. "No response, and all channels are open."

Dax added, "The Klingon ships are renegades. The Klingon High Council is offering rewards on the captains' heads. Higher if you turn in *only* their heads."

Sisko sighed bitterly and muttered, "It's all over. Like that. As soon as it's safe, we have to look for survivors."

Then his dark eyes brightened with a new thought. "You know, I don't think even a Bird-of-Prey can go very fast towing a tanker with a tractor beam. We could dog them a little."

He looked around at his command officers, many of whom he was still getting to know. He certainly didn't know any of them well enough to send them on a suicide mission. "I'm taking the runabout," he declared. "Is anyone fool enough to want to come with me?"

Dax nodded resolutely. "I want to go."

Sisko smiled. "All right, old man," he agreed. "Anybody else?"

Odo put his hands behind his back and stepped forward. "May I go?"

The commander smiled puzzledly. "Odo, I'm not sure this is such a bright idea—chasing two Klingon Birds-of-Prey in a runabout. Do you want to reconsider?"

"No, sir. I was the first one who predicted there would be trouble over this antimatter shipment. I feel as if this is my case. Besides, I want to see if there are any Ferengi involved."

"Okay." Sisko nodded.

"Count me in, too," said O'Brien.

Sisko shook his head. "I'm sorry, Chief, but I need you here. If Dax and I were—delayed—we would need at least one ranking Federation officer here. Besides, I don't think DS9 can operate without you."

He turned to Kira. "That's it. Major, you are in charge until we get back. You might want to prepare another runabout to look for survivors."

"I will, Commander." The Bajoran smiled. "Good luck, and get our antimatter back."

"We'll try." The commander motioned to his tiny crew and headed for the turbolift. He was almost out when he heard O'Brien yell.

"Commander! They were playing possum!"

The crippled cruiser suddenly came alive with a vibrant surge that lit it from stem to stern. It raked the nearest Klingon ship with an array of photon torpedoes at point-blank range. Because the Bird-of-Prey had been using its tractor beam, its shields were down, and it sparkled like a pigeon hitting a live wire. Just as suddenly, the second cruiser came out of warp drive, its phasers blazing. The other Bird-of-Prey went reeling under the blast, and the battle was rejoined.

Sisko, Odo, and Dax dashed to the turbolift.

The runabout *Mekong* shot away from the dock with Sisko piloting, but they had only gone a thousand kilometers when they saw something that horrified them. One of the Klingon vessels had backed away from the main battle and was steadily emptying its phasers into the tanker. Her shields were holding, temporarily, but such an action was the height of lunacy.

"Those idiots!" growled Sisko. "If even one blast gets through to those storage pods, we'll all be space junk!"

He opened all channels and calmly said, "This is Commander Sisko of *Deep Space Nine*. Come in, Klingon vessel."

There was no answer, so he remarked, "Klingon vessel, if you continue firing at that tanker, our families will be screaming the death howl tonight."

On his small screen, the brutal face of a Klingon appeared. His bony brow was crosscut with a variety of ancient scars, and he wheezed a sickly laugh. "My family screams the death howl every night, for they have been told of my death a thousand times. By lying scum like you!" He spit in contempt. *"vIjonta!"*

"You may not care if you die," said Sisko, "but what about your crew? The Klingons on the other ship?"

"We want one thing, human," scowled the Klingon. "We want the tanker to lower her shields. Tell her, or we keep firing."

Benjamin Sisko looked to Dax, sitting beside him, but she could only shrug. A civilized Klingon wasn't easy to deal with, and a renegade Klingon was a hundred times more reckless. Both of the Starfleet cruisers were idle in space, spent by the battle, diverting all their power to their shields and life-support. The second Klingon cruiser was limping away at impulse power, but the first one kept firing at the tanker. It was a standoff, thought Sisko, except for the fact that one of the participants was holding a loaded grenade.

"This is crazy," muttered Sisko. "They're committing suicide."

"Who is committing suicide?" asked Odo, standing behind him.

"Everybody, including us."

Dax sat forward, studying her readouts on the Ops console. "The tanker's shields are weakening. They're either going to have to put them down, or—"

She was cut off by a static-filled audio transmission. "Mayday! Mayday!" came a distraught voice. "This is the Starfleet tanker *Phoenix,* carrying two thousand cubic meters of antimatter. We've been attacked near *Deep Space Nine,* and we're going to have to lower our shields or risk complete destruction!"

"Can you get us visual?" asked Sisko.

Dax shook her head. "No, only audio."

Anguished cries suddenly echoed over the speaker system. "We're being boarded! All hands, repel invaders! Repel . . ." A phaser pistol roared, and the captain's voice degenerated into a mangled scream. It was followed by the awful din of hand-to-hand combat, with shouts, screams, and blunt weapons striking targets of flesh. The audio crackled with static, but not enough to drown out the cries of people dying.

"Bastards!" growled Sisko, banging his fist on the console.

Odo leaned forward. "Can we do anything to help them?"

The commander shook his head. "I'm afraid not, Constable. We can't fire on the tanker, and we don't want to trade phaser volleys with that Bird-of—" A gut-wrenching scream cut him off.

They listened as the battle subsided in intensity. The cries faded into moans, and somebody shouted, "Ship secured for Bajor!" That declaration was followed by cheers, just before the transmission went dead.

"Bajor?" asked Sisko. "What does that mean?"

Dax reported, "Both Klingon vessels are backing off. The tanker has put up shields again, and it's beginning to move under impulse power."

Sisko nodded glumly. "Following the Klingons, I suppose."

"No." Dax lifted her expressive eyes and stared at Sisko. "The tanker is headed for the wormhole."

Major Kira couldn't believe the viewscreen—the battle had abruptly ended, and the Klingons were breaking off. The Starfleet cruisers had fought valiantly, especially in their counterattack, but they had never recovered from the initial ambush. They were both dead in space. So why were the Klingons running? They couldn't be afraid of the *Mekong,* the little runabout from the station, because it wouldn't even be a mouthful for a Bird-of-Prey. The counterattack had foiled the Klingons' attempt to haul the tanker away with a tractor beam, but that didn't explain why they were giving up. Kira had caught bits and pieces of the Mayday issued by the tanker, but she wasn't sure what the final outcome had been. The tanker appeared little damaged by the skirmish, and it was on the move.

But why was it headed for the wormhole? She opened the standard channels and hailed them. "*Deep

Space Nine to Federation tanker *Phoenix.* What is your status?"

There was no answer, so she added, "You cannot enter the wormhole without clearance." She wanted to explain that warp engines had to be tuned a certain way to enter the wormhole, but this was a Federation ship. They knew the proper tuning.

After three more failed attempts at contact, she turned to the runabout, which was also streaking toward the wormhole. "Kira to *Mekong.* What is going on?"

"Dax here," came the reply. "We think that an armed party took over the tanker in hand-to-hand combat. Why they're headed toward the wormhole, we don't know. Can you stop them with a tractor beam?"

"Negative," answered Kira. "They're staying out of range. I estimate they'll hit the wormhole in . . . fifty-nine seconds."

A voice peeped up behind her. "What will happen if the antimatter explodes in the wormhole?" asked Amkot Groell.

Miles O'Brien took a sharp breath. "That's not something we want to think about. Let me assure you, starships powered by antimatter have gone through before. The tanker just happens to be a little starship that is packed to the gills with antimatter."

Kira leaned over her console and said, *"Mekong,* we can't do anything to stop the tanker. The Klingons are gone—at least they're out of sensor range. So we're going to concentrate on helping those two cruisers and getting them into our docks. What will you do?"

There was a tense moment, and Dax finally replied, "We're going after them."

Sisko broke in. "Major, just hold down the fort

until we get back. We're going to drop down to match their speed and trajectory, so maybe they'll think we're just an echo on their sensors. Neither this ship nor the tanker has much in the way of armaments, so we won't be risking a shoot-out."

Kira exchanged a look with Amkot Groell, and they were both thinking the same thing. "Commander," she said, "if you can get that antimatter back, we'll all be very happy."

"Understood," said Sisko. "Please explain to my son that . . . I'll be back."

"I'll handle it," said Kira.

The wormhole opened up like a giant blue-and-white iris, and the antimatter tanker was no bigger than a speck against its swirling depths. After the tanker was consumed, the wormhole blinked out of existence for thirty seconds; then it opened again to swallow the *Mekong*. When the wormhole closed, the open channel to the *Mekong* sounded a strange hum, and Kira knew that all contact between the station and the runabout was over—at least until they returned, or another ship went after them.

"Good luck, Commander," whispered Kira, although she knew he couldn't hear her.

She turned to see a gloomy white-haired Bajoran standing beside her. "Good luck to *him?*" muttered Amkot Groell. "We have the hard job—we have to explain all of this to Minister Roser, the assembly, and the Federation!"

"Yes," agreed Kira, sinking a few centimeters in height. "That won't be easy. Chief O'Brien—"

The chief was already headed toward the turbolift. "I'll grab Dr. Bashir and a runabout, and we'll see what kind of shape those cruisers are in."

"Thank you, Chief."

After O'Brien left, Major Kira felt very alone in the suddenly depleted Operations Center, despite the presence of Director Amkot and an experienced relief crew. Kira knew she could run *Deep Space Nine,* and she had often resented Benjamin Sisko, despite her respect for him, because he stood in her way. But this wasn't how she wanted to get the job. She wanted to earn it. She wanted her promotion to commander to be obvious to everyone, from the provisional government to the Federation. She wanted it to be a happy day, a day for celebration—not a troubling day, a day when Bajor had once again shown that it was unstable, perhaps unfit to govern itself. By her actions, she would have to provide a contrast, to show that Bajorans were ready to take over.

But were they?

Inside the wormhole's unearthly swirl of colors, the little runabout was bounced and battered. Panel doors popped open, and sparks shot out of one of them. Sisko couldn't remember two ships ever going in so closely together, and he wondered if that might have resulted in the unusually bumpy ride. Well, he thought, there wasn't anything anybody could do but hang on and wait it out. He noted that even the stoic Odo scrambled to find a seat.

After a handful of seconds that seemed much longer, the turmoil ceased, and the wormhole deposited them in the Gamma Quadrant with a last burst of blinding light. Sisko grabbed the controls.

"Can you find them?" he asked Dax.

"Yes, sir. Bearing two-mark-nineteen. Traveling at warp three."

"Good, we can match that," said Sisko, working the

conn. "Remember, we want to shadow them so closely that they think we're an echo. Also, let's have the computer make an automatic log of our course changes, so we can find our way back."

On the face of it, the Gamma Quadrant didn't look any different than the Alpha Quadrant—stars and nebulae as far as the eye could see. But there was a big difference, and Sisko knew it. Except for a few unremarkable planets and solar systems near the entrance to the wormhole, the Gamma Quadrant was virtually unexplored, uncharted, and unknown. Several Federation, Klingon, Ferengi, and other vessels had gone through the wormhole, but not many of them had returned yet to report their findings. Some that had returned were keeping their secrets.

A handful of spacefaring races from the Gamma Quadrant had emerged on *Deep Space Nine's* side of the wormhole, but most of them had taken a quick look around and gone home. Despite the galactic shortcut, explorations on both sides were proceeding slowly and cautiously. Sisko glanced at his navigational charts and knew why—if the wormhole ever closed, it would take the explorers a lifetime to get back to their home quadrant, even at warp nine.

Yet here he was, chasing a stolen tanker full of antimatter across untold parsecs of uncharted space. He knew perfectly well how he had gotten into this mess, but he didn't know how he was going to get out of it. How were the three of them, in a tiny runabout, going to recapture a tanker that twenty crew members hadn't been able to hold?

Odo wasn't telepathic, but he seemed to read Sisko's mind. "Commander?" he asked. "Where are we going?"

Sisko frowned. "Damned if I know, Constable. For the time being, we're just following that tanker straight into the unknown. Do you think we ought to turn back?"

Odo's jaw jutted forward. "I don't enjoy letting lawbreakers escape. However, it would be reassuring to know our destination."

"I can tell you our heading," said Dax, "although that won't help much in determining our destination. We basically don't know where we're going."

Odo cleared his throat. "I suppose I was really asking—how far are we going to pursue these buccaneers?"

"They've just shot up a Starfleet convoy," answered Sisko through clenched teeth. "And they probably killed everybody on board that tanker. Plus, they stole two thousand cubic meters of antimatter out from under our noses."

"Which I predicted would happen," Odo added.

The commander nodded grudgingly. "Yes, I know. But you thought they might steal a couple of pods off the station. This is bigger than that. What did those Klingon renegades get out of it? Not the antimatter. So we have to assume that they were paid for their participation."

Odo sniffed with disdain. "Yes, this whole operation reeks of Ferengi involvement."

"Bajorans too," Dax reminded him. "At least one of the attackers claimed they were doing it for Bajor."

"Well," muttered Sisko, "they've come over here for a reason. Let's tail them long enough to find out why. Dax, do they suspect we're following them?"

"Not by their actions," said the Trill. "That tanker is capable of outrunning us, if they wanted to. They haven't made any course changes for a while, so I suspect they have a destination in mind."

"Maybe this was their plan all the time," said Odo. "Sources of antimatter may be scarce in this quadrant, so they can get higher prices."

"Or trade it for something," Sisko replied. "Damn it, why don't they stop?"

Dax leaned forward and studied her instruments. "Benjamin, I think they heard you. They're coming out of warp drive."

"Let's correct our course and speed to match theirs," said the commander. His long fingers played over the console as he made the adjustments himself.

"They've just entered a solar system," observed Dax.

"Computer," said Sisko, "do we know anything about the solar system that is currently in our sensors?"

"There is no record of this solar system," answered the flat voice of the computer.

"Figures," muttered Sisko. "Dax, can you make their destination?"

"Third planet from the sun," answered the Trill. "We're too far away to tell for sure, but it could be class-M. It's about the right size and clearly has an atmosphere."

"They'll have to establish orbit," said the commander. "Let's set up our orbit as far away as we can and still be in sensor range." With consummate skill, he adjusted the course and speed of the *Mekong*.

"Now what?" asked Odo.

Sisko managed a smile. "Constable, I wish you would stop asking me questions I can't answer. We're going to go into orbit around a strange planet nobody in the Federation has ever heard of. If somebody from that tanker beams down to the planet, *we're* going to beam down."

"Fine," said Odo sarcastically. "I just wanted to make sure we had a plan."

Slowly a planet was coming into visual range on the *Mekong's* viewscreen. The sphere was lime green, with dense but not unpleasant-looking clouds surrounding it. As they drew closer, gaps could be seen in the clouds, and the planet's surface appeared to be a dark green color, broken up by splotches of salmon-colored seas. Or perhaps they were deserts, Sisko thought. He would have liked to gaze at the mysterious planet, but he had to monitor the tanker's every movement and match it as closely as he could. Thus far, the tanker had shown no evidence that its operators knew they were being followed, or cared. If they spotted the runabout at this range, he decided, they might not be too concerned with such a small craft.

"They've taken an orbital trajectory," announced Dax.

"All right," said Sisko. "Let's match them."

"And they're not the only ones," she added.

"What?"

"There are three other ships in orbit," she replied. "The tanker and ourselves will make a total of five ships orbiting the planet."

"Can you get an identification on any of the others?" he asked.

Dax spent a few seconds manipulating the runabout's scanners. "One of them is a Ferengi Marauder that went through the wormhole three weeks ago."

"I knew it!" crowed Odo.

"The others?" asked the commander.

Dax shook her head. "They don't correspond to anything we know."

Sisko shrugged his large shoulders. "Well then, what's one more? I'll take us into standard orbit, and to hell with them if they see us."

"I can go for a space walk," said Odo, "and disguise the Federation markings. If that is acceptable to you, Commander?"

"It wouldn't hurt," answered Sisko. "Until then, we'll keep our distance. And keep our shields up."

There were several moments of silence as Commander Sisko piloted the compact runabout into a standard orbit. He waited to see if they would be hailed by any of the ships, but nobody seemed to mind another one joining the party. Now the curve of the planet filled the small viewscreen, and they could see immense green continents, broken up by irregular salmon-colored seas. The shape of the seas reminded Sisko of the Great Lakes back in North America, but he had no idea how they got their odd coloring. Dark spidery blotches on the surface of the planet could be population centers, he thought, but there wasn't time to do a full scan.

"What are they doing?" he asked Dax.

"A small party just beamed down to the surface," she answered. "I've got their transporter coordinates."

"Is it class-M?"

"Yes, breathable atmosphere."

Sisko stood and stretched his arms, weary from the long chase. This was the deepest he had ever penetrated into the Gamma Quadrant, and he wasn't enthused to think that nobody in Starfleet or *Deep Space Nine* had any idea where they were. But there was a secret thrill in thinking that soon he would be beaming down to a planet that was unknown to the Federation, a complete mystery. Given the incredible distance they were from Federation space, there was no mistaking the fact that they were absolutely on their own. They couldn't count on backup or help—they had only their wits and a tiny runabout.

"Okay," he said, "I'm beaming down. One of us should stay with the runabout to discourage boarders and run the transporter. Would you like to stay here, Dax?"

"No," the Trill answered quickly. "I want to experience whatever there is to experience."

Sisko gave her a cockeyed grin. "Okay, old man, I guess you know what you're doing. After all, this is a volunteer mission. Constable, you stay here and hold down the fort. I think it's a good idea to disguise our markings."

"If you don't return?" asked Odo.

"Then go home," said the commander. "The computer has analyzed our course. We'll report back every two hours. If we lose contact and you can't raise us, assume the worst."

"I always assume the worst," muttered the shapeshifter, slipping into Sisko's vacated chair. "I would like relief in approximately six hours, because I will have to assume my liquid shape."

The commander nodded. "Six hours ought to be enough time to figure out what's going on." He glanced down at his Starfleet uniform and insignia badge. "Maybe we need to remove a few of our own markings."

Dax headed for a storage compartment. "We've got unmarked jackets," she said, "and we can take off our comm badges and our rank insignia."

She fished around in their stores for a large jacket and a small one. Sisko put on the jacket and plucked his badge off his chest, then took the three gold buttons off his collar. He felt oddly undressed without his rank insignia, but there wasn't much choice. He put the badge in his jacket pocket, and Jadzia Dax did the same.

"What about weapons?" she asked.

"Hand phasers," said Sisko. "We can hide them in our pockets."

The Trill handed him a phaser and took one herself. Together, they strode toward the transporter platform.

He smiled at her. "Seems like old times."

She smiled back. "And new times."

Sisko nodded to Odo. "Lower the shields just long enough to beam us down, then put them back up. Call us if there's trouble."

"Likewise," said Odo. His slim fingers touched the console. "Energizing."

In twin columns of blazing light, Jadzia Dax and Benjamin Sisko left the *Mekong* for parts unknown.

CHAPTER
4

COMMANDER SISKO and Lieutenant Dax materialized inside a small room. To the commander, it looked uncomfortably like a holding cell, or perhaps a very sturdy vault. There was no furniture in the room, except for a desk of adjustable height, upon which sat what was unmistakably a computer terminal. Sisko took a step toward the computer and halted when he noticed several large winged bugs scurrying across the floor. At his footstep, some of them fluttered toward the ceiling and disappeared into tiny vents. He gasped and jumped back.

Dax smiled. "Benjamin, are you still scared of bugs?"

Sisko gulped. "Old man, you may be a different person, but I'm not. Besides, I seem to recall that you don't care for spiders much."

"Spiders are arachnids," Dax observed dryly, "which are more venomous than arthropods. Besides, they may be keeping this area clean, or performing some other useful function. Don't judge a creature by its appearance."

Sisko smiled gamely but didn't look convinced. "Right."

The computer screen blinked on, and a synthesized voice said pleasantly, "Welcome, travelers, to the planet of Eco, Hive Three. For your safety and convenience, your transporter beams have been redirected to this chamber. Our scanners indicate that you are humanoid, and our records indicate that you are first-time visitors. Do you understand this idiom?"

"Yes, we do," answered Sisko. He wondered how these Gamma Quadrant aliens could know the Standard language, but then he remembered that the Ferengi were already here, in addition to the hijackers of the tanker.

"May we ask your purpose?" the computer said.

Sisko shrugged. "Business."

"Then you have certainly come to the right planet," said the synthesized voice. "Eco is the home of the Ecocids, who, in your idiom, would be called insects. Individually, as you see us on the floor or in the vented passageways above you, we are rather unremarkable. But together we form a hive mind that is every bit as advanced as your own. Probably more so. We try to confine our movements to the overhead passageways, but occasionally we must use the floor. You are rather clumsy creatures, and if you accidentally take the life of one of our individuals, we will understand. But please endeavor not to step on us. You may communicate with us through any of these interfaces, which you will find located throughout the hive.

"We regret," continued the voice, "that not all areas

of Hive Three are suitable for humanoid occupation. You will be restricted to certain levels. Also, we are a peace-loving race, and we require that you leave your weapons in this chamber."

"Weapons?" asked Sisko, trying to sound nonchalant. "We only have a few electronic devices."

"Our scanners indicate that each of you has an electronic device which is also a weapon. Please leave it on the table if you wish to leave this chamber."

Sisko looked around the windowless vault and decided that yes, he wished to leave it. He took his hand phaser out of his pocket and deposited it on the table. Dax did likewise. If this rule was strictly enforced, thought Sisko, it was really a benefit to them, since they were considerably outnumbered.

"Will these devices be returned to us?" he asked.

"No," answered the voice. "We wish to purchase them—in order to study them. Each of you will be given ten bilbok for your weapon. Since we detect that you are carrying no bilbok, we presume that this sum will be useful in your stay here. Do we have a deal?"

Sisko smiled in spite of himself. No wonder the Ferengi liked it here. "Agreed," he said.

In a flash, the weapons disappeared from the table, to be replaced by two stacks of black rectangles, ten in each stack. Dax walked to the table and picked up the bilbok.

"Well," she said, "let's see what they buy."

The voice interjected, "Your most valuable purchase would be a guide to the color-coded passageways of Hive Three. You can obtain one here for only twelve bilbok."

Sisko frowned at the interface. "A map costs more than one of our weapons?"

"It has been specially translated into your native idiom," said the hive mind cheerfully. "On the other hand, you may prefer to explore at your leisure."

"Yes, I think we'll do that," said Sisko.

"Have a profitable visit," the voice intoned. The table rose in the air to a height matching Sisko's height, and a door whooshed open behind it.

Carefully stepping around an Ecocid on the floor, Sisko followed Dax out of the chamber. They entered a corridor that branched haphazardly into other corridors, some climbing up, some trailing down. In the distance, they could see more corridors crisscrossing those in front of them. The only signposts were numerous colored stripes that ran horizontally along the walls. The junction where they were standing had at least a dozen of these stripes, but some of the corridors had only two or three colored stripes, stretching off into the distance.

Sisko muttered, "This looks like . . . well, like a hive."

Dax studied the colored stripes on the wall. "These must be directional indicators," she said. "Unfortunately, even if we bought a guide, it wouldn't tell us where the hijackers went. Where do you want to go, red, yellow, or green? How about magenta?"

The commander shrugged. "I like blue myself. That seems to be a popular place—there are at least three corridors leading there."

Dax nodded. "Let's go."

The blue-striped corridor led upward, which was also somewhat reassuring, although Sisko doubted that any of the pathways opened onto the surface of the planet. He wouldn't be surprised if Hive Three was entirely subterranean. He spotted a few Ecocids scuttling along the walls, so he stuck squarely to the center of the corridor. Except for the colored stripes, the only distinguishing features of the maze were the small vents in the ceiling, which carried air and also Ecocids. The commander swallowed and plodded onward, wondering if he could possibly get used to a planet run by insects.

"Wouldn't it be wonderful to study this culture?" asked Dax. "Spend a couple of years here?"

"I'd rather spend a couple of years with the Cardassians," answered Sisko. "You know, the Ecocids couldn't have built these corridors by themselves. Who built them?"

"The Ecocids must be wealthy," answered Dax, "if bilbok is a widely accepted form of currency. The question should be, how did they amass their wealth?"

There was no immediate answer, just a blue stripe that the two visitors followed through the rambling maze. They slowed when they saw two short bipedal individuals headed their way. The two creatures were covered with hair and wore green smocks, and they pushed small devices that were apparently cleaning appliances. Sisko thought about speaking to them, but the two creatures, who were marginally humanoid, were so intent on their task that he didn't want to interrupt them. They passed each other, exchanging barely a glance.

When they were out of earshot, Dax remarked, "Those creatures may be hired help."

"Yes," agreed Sisko. "Although they may be saying the same about us."

He was relieved to hear the sound of voices in the distance, and both he and Dax quickened their step.

The blue stripe blossomed into a wide triangle that ended at what appeared to be a darkly lit restaurant. At least there were tables and booths, with a staggering variety of creatures sitting at them. Several of the squat hirsute beings they had seen before were bustling around, carrying trays and attending the tables. Overheard, the ceiling blinked with a procession of illuminated markings that crawled from one end of the restaurant to the other, affording all of the diners a chance to see them. Indeed, many of the diners stopped their conversation to study the queer figures, and a few pounded their tables in disgust.

Dax drew close enough to the commander to whisper, "Are they gambling?"

Sisko squinted at the endless readouts in the ceiling. "It looks like something they used to have on Earth, called a stock-market ticker."

The Trill gave him a quizzical expression, and Sisko shook his head. "Never mind. Let's concentrate on our mission. We'll take a quick look around for Bajorans, Ferengi, or anyone who looks they came from our neighborhood."

Dax nodded, and they made a quick tour of the establishment, not finding any species they could identify. Several of the aliens eyed them curiously, especially Dax.

They soon found themselves at another doorway, confronted by the same array of colored stripes. Sisko was afraid they could spend days roaming Hive Three in this fashion. A short hairy servant wandered past with a tray of empty glasses, and Sisko held out his hand to stop him.

"Excuse me," he said, "have you seen anyone from the Alpha Quadrant? People with big ears?"

The servant shook his head. In a guttural voice, he replied, "Interface." He pointed to a small alcove that contained a computer identical to the one they had found in the holding chamber.

Sisko shrugged and said, "Thank you." He and Dax made their way over to the terminal.

"Well," said the commander, "it understood us before." He pressed a button on the alien keyboard to get the machine's attention. "Computer," he said, "can you help me?"

"I am not a computer," came the synthesized reply. "I am the interface to the hive mind. What is your problem?"

"We're looking for friends of ours, people we were supposed to meet. They are Ferengi—humanoids like us, but with large ears. There will also be Bajorans, other humanoids who have recently arrived from the Alpha Quadrant."

"We welcome visitors from the Alpha Quadrant," the device said cheerfully. "Your friends are in the Redemption Center. Simply follow the cyan pathway."

"Thank you," Sisko replied. He didn't know what else to say to a collection of insects.

Dax had already moved toward the array of stripes, and she quickly picked out a light blue one. "You were close when you picked blue," she said. "Does this look like cyan?"

Sisko nodded without much certainty. "Let's try it."

They walked downward along a meandering corridor, passing several unusual species who were headed toward the restaurant with the ticker-tape displays. Everyone seemed to be on holiday, thought Sisko, judging by the happy chattering from the revelers they passed. He might have understood some of the conversation if his comm badge had been pinned to his chest, thus activating the Universal Translator; but with his comm badge in his pocket, he heard nothing but gibberish.

Before they reached the Redemption Center, three burly humanoids dressed in rugged leather garments stepped into the corridor just ahead of them. Sisko motioned Dax to stop, and they froze in place, fearing that the newcomers would turn to look at them. From the back, he couldn't tell for sure if they were Bajorans —or the hijackers—but their uncertain actions identified them as strangers. They appeared weary as they slouched down the corridor, peering at the stripes, and one of them had a streak of blood on his sleeve. They walked in silence, too tired to talk.

He and Dax followed them in silence. The cyan stripe ended in a large triangle, and the corridor opened into what might be called a store. There were gleaming cases from floor to ceiling, containing the most diverse assortment of merchandise Sisko had ever seen in one place. The shelves kept revolving, displaying tools, canteens, cushions, jewelry, clothing, and works of art. Each item had a number posted beneath it, which he assumed was the price in bilbok.

When he saw that their quarry had stopped to inspect the unusual surroundings, he allowed himself to take a closer look at one of the display cases. Passing within view were several clear globes that contained miniature ecosystems—delicate spiral mountains, strange plants, oceans of different colors within which tiny creatures cavorted—all in worlds that were about ten centimeters in diameter. They were unspeakably beautiful. They passed out of sight to be replaced by even stranger souvenirs—dead ecocids mounted and frozen in curious tableaus, such as mating, fighting, giving birth to larvae. He gulped, thinking it was a bizarre species that would sell its dead to intergalactic tourists. Another shelf came into view, displaying unfathomable objects that could be anything from engine parts to alien sex toys.

"Benjamin," whispered Dax, "they're looking for someone."

Reluctantly, Sisko turned away from the display case to take in the entire establishment. Beyond the shop were a number of tables in a smaller version of the restaurant they had passed through before. As in the other place, unusual symbols marched across the ceiling, capturing the attention of the scattered diners. One of the three leather-garbed men turned to look around, and Sisko could see in silhouette the ridges on the bridge of his nose that marked him as a Bajoran.

"Over here!" someone shouted.

Sisko pushed Dax back into the shadows of an alcove, while keeping the Bajorans in sight. He saw them stride toward a table, where two Ferengi were waving them over. His rear end bumped against a table, and he turned to see another one of the Ecocid interface devices.

"I see you have found your friends," the synthesized voice remarked. "Why don't you greet them?"

"I don't think that's any of your business," Sisko whispered.

"Nonsense," replied the hive mind, "everything on Eco is my business. Perhaps this transaction requires delicate handling. May I be of assistance?"

Sisko was about to reply in anger when one of the

Ecocids fluttered toward his face; he gasped and slapped at it without thinking.

"We don't require your assistance at the moment," Dax interrupted. "But thank you, anyway."

"Remember," the voice replied, "we offer a variety of services—for the right price."

"We'll remember," said Dax.

Sisko took several deep breaths and tried to compose himself. He wanted off this buggy planet and back to the relatively safe confines of *Deep Space Nine*—with the antimatter in tow. More immediately, he wanted to hear the conversation between the two Ferengi and the three Bajorans at that distant table. But how?

"Benjamin," said Dax, reading his mind like the old friend she was, "I have an idea."

"I'm listening."

She took her Starfleet insignia from her pocket. "If I activate my comm badge and drop it under their table, we ought to be able to listen to them on your comm badge."

"Good idea," answered Sisko. "Let's do it."

"But we need a diversion. Something to distract them."

Sisko looked down at the beautiful raven-haired woman standing in close proximity to him in the tiny alcove. He smiled. "Old man, I know you haven't been a woman for very long, not recently anyway, but do you think you could walk like one of the Dabo girls from Quark's Place?"

She smiled with amusement. "You mean, jiggle my rear end back and forth?"

"Yes," he admitted, "that's the general idea. To jiggle whatever you've got to jiggle."

"Like this?" she asked, shifting rapidly from one foot to another.

"More slowly," answered Sisko. He tried to demonstrate, but he was ill-equipped to jiggle. "Look, just hand me your jacket. I think it'll come naturally once you get started."

She took off the bulky jacket, revealing the tight-fitting uniform underneath. "Do you really think that my merely walking by them—jiggling—can cause a sufficient diversion?"

Sisko took her jacket and smiled. "I think so." He took the comm badge out of her pocket. "Now, open a channel to me."

She squeezed her comm badge and said, "Dax to Sisko."

His comm badge beeped plaintively in his pocket, and he took it out. "Sisko here. Keep this channel open." He dropped his comm badge back into his pocket and held out his hand. She nodded and dropped her comm badge into his dark palm.

"Now," he said, "just walk past their table, very slowly. I'll be right behind you."

Dax nodded and straightened her shoulders. "I'm looking at this as an experiment."

She set off at a gait that was very slow and properly distracting. Sisko had to walk slowly to keep behind her. As she approached the table where the five conspirators were hunched over in conversation, her movements became even more exaggerated and seductive. Sisko couldn't see Dax's face, but he could see the faces of the two Ferengi and the three Bajorans —their conversation was short-circuited as she sauntered past. One of the Ferengi actually drooled through his snaggled teeth, and Sisko smiled to himself as he tossed the comm badge under their table. Of course, none of them paid him the slightest bit of attention. As far as they were concerned, he might have been an incorporeal energy creature.

The drooling Ferengi rose to his feet and croaked, "Darling, don't go away!"

"Leave it, Gimba," snapped the handsomest of the Bajorans. "There's time for that later."

"Always time for that," agreed the Ferengi.

That was the last Sisko heard of the conversation until they rounded the corner and stopped in a corridor, out of sight of the hijackers.

"How did I do?" asked Dax.

"Don't you know?"

She smiled. "Yes, I do know. That effect on males is so simple to attain. Was I that simpleminded when I was Curzon Dax?"

"Yes," admitted Sisko. He handed the Trill her jacket and took his comm badge out of his pocket. The conversation was so clear, they might have been sitting at the table with the hijackers.

"Gimba," said an irritated voice, "are you listening to me?"

"Of course I'm listening to you," answered a snide Ferengi voice. "But what you were saying doesn't make any sense."

"I said, I want to renegotiate our deal."

"No!" A fist pounded on the table. "Listen, Rizo, you got what you wanted—the shipyard is out of business, the government is embarrassed, and the Federation is angry. Now it's time for us to get what we want—the antimatter."

"But we need funds!" protested the Bajoran. "The revolution has only started."

"Funds shmunds," said Gimba. "This was a robbery, a heist, nothing more. It wasn't a revolution. Listen, we're out a lot of money to those Klingons. The only way we can recoup our investment is to sell the antimatter on this side of the wormhole."

"What about the tanker?"

There was a pause, and the Ferengi answered, "That's our profit."

"Too much profit," said Rizo. "We're the ones who lost seven lives taking that tanker. And we're the ones who now control it. You want the antimatter, you start negotiating."

"That wasn't our deal!" screeched the Ferengi, banging repeatedly on the table.

"We can have a new deal," said the Bajoran, "one that takes into account the needs of Bajor."

"Hey," drawled the other Ferengi, "I always heard Bajorans were idealists. It turns out they're just as greedy as Cardassians."

There were muffled shouts and the sound of chairs scooting back. Sisko and Dax peered around the corner in time to see the smaller Ferengi snarling like caged rats at the hulking Bajorans. In the absence of weapons, a fistfight seemed imminent. The last thing Sisko wanted was for the Bajorans to pack up and run off with the antimatter, so he strode toward them, wondering what he was going to say.

"What's this?" he asked pleasantly. "A fistfight? There aren't many of us from the Alpha Quadrant here—can't we all be friends?"

The combatants were about to ignore him, until Dax appeared at his side. "What's the problem, boys?" she asked seductively.

At once, fists began to unclench, and Gimba bowed

as low as his pot belly would allow him. "Hello, my fair lady. And what brings you to this side of the wormhole?"

"You don't recognize us?" asked Dax.

"No," said Gimba, "have we had the pleasure of meeting?"

Sisko studied the five humanoids, and he couldn't recall any of their faces. Of course, he didn't meet every person who came through *Deep Space Nine,* and the Bajorans were terrorists—they wouldn't have set foot on the station except to sabotage it.

"You don't know us?" he asked incredulously. "Why, I am Marcus Garvey, and this is Jade Dixon. We are known throughout the galaxy as accomplished private arbitrators."

The handsome Bajoran stepped forward, looking at them suspiciously. He reserved his longest look for Dax. "You're human," he said finally, "but what is she?"

"A Trill," she answered, fluttering her eyelashes. "And what are you?"

The Ferengi guffawed. "A Bajoran," said Gimba. "A decidedly minor race, but they do control the other side of the wormhole. Didn't you come that way? You couldn't have taken the long way to get here, unless you're a lot older than you look." He gave her a lengthy examination to make sure she wasn't older than she looked.

"Of course we came through the wormhole," answered Dax. "We were in a hurry, so we didn't meet any Bajorans."

"It was a delicate matter," Sisko assured them. "We had to, shall I say, disappear for a while. A tour of the Gamma Quadrant seemed a suitable diversion."

The handsome Bajoran turned away and muttered, "That's nice, but we've got business to discuss." From his voice, Sisko recognized him as the one called Rizo.

The commander leaned forward and lowered his voice. "We know you've got business to discuss, because you were discussing it rather loudly. As I said, we are private arbitrators, and we are very discreet. Perhaps we could be of assistance in resolving your differences."

"Leave us alone," growled Rizo.

"Now, now, let's not be too hasty," said the chubby Ferengi. "We obviously cannot resolve this problem by ourselves. You say you want to renegotiate—perhaps an objective third party could be helpful."

The Bajoran glowered suspiciously at Dax and Sisko. "How do I know this isn't some trick? How do I know these people aren't working with you, Gimba? For that matter, how do I know they didn't follow us through the wormhole—they look like they're wearing some kind of uniform."

"Simple," answered Gimba, "ask the proprietor of this place. The hive mind. It knows everyone and everything that goes on here, believe me. We've been here two days—ask it how long they've been here."

Rizo peered over his shoulder at the interface terminal in the alcove, the same one Sisko had bumped into. He nodded. "All right."

He strode toward the device, and Sisko trailed after him, trying to appear only mildly interested. In his mind, he was formulating excuses for how they had managed to arrive minutes after the Bajorans, but none of them sounded very convincing. He noticed that Dax stayed with the other Bajorans and the two Ferengi, keeping up her charming but saucy facade.

He stood near the alcove with a pleasant grin on his face as Rizo approached the machine.

"Uh, hive mind?"

"Yes, may I be of assistance?" asked the synthesized voice.

"This human beside me is named Marcus Garvey," said Rizo, casting a suspicious eye at the human. "And he has a female with him named Jade Dixon. How long have they been here?"

"By 'here,' do you mean this room or Hive Three?"

"Hive Three."

"And do you wish this time interval to be expressed in solar days, sidereal time, light-years, or some other measurement?"

"Dammit, just answer me," growled Rizo. "How many days?"

"Six days," answered the Ecocid collective mind.

Sisko tried not to show any surprise at the lie. He merely smiled accommodatingly when Rizo glared at him.

"All right," said the Bajoran, "do you know what kind of business he's in?"

"We wouldn't care to pry," replied the voice, "but he has offered his skills as an arbitrator and negotiator."

"Yeah, he has," muttered the Bajoran. "Thanks."

"Yes, thank you," said Sisko with heartfelt gratitude.

"Glad to be of service."

When they returned to the table, Rizo explained, "That thing over there says they've been here for six days. But I still don't know if I want to include anybody in this deal. You know, what we did isn't exactly legal."

Sisko held up his hands. "Believe me when I say we are the soul of discretion. We represent no power but ourselves. Each side can submit its case to us, and we will use our proven formulas to find an equitable solution. That is what we offer, no more, no less."

"For our own reasons," added Dax, "we're in no hurry to go back to the Alpha Quadrant."

The Ferengi smiled lasciviously at the Trill. "You intrigue me, Jade. May I call you Jade?"

"You may call me anything you like." She glanced at Sisko. "I am accustomed to using various names."

Gimba chuckled. "I bet you are."

"How much do we have to pay them?" asked one of the Bajorans.

Sisko made a magnanimous gesture. "We don't ask for much—just a few bilbok to make our stay here more pleasant."

"You will be amply rewarded," promised Gimba, looking Dax up and down approvingly.

"Don't promise them anything yet," snapped Rizo. "I need to talk this over with the others."

"Especially Elaka," said one of his comrades, giving the third Bajoran a knowing smile.

"Then let us arrange to meet later," offered Sisko, "and if everything is agreeable, we can talk about how to proceed. Do you know the restaurant at the end of the dark blue stripe?"

"It doesn't matter where we meet," snarled Rizo. "It's very simple—we've got something they want, and they refuse to pay for it. They think we should do their dirty work for free."

Gimba wrinkled his bulbous nose. "We've taken a considerable financial risk already, and they're trying to back out on the terms of a previous agreement!"

Rizo snorted. "As if no Ferengi ever did that."

"Now, now, boys," said Dax soothingly. "Let's not hash this out in a public place. Marcus and I will arrange with the hive mind for a private meeting room. The two of you prepare your cases, with all the particulars. Let's meet back here in four standard hours. Will that be enough time?"

"I suppose," muttered Rizo. He pulled a Starfleet comm badge out of his pocket, and Sisko's jaw tightened with anger, knowing how he had gotten it. But he said nothing. "Can you beam out of this place?" asked the Bajoran.

"We have," replied Gimba. "Once the hive mind has met you, they don't seem to care what you do."

"With the exception of carrying weapons," Sisko added.

Rizo nodded and squeezed the comm badge until it beeped. "Rizo to Elaka," he said.

"Elaka here," came a no-nonsense female voice. "Are you ready to beam back?"

"Yes. Can you lock on to us?"

"We can," she answered. "And we're just about done converting more comm badges to our frequencies."

"Good," said Rizo. "Get us out of here." He stole a final glance at Dax before his molecules were disassembled, along with those of his comrades.

Gimba grinned at Dax and took her delicate hand in his pudgy fist. "Now, my darling Jade, we have four hours to go somewhere and, um, get to know each other more intimately."

"I think not," said the Trill, politely pulling her hand away. "We are serious about the services we offer, and we must remain objective." She smiled flirtatiously. "But when the negotiations are over—"

73

The Ferengi grinned and made a portly bow. "All the more reason for us to conclude them quickly."

"Excuse us now," said Sisko. "We must speak to the hive mind—about that private meeting room." He bowed formally. "Until later, gentlemen."

"Yes." Gimba grinned, never taking his rheumy eyes off Dax. "I am a gentle man. Very gentle."

The two Ferengi reclaimed their seats at the table and signaled a passing server, while Sisko and Dax returned to the alcove containing the hive-mind interface.

"I've got a few questions," Dax whispered.

"So do I," answered Sisko. "Like, are we crazy? We mustn't forget that these people are as dangerous as that antimatter they're carrying."

He stopped in front of the by now familiar terminal. Glancing around to make sure nobody was in earshot, he leaned over the terminal and said, "This is the person you know as Marcus Garvey."

"Hello, Mr. Garvey," replied the voice.

"I want to thank you for, uh, lying about us."

"You're quite welcome," said the collective mind. "You are probably wondering why we did so. You see, we consider it our mission in life to facilitate the conduct of business under ideal circumstances. Obviously, your two groups of friends need someone who is offering your type of service. Your apparent aim is to conclude the business between these two disagreeable parties without them resorting to violence, and that is also our aim. Simply put, the planet of Eco is a peaceful haven for commerce. If you support that goal, we will help you in any way we can."

Before Sisko or Dax could think of anything to say, a small shiny object came skittering out from behind the screen. It took the commander a moment to realize it was the comm badge he had tossed under the table. He wondered how it could be moving until he saw the dark antennae sticking above the metal and the black legs scurrying underneath it. Sisko drew back, but Dax reached out to retrieve her comm badge, uncovering a large Ecocid.

"Thank you," she said. "We need a private meeting room. Can you arrange that?"

"Certainly," answered the hive mind. "The yellow pathway leads to private conference rooms. You may use room number nine for as long as you need it, and a modest charge will be billed to you. May I also arrange sleeping quarters?"

"No, thank you," said Dax. "We're sleeping on our ship."

"If your ship needs maintenance or refueling, we have full facilities."

"Thank you," said Dax, "I think we're all right in that regard."

"Thank you for your help," Sisko managed to say.

The synthesized voice concluded, "Good luck in your endeavors."

Sisko stepped away from the interface with more questions than answers churning in his mind. He wondered how far they could go with this charade. He wondered how they could overcome both a shipload of greedy Ferengi and a shipload of bloodthirsty Bajorans. Most of all, he wondered about the Ecocids. If they had lied so glibly to Rizo, they were quite capable of lying to him and Dax as well.

Finally he shook his head, knowing there were no answers, only actions. Under the circumstances, they had very little choice but to wing it. After making sure that the Ferengi were still occupied at their table, he took out his comm badge and tapped it.

"Sisko to Odo," he whispered.

"Yes, Commander?"

"We're ready to beam back."

"Yes, sir. I'm locking on."

So deep in thought was Commander Sisko that he failed to notice that the Ecocid which had fetched the comm badge suddenly leaped off the table, landed on his jacket, and burrowed inside his pocket.

"Energizing," said Odo's calm voice.

CHAPTER
5

DR. JULIAN BASHIR quickly loaded another hypospray with painkiller and administered it to the wounded ensign lying on the deck of the bridge. He and Chief O'Brien had already spent an hour aboard the *Valor*, the more damaged of the two cruisers, and Bashir had just beamed over to the *Regal*, where there were half a dozen wounded crew members. The only death had been aboard the *Valor*—a radiation burn—and thus far none of the others required immediate hospitalization. For the time being, Bashir had been able to patch up their contusions and fractures. He hoped his handiwork would suffice until they could be transferred to the station, whenever that would be.

The young doctor yawned, fighting fatigue. Every moment since leaving the station on the runabout had been a blur of activity. He was beginning to wish that he weren't the only medical practitioner in this part of space. The cruisers were too small to have their own doctors.

"When is Chief O'Brien getting here?" growled an angry voice.

Bashir looked up from his patient, who was mercifully falling asleep, to see a handsome young man in a cranberry-colored uniform. At first, he had been glad to meet Captain Jon Rachman, thinking their similar ages would make them compatible, but now he was finding the *Regal*'s young skipper to be rather tiresome.

"I don't know," he muttered as he cauterized the wound.

"What do you mean you don't know?" snapped Captain Rachman. "Aren't you coordinating with him?"

"Not really," answered Bashir. "I'm patching up the people, and he's patching up the impulse engines. I'm sure he'll be here as soon as the *Valor* can make it to the station under its own power."

"What about tractor beams?"

The doctor sighed and turned off his cauterizing instrument. He stood and looked Captain Rachman in the eyes, wishing the young officer weren't several centimeters taller. "You came in too far away from the station for us to be of any help," he explained. "If you had come in closer, none of this might have happened."

Rachman's lips thinned. "So now you're telling me my business. We were ordered to avoid the wormhole. Why is your station sitting right on top of it?"

"To monitor traffic going in and out," Bashir replied. "Listen, Captain, I have patients who need me. If there's nothing else . . ."

"There's plenty," snarled Rachman. "I want to know who attacked us, and where to find them!"

When Bashir looked past him, scanning the bridge for more wounded, the captain's attitude softened. "Take a look at my first officer, will you. Over here."

The doctor nodded and followed the captain to the navigation console, where an attractive blond woman sat, grimacing in pain. With his long fingers, Bashir unsnapped her collar, noticing her lieutenant's buttons. He quickly opened his tricorder and made a preliminary examination.

"Broken ribs," he announced. "I don't find any internal injuries. Lieutenant, I want you to remain perfectly still. Don't move around at all. I can give you a painkiller."

"No," she said through a grimace. "I have to remain alert." She looked up at her captain. "We're going after them, aren't we, sir?"

"Damned right," snapped Rachman.

"Not for several days," said Bashir. "At least *she's* not going anywhere, except to bed. By the looks of this ship, I don't think the rest of you are going anywhere either."

Captain Rachman's pink cheeks were turning red. "Don't tell me what to do, Doctor. We were ordered to protect that shipment of antimatter, and I intend to fulfill those orders. I'll pursue our attackers to the ends of Federation space!"

"You *are* at the ends of Federation space," countered Bashir. "All around us is the Cardassian Empire, and through the wormhole is a whole quadrant we know nothing about. Plus, this sector is full of Ferengi and renegade Klingons who don't owe allegiance to anyone but themselves. I don't know what you were told to expect, Captain."

"We weren't told this was the Wild Frontier, where we were going to be shot up the moment we arrived!"

Bashir smiled. "Then you were misinformed."

"Starfleet will hear about this!" Rachman threatened.

"I certainly hope so," answered Bashir as he strode away.

"Minister Roser Issa would like to speak with you," said the Bajoran officer at the communications console.

"Soon," answered Major Kira. "Tell her to wait."

"Director Amkot is waiting for you in his quarters," the officer reminded her.

"Yes, I know," answered the attractive Bajoran.

"And we're being hailed by the council."

Kira nodded. "I expected that."

"They would like to see you on Bajor immediately."

"Would they now?" asked Kira. "Tell them all that I have an urgent appointment to keep first, and then I will contact them. In fact, why don't you tell them all to talk to each other, if talking will make them feel better. I've made my report, and I haven't got anything to add!"

The Bajoran officer looked quizzically at her. "Shall I tell them that?"

Kira shook her head. "No." She squared her shoulders and took a deep breath. "Where is he?" she muttered.

As if in answer, the turbolift doors slid open and a gangly adolescent walked into Ops. She looked at him and smiled, thinking that he looked more like his father every day. She had often had her differences with Commander Sisko, but she couldn't fault him for the way he was raising his son. He was doing a stupendous job in her estimation, and she doubted if she could do as well, especially as a single parent.

"Hello, Jake," she said.

The boy shifted uneasily from one foot to another. "Hello, Major Kira. I'm sorry I took a while to get here, but we were having an exam. We had to stay late because of the alert."

"That's all right," answered the Bajoran. "I wish we were meeting under better circumstances."

He looked at her puzzledly. "Where's my father?"

She sighed. "That's what I wanted to talk to you about. Would you like to go into your father's office?"

"Where is he?" the boy asked, suddenly alarmed.

"As far as we know, he's fine," Kira replied. "But we don't know where he is. He went through the wormhole with Dax and Odo almost two hours ago, pursuing an antimatter tanker that was hijacked."

The boy nodded, squinting at her. He was a bright young man, she knew, but that was a lot to take in in one blunt sentence.

"Uh, when is he coming back?"

"We don't know," she answered. "As you know, we can't communicate with the Gamma Quadrant. He asked me to tell you that he will return as soon as he can."

"Who was he pursuing?" asked Jake.

Kira's lips grew thin, and she looked down. "We think it was Bajoran terrorists, working with Klingon renegades."

The boy turned away from her, and she could tell he was fighting his emotions. "Damn it," he muttered, "why did we have to come here? Why couldn't we go back to Earth, where we *understand* the people? Why can't Bajorans stop fighting?"

Kira stepped down from the Ops command table and approached the boy. He was already taller than her, and she could swear that hadn't been the case a few months earlier. She put her arm around his thin shoulders.

"Do you want me to explain what makes Bajorans tick?" she asked. "What makes us tick is half a century of brutal occupation at the hands of the Cardassians. That's the only thing all of us have in common. Some of us were collaborators, to one degree or another; others were resistance members and patriots. Some of us can't stop resisting, can't stop fighting. We're like that antimatter that everyone is chasing—we can't change our reactions—we explode when anything, including peace, gets too close."

She shook her head. "I don't know how many generations it will take before we're normal. You study us in school—you know what we were like before the Cardassians invaded."

Jake nodded. "You were peace-loving."

"Yes," Kira agreed. "And now we're war-loving. We're vengeful, we're distrustful. But we're also hopeful. That's why we're building a starship for the Federation, because we want to show that we can build things again."

She managed a smile. "I've been reading a little bit about Terran history lately, and you've gone through all of these same stages. In your case, it was worse, because your cruelty came from within. You overcame it, but it wasn't easy. Your father is helping us and trying to set a good example. Please don't hold it against him for helping us."

Jake frowned. "Will you let me know . . . when there's any news?"

"Of course," said the major. "I have a lot of faith in your father. You should, too."

"Yeah," mumbled Jake. He smiled gamely. "Thanks for telling me in person, Major."

"That's okay."

Jake slouched toward the turbolift, and the doors whooshed open. Kira watched him until he was gone, then shook her head.

"Well," she muttered, "I guess if I can get through that, I can get through the other meetings. Contact the council, the ministers, and whoever else wants to see me, and tell them that I'll go to Bajor as soon as Chief O'Brien returns to DS9 with the cruisers."

"Yes, sir," answered the subordinate.

"What is your plan?" asked Odo with his usual directness.

The shapeshifter looked well rested, thought Dax, after spending three and a half hours as a blob of liquid at the bottom of a portable lavatory aboard the *Mekong*. Since she and Benjamin were about to return to the planet, they had requested that he cut his rest period short.

"I don't know," sighed Sisko. "We've got to get aboard the tanker, but we've got to do so with a chance to take it over."

"In other words," said Odo, "we've got to hijack it back."

"With three people," Dax added. "Really, two people, because one of us has to pilot the runabout. I don't know what we're doing exactly, but I think we're on the right track in winning their confidence." She gave them a wry smile. "I'm using a few skills I very seldom use."

Odo cocked his head curiously. "I see. From what you've told me about the planet, there are no authority figures to whom we could appeal for help."

"No," said Sisko, "there's only the hive mind of the Ecocids, and it only seems interested in business-as-usual. Weapons are outlawed, but we haven't found much else that is."

"I don't suppose," Odo said thoughtfully, "that you saw anyone who might be of the same species as myself?"

Dax shook her head. "Who knows? We saw a lot of unusual aliens, but nobody in a liquid state."

Odo frowned. "Of course not. If I am modest about my natural state, I suppose they would be too. I see that we have no choice but to remain here and try to pit the Ferengi against the terrorists, hoping they will rely upon us for a solution."

"That's about it," agreed Sisko. He slapped the armrests of his chair, then stood. "Marcus Garvey and Jade Dixon have a meeting in a few minutes."

Dax smiled puzzledly. "I understand the correlation between Jadzia Dax and Jade Dixon, but who is Marcus Garvey?"

"You need to study more Terran history," answered Sisko. "I'll loan you some reading materials as soon as we get back. Let's put it this way—he has something in common with Hannibal."

Odo and Dax glanced at one another, but neither one could enlighten the other. Odo swiveled around in the Ops chair and ran his fingers over the controls. "Should I return you to the same coordinates where I picked you up?" he asked.

"Yes," said the commander, striding to the transporter platform. "Coming, Jade?"

"Yes, Marcus," she answered. Dax had been counting the stack of black rectangular coins, wondering exactly what twenty bilbok would purchase, other than an overpriced map. She scooped up the coins and stuffed them into her jacket pocket before joining Sisko in the transporter. "I want to make sure we don't run out of money," she explained.

"If there's a bill, I'll make sure you get it," said Sisko. "Okay, Constable, energize."

Their molecules were dispersed across several thousand kilometers of sunny planetary atmosphere to be reassembled inside a dark subterranean emporium. As before, the Redemption Center was sparsely crowded compared to the larger restaurant they had visited, but the odd illuminated symbols continued to march across the ceiling.

Dax looked around the room and didn't see any of the parties they were supposed to meet. Suddenly, her eyes struck something in one of the display cases, something she would not have looked at if she hadn't been thinking about how to play the part of Jade Dixon. Draped over a curvaceous form in the display window was a shimmering, low-cut, golden dress. She walked toward it, wondering how it would look on her.

Even before joining with the symbiont named Dax, the young woman named Jadzia had been a serious person, little given to frivolity. The path to becoming a host was demanding and unforgiving—only the most determined were selected, fewer than ten percent of the total population. That Curzon Dax had turned into such a roustabout was still amazing to her, but Jadzia Dax had completely different priorities. At the moment, one of them was to try on the shimmering gold dress.

Jadzia had not been a sensual person, and she had had no desire to be one. However, that facet of life had been fully appreciated by Curzon Dax, and the power she wielded over the masculine sex—just by jiggling a little and batting her eyes—was for part of her a new experience. It required further study, and these circumstances were ideal. No one from Starfleet or DS9 was present to witness her "study," except for the one person who knew her best, and he would forgive her under the present circumstances. Yes, thought Dax, the dress must be part of this experience.

Sisko followed her without knowing where she was headed. "Just like Ferengi and Bajorans to be late," he muttered. "What are you looking at?"

"That dress," she answered. "I'd like to buy it."

He laughed. "You're not serious!"

"Yes, I am."

Sisko suddenly got serious too. "That's not something you would wear."

"I know," she answered, transfixed by the dress. "But it's something Jade Dixon would wear."

"I don't think so," he grumbled.

"Listen, Benjamin, we have to keep them distracted and off-balance. Can you think of anything that would do it better than that dress?"

Before he could answer—if he had an answer—the dress shifted to the right on a pulley system that revealed another dress. Afraid it would disappear forever, Dax reached out to touch the case, and the glasslike substance vanished at her touch.

Touching the forcefield activated a synthesized voice, which informed them, "The apparel costs eighteen bilbok."

"Eighteen bilbok!" scoffed Sisko. "That's almost all we have!"

She ignored him and reached for the dress. It tumbled off the form into her hands.

"What if it doesn't fit?" he asked.

She smiled. "I haven't paid for it yet. You keep watch for our friends."

"The fitting room is to the right of this case," said the voice.

Dax gave Sisko what she hoped would be a comforting smile. "I'll only be a minute."

Commander Sisko paced in front of the display case, occasionally slamming his fist into his palm. He didn't know who he was less anxious to see—the surly terrorists and their Ferengi partners, or Dax in that dress. He tried very hard to think of Dax as his chum and mentor, Curzon, and most of the time that wasn't difficult. Jadzia had all of Curzon's memories and experience, and the levelheaded wisdom she brought to every occasion was a reassuring reminder of who she was. But she wasn't the old man. She was a different person, like someone who had been through a very traumatic experience and had been forever changed. She was perfectly calm about being a beautiful young woman, and that kept him calm about it. Most of the time.

Sisko's traumatic experience came a moment later, when Dax emerged from the fitting room, wearing the revealing floor-length golden dress. His mouth hung open, and his throat got dry, and he tried to stop his eyes from wandering down the neckline. He knew she had breasts, but he had never seen quite so much of them before. Her cleavage was accentuated by the delicate brown spots that wandered from her shoulders deep into the glittering fabric.

Sisko forced himself to look farther down the dress, but that wasn't any better. It flowed around her hips and thighs like a shimmering coat of paint, and the fabric was transluscent enough to reveal the shape of her legs underneath. He finally had to look away entirely.

"You're not wearing that dress," he declared.

"Please, don't act like my father," Dax said. "I'm old enough to be *your* father several times over, and I think this dress will be very effective."

Sisko couldn't argue with that. While he tried to think of some *good* reason to forbid her from wearing the dress, she shoved a box into his hands. "Those are my old clothes," she said, "and I think I see our first guests arriving."

Swaggering through the room came the Bajoran, Rizo. He was dressed in his same rough leather garments, wearing the same distrustful scowl, only this time he was accompanied by two Bajoran females. Sisko felt that Bajoran women were as attractive as any other, when they tried to be, but the contrast between these two rugged terrorists and the shimmering apparition beside him was rather amazing. Perhaps if they had been wearing the same dresses . . . No, he decided, they still wouldn't look as good as Dax.

The contrast was not lost on Rizo either, or his escorts. He smiled bemusedly at Dax, and the two women glowered at her. To her credit, she looked as calm as usual, as if she wore such exotic outfits every day of the week.

"Welcome," she said with a smile.

"Hello," muttered Rizo. "Sorry we're late. If you come down here with any sort of weapon at all, you get whisked off to some damn holding cell. Even a little knife."

"How unfortunate," said Sisko. He nodded to the

Bajoran women. "I am Marcus Garvey. It's a pleasure to meet you."

"Elaka," said the taller and more forceful of the two women. Her light brown hair was dirty and cut raggedly, and her clothes were no cleaner than Rizo's. She considered Dax with disgust. "I thought we were coming down here to discuss business, not have an orgy."

"Actually," said Dax, "I was thinking more of dancing."

Rizo snapped at Elaka, "Leave her alone. We were at each other's throats until they came along and offered to help. Maybe we can get this resolved and get on with the things we have to do." He leered at Dax in a way that made Sisko feel both protective and jealous. "I think Jade's approach will work very well with Gimba. Put him in a good mood, if you know what I mean."

Elaka's eyes narrowed, as if she wasn't convinced that he was thinking about Gimba. Sisko wondered how involved the relationship was between her and Rizo.

"I am Petra," said the third Bajoran, and Sisko's attention was diverted to the younger woman. "We are freedom fighters, and we don't have many resources," she explained. "Anything you can do to help us will go a long way toward freeing Bajor from oppression."

Petra reminded him of what Major Kira might have been like, say, five years ago, before her idealism was tempered by pragmatism. He knew he shouldn't say anything political, but he couldn't help but state the obvious. "I thought Bajor *was* free? At least, I heard you had gotten rid of the Cardassians."

"Cardassians?" scoffed Rizo. "At least they were honest about their intentions. Now we have a puppet government set up by the Federation." He looked suspiciously at Sisko. "You aren't a Federation sympathizer, are you?"

"I do most of my work *outside* Federation influence," he answered, somewhat honestly.

"By the wonders of Zot!" bellowed a voice behind them. "What a scrumptious vision!"

There was little doubt what Gimba and his two retainers were staring at and slathering over. The Ferengi rushed forward to kiss Dax's hand, and she smiled as if she enjoyed the slobbery attention. The other two Ferengi stood bouncing on their feet, waiting their turn to get close to Dax, but Gimba wasn't going to give them the opportunity.

"Jade," he purred, "looking at you in that beautiful dress makes me wonder if we aren't mistaken in keeping our own women naked. But then, one has to maintain tradition. You are indeed a delicious vision, and I am gratified that we made your acquaintance."

"Can we get on with this?" snarled Elaka.

Gimba surveyed the Barjoran female with disdain. "I suppose fifty years of Cardassian rule would make anybody coarse," he sneered.

Rizo looked torn between defending Elaka and joining the others in their unabashed fawning over Dax. Finally, he heaved his big shoulders and said, "I suppose we must get on with it. Do you have a meeting room for us?"

"This way," said Dax, pointing to the corridor. "We must follow the yellow pathway."

The odd party made their way slowly through Hive Three, passing a number of small doors that might have been private quarters, then past what appeared to be a recreation room, complete with clanging bells and excited shouts. Gimba told his comrades to remember what color would get them back to the gaming room. Otherwise, he was content to make aimless small talk with Dax. Sisko found himself walking between the two Bajoran women.

Elaka wore a perpetual frown, but Petra seemed genuinely excited to be on the strange planet of Eco. "I've never seen anything like this," said the younger woman as they passed the gaming room.

"You should go to *Deep Space Nine*," said Sisko.

Elaka glared at him. "I thought you had nothing to do with the Federation?"

"I didn't say I had *nothing* to do with it," answered Sisko. "I don't know how you come to be in the Gamma Quadrant, but most ships have to stop at *Deep Space Nine* before they can go through the wormhole."

"Hmm," she grunted, granting him that small concession. "One day *we* will control *Deep Space Nine* and the wormhole, and we'll blast any Cardassian or Federation vessels to pieces!"

It was difficult, but Sisko held his tongue. "What possessed you to become a freedom fighter?" he asked.

For a moment, Elaka's hateful expression was replaced by one even more terrifying. "You don't want to know."

"Yes, I do," Sisko insisted.

It was Petra who replied, "Our comrade, Elaka, was buried alive in a ditch by the Cardassians. The bodies of her parents were thrown on top of her. She had to claw her way through them to get out." She said it in a matter-of-fact tone that was chilling, as if such histories were commonplace among their band.

A breath escaped from Elaka, like the hissing of an airlock. "Death is the punishment for those who oppose us," she said. "They deserve no mercy."

Sisko nodded and could think of nothing else to say. He was familiar with unbridled hatred—he had felt it himself, against the Borg and their conduit, Captain Jean-Luc Picard. But hatreds so deep had to be treated, had to be replaced with duty that benefited others rather than destroyed blindly. Despite his sympathy for Elaka and her kind, he had to remember that they had massacred the crew of the tanker and endangered the lives of thousands of people. They were warped and unstable, like the antimatter they had so recklessly stolen.

It was with relief that he saw the yellow line widen into a triangle, leading them into a circular lounge with several numbered doors surrounding it. Dax led the group to the room assigned them, and the door whooshed open at her approach.

They entered a brightly lit room containing a massive table of what appeared to be natural amber, a dozen comfortable chairs, and two food slots. At the sound of their voices, one of the food slots began producing delicate pastries, and the other slot produced several cups of steaming liquid.

Sisko walked over to the food slot and picked up one of the steaming cups. He held it to his nose and took a long sniff. "Coffee!" he marveled.

"Coffee," echoed Gimba, strolling over toward the machine and taking a cup. "One of the few Terran refreshments that I can tolerate."

But Sisko was frowning. "How do they know how to make coffee?" he asked. "Or that we even drink it?"

"*We* don't drink it," said Rizo, looking in disgust at the dark fluid. "I'll have a Regulan ale."

"That is not in our memory," answered the machine.

Rizo balled his hand into a fist. "You can make coffee, but you can't make ale?" He looked as if he was about to smash the machine; then he glanced at Dax and thought better of it. He finally grabbed one of the cups of coffee and took a seat at the handsome table.

Sisko sat at the head of a table. "Shall we begin?" he asked pleasantly.

"Yes," said Gimba, who continued to pace near the food slot, consuming pastries as quickly as the machine could make them. "The Bajorans were partners of ours in a rather risky business venture. All the arrangements were made in advance, and now they want to change them."

"Lies!" snarled Elaka, slamming her fist on the table. "It was harder taking that tanker than they told us it would be. We deserve more!"

"Let's stay calm," said Sisko with determination. "What was this business venture?"

Gimba smiled. "Shall we say, we relieved the Federation of several storage pods of antimatter."

His fellow Ferengi chuckled, and Gimba went on, "They weren't our only partners—we also used certain Klingons who don't care much for the Federation. There's our problem. The Klingons got paid hard currency for their part in the activities, currency which we planned to recoup when we sold the antimatter. Now Rizo and his crew refuse to turn the antimatter over to us."

Rizo banged his coffee cup on the table. "We risked our lives for that antimatter! We lost many brave people, people we can't replace. All these fat Ferengi did was sit around and wait for us to do all the dirty work!"

"I resent that!" snapped Gimba. He looked down at his protruding stomach and tossed the last bite of pastry into his mouth. "We organized and planned the entire heist. It was our contacts and our secret intelligence that made it possible."

He shook a chubby finger at Rizo. "He wouldn't have been able to get within a parsec of that tanker without our help. He's just an ungrateful fool!"

As fast as a Regulan eelbird, Elaka jumped behind Gimba and whipped a cord around his neck. As her sinewy forearms pulled tight, his cheeks bulged and chunks of pastry shot out of his mouth. Gagging, the Ferengi dropped to his knees and clutched at his throat.

Sisko leaped up and started toward her, along with the other two Ferengi, but Elaka murmured, "One more step, and he's dead. Rizo can tell you—I've garroted much stronger men than this weakling. You won't hear his lies until you've heard us first!"

CHAPTER
6

ALL EYES TURNED toward Rizo, and the big Bajoran rose slowly to his feet. His cautious movements made it clear that he knew Elaka was capable of strangling Gimba in an instant. That didn't keep him from glaring at her.

"Let him go," he said evenly. "We're not here to fight—we're here to negotiate. The Ferengi were a help to us, and they deserve to get something. Let him go!"

Elaka looked chastened, as if she hadn't counted on Rizo turning against her. Sisko looked over at Dax, and he could see through her tight gown that she was holding her breath. He fumbled in his pocket for his comm badge and felt better once he had found it. If worse came to worse, they could beam out of that stifling room.

Elaka grimaced in disgust and released the cord. Gimba slumped forward, gasping for breath, and his retainers rushed to help him. Elaka prowled the room like an angry cat, until she came to rest in the corner farthest from her victim. Despite the way everyone glared at her, she exhibited no remorse.

Sisko knelt down beside the strickened Ferengi. "Can you continue?"

"Yes, yes," croaked Gimba. He glanced at the Bajoran in the far corner. "They're rather forceful about making their points, aren't they?"

"Excuse me," said Dax, "but I don't believe this method is going to work. Whenever one of you tries to give his case with the other one present, we'll have an argument. There are two of us, Marcus and myself, and I think it might be better if we heard your cases separately. Then we could confer and reach a decision."

"I would agree to that," said Rizo. He looked pointedly at Dax. "I think we can tell our story to Jade, and she would understand."

Sisko was about to protest—he didn't want Dax alone with those lunatics—but then he realized that she would probably be even less safe alone with the Ferengi.

Elaka didn't look pleased by the prospect either. "I don't want her to come aboard the ship," she declared.

"Of course not," said Rizo. "Nobody gets aboard that tanker but us."

"You can stay here," rasped Gimba. "We'll take Marcus Garvey aboard our ship and talk to him there. It is agreed then." The Ferengi staggered to his feet and massaged his neck.

"May I confer with Jade for a moment?" asked Sisko.

Both Rizo and Gimba nodded, and Sisko led Dax to

a neutral corner. "Have you got your comm badge on you?" he whispered.

She smiled. "Yes, although it's not anywhere I would want anybody to look for it."

"At the first sign of trouble, you call Odo and get back to the runabout."

Dax whispered, "I may look stupid in this dress, but I'm not. I thought, by splitting up, maybe one of us could get aboard the tanker. Maybe that won't happen now, but it's got to happen sometime. I'll stay here with them, and we'll meet back at the runabout as soon as possible."

"All right," agreed Sisko. "I suppose you'll be safe here." He knew he didn't have to tell her to look out for Elaka.

He gazed at Rizo as he strode past him. "I'm depending upon you for the safety of my associate."

"Don't worry," said the Bajoran. "No harm will come to her, I swear it."

Sisko nodded. "I'm ready to go," he told Gimba.

The Ferengi gave him a sly smile. "I trust you will enjoy this little visit to our ship. There are some people I would like you to meet." He touched an ornate bracelet on his wrist and spoke loudly, "Four to beam back instead of three. Please prepare a special welcome for our guest, Marcus Garvey, who is standing on my right."

"Aye, sir," came a raspy voice. "Getting ready to transport."

Sisko tried to conceal the worry in his eyes as he gave Dax an encouraging smile. A second later, he felt the tingle of the transporter beam along his spine, and the conference room faded from view.

It was replaced by a garish silver-and-gold transporter platform that had twin arches crossing over it, each embedded with glittering jewels. The walls of the room were made entirely of mirrored surfaces and colored lights, which made the room look bigger than it was. Eerie music and some sort of perfumed scent wafted about the place. It reminded Sisko of one of Quark's more obnoxious holosuite programs, and this was only the transporter room.

He had seen a number of Ferengi Marauders, and he knew the unihull vessel had the approximate shape of a horseshoe crab, with its propulsion system in the tail. He also knew the Marauder was a very sophisticated starship with technologies stolen and bought from all over the galaxy, plus a crew of several hundred. He assumed the transporter room was in the larger forward section, and he wondered where the weapons were, as well as what they were.

Gimba let out a large sigh and stepped off the platform. "I think you can see the difficulty we have dealing with those barbarians," he told Sisko.

"Yes," said the commander, following his host, "some of them are rather unpleasant. But that doesn't mean they don't have a valid claim."

"They have no claim," grumbled Gimba, "all they have is the antimatter." The Ferengi motioned to his retainers to remain behind, and Sisko followed him into a turbolift. When the doors closed, he found himself alone with the Ferengi chieftain.

"Deck six," ordered the Ferengi, and the turbolift lurched downward. Gimba smiled at Sisko. "You're surprised I asked you to accompany us instead of your lovely associate, Jade."

"Well, yes, I am," the commander admitted.

"We're reasonable men," said the Ferengi, "with

reasonable wants and desires. What are your desires, Marcus Garvey?"

Sisko smiled. "Are you attempting to bribe me?"

Gimba shrugged. "But of course. We Ferengi have a saying—an angry man is an enemy, and a satisfied man is an ally."

"Satisfied?" asked Sisko suspiciously.

The turbolift thudded to a stop, and the commander felt his stomach sag. He was first off the decrepit lift, and he could hardly believe the sight that greeted his eyes. The turbolift opened into a luxurious bedroom, with pillows piled high in every corner and striped sheets adorning the walls. On the other side of the room, a door opened, and the sight got even more amazing as five naked Ferengi women strutted into the giant boudoir.

Sisko tried to find somewhere else to look, but he was unable to avert his eyes. The Ferengi women were entirely comfortable with their nudity, and they took his wild-eyed stare as a compliment. Two of them giggled.

Though there were only five of them, they represented every imaginable shape and size. There was a tall one with a sleek tanned body; a squat rotund one who laughed a lot; another with mammary glands that sagged to her navel; and a haughty creature who would have looked presentable in Dax's new dress, despite her enormous ears. The last one was disgustingly young, barely older than his son, Jake, and her body was still forming.

Sisko cleared his throat and tried to find his host, but Gimba had stepped back into the turbolift. "This is my harem," he explained. "And my harem is your harem. We'll talk later." The turbolift door clanged shut.

"No, no!" shouted Sisko. But the naked women were already converging upon him.

"Can we get some real food out of this thing?" muttered Rizo, staring forlornly at the food slot in the conference room.

Dax stole a sidelong glance at Elaka, wondering what else might send the unbalanced woman into attack mode. Dax was beginning to regret buying the body-hugging dress, but there was no turning back now. She had a part to play, and the dress helped her play it. Luckily, Benjamin had left the box containing her regular clothes, so she could change if things got too sticky.

She told Rizo, "There was a wide variety of food in the dining hall we saw earlier. All we have to do is follow the blue stripe."

"Fine," said the Bajoran. He looked pointedly at Elaka and Petra. "Just Jade and I will go."

"No!" protested Elaka. "We all go."

Rizo shook his head sternly. "No, Elaka, not after the trick you pulled. You're going back to the ship."

Dax held her breath, thinking that the insane woman was going to attack Rizo with her bare hands. Instead, Elaka rushed to him and hugged his broad chest fiercely. "Don't ever leave me. Ever."

He gently but forcefully pushed her away. "You and Petra go back to the tanker. Double the guard, and keep the shields up. These negotiations may not work, although I hope they will." He glanced at Dax.

Elaka looked at Dax, too, as she drew her stolen comm badge from her pocket. Her look told the Trill that a cord would find her neck if she tried to steal Rizo from her. Dax returned the woman's spiteful gaze with what she hoped was a guileless smile.

"I have my eye on you," said Elaka.

"Understood," answered Dax. "I only want what's best for all of us."

Rizo strode toward the door, and it whooshed open. "Come on," he ordered. Dax grabbed her box from the table and followed him out.

As soon as they were in the corridor, the Bajoran seemed to relax, although Dax saw him glancing over his shoulder to make sure Elaka wasn't following.

"She is a great fighter," he explained. "Very loyal. But she doesn't understand that not everything needs to be won by force. If we are to succeed, we must learn to lead our people."

"What is your goal?" asked Dax.

"A Bajor for Bajorans, not for anyone else. We've earned the right to map our own destiny, and we don't need that pompous Federation to tell us what to do. Do you know what they are doing on Bajor right now? They are building a starship—for the Federation! Not for Bajorans. Not for our use or our commerce. First it was the Cardassians, now it's the Federation. We must expel them all."

"Is that why you stole the antimatter?" Dax asked innocently.

"Yes. It was destined for that starship. Originally, we did agree to steal the antimatter in order to stop the launch and embarrass the puppet government. But now we have both the storage pods and the tanker, and we paid for them with our blood! Why should we give them up to a bunch of money-grubbing Ferengi?"

Rizo chuckled, and Dax found it a pleasant sound. She liked the way his scowl vanished and a warmth came over his rugged features. She had to remind herself that he was cold-blooded murderer.

"I guess I'm not presenting my case very well, am

I?" he asked. "I shouldn't say I agreed to one thing and now want to renege. But we need either cash, the tanker, or a good portion of the antimatter. We can't count on Klingons and Ferengi to help us—we have to become stronger on our own. There used to be a dozen rebel enclaves, until the Federation came along and fooled most of them into laying down their arms. We have to bring them back into the fight! What we did is only temporary—we know the Federation will send more antimatter, and they'll try to claim their ship. We have to stop them. That ship was built on Bajor, and it belongs to Bajor."

As if making small talk, Dax remarked, "The Federation is pretty stubborn. How can you hope to get rid of them for good?"

Rizo's eyes narrowed as he stared down the winding corridor. "By destroying the wormhole. That's the only reason they're around. When the wormhole is gone, the Federation will follow."

A naked Ferengi woman towered over Benjamin Sisko, flaunting her voluptuous body. "What's the matter?" she sneered. "Don't you like what you see?"

Another woman had pushed Sisko onto a pillow, and a third was insistently massaging his neck—he felt he was in immediate danger of being raped. Two of the women, including the youngest one, showed little interest in him, but the other three appeared determined to have their way with him, or at least have a good laugh at his expense.

"He must like boys," said the chubby one with a snicker.

"We'll cure him of that," cooed the one massaging his neck. Her hands worked around to his chest and started downward.

"No, no, you don't understand," said Sisko, gently removing her hands. "I am a . . . a Vulcan. And we only mate during *pon farr.*"

"A Vulcan?" said the statuesque nude. "You don't look much like a Vulcan."

"Plastic surgery," said Sisko. "I didn't want to be mistaken for a Romulan."

"Gimba will be displeased," said the woman behind him.

"Why does Gimba have to know?" asked Sisko. "Let's give ourselves a short amount of time, then we'll contact him."

"I suppose so," the tall one pouted. "But it's so boring here in the Gamma Quadrant—we were hoping to have a little fun."

Gradually, Sisko was becoming accustomed to the unabashed nakedness of the Ferengi women—it reminded him of a Betazoid wedding he had once attended. As long as he could keep them talking, he decided, maybe they wouldn't try anything else.

"Why do Ferengi women always go around naked?" he asked.

The chubby gave him a toothy grin and slid her hand along her corpulent waist. "Because we have such great bodies."

"And our men like us this way," the tall one added.

"But do you like being naked?" he asked.

The voluptuous one stared at him puzzledly. "Do I like being naked? What a queer question. Do you like being clothed? Aren't clothes hot and uncomfortable?"

"Zot gave us skin. Zot didn't give us any clothes," said another.

This conversation was going nowhere, thought Sisko, and it could take a dangerous turn any minute.

He stood and started backing toward the turbolift. "I promise that, when *pon farr* overcomes me, I will seek out your ship. Will you please tell Gimba that I would like to see him now?"

"What a pity," said the chubby one. She lifted a pillow and suggestively stroked the panel underneath it. The turbolift door opened, and Sisko hurried inside, slumping against the wall.

"Take me to the bridge," he sighed.

The turbolift shook for a moment, then rumbled upward. When it stopped, the door opened, and he was greeted by a frowning Ferengi with his arms crossed.

"What's the matter?" asked Gimba. "Didn't you like my women?"

"Quite lovely," said Sisko. "And charming. It's just that I, uh, couldn't . . ."

"You like boys?" asked Gimba. "I can arrange that." He clapped his hands. "Maalo, Pixo! Come here!"

"No, no," said Sisko, "I'm content just to talk. If you're trying to buy my help, the use of your harem isn't necessary. I'm predisposed to help you, anyway."

Gimba grinned. "You are?" Then he frowned suspiciously. "Why?"

Sisko lowered his voice, as if revealing a confidence. "As I told you before, Jade and I can't go back to the Alpha Quadrant for some time. Until some trouble blows over. We would like to explore the Gamma Quadrant for a bit, but we don't have enough antimatter to get us very far. That's what attracted us to your conversation, when we heard you arguing over antimatter."

Now Gimba really grinned, and he ushered Sisko

back into the turbolift. The doors jarred shut behind them. "Deck four," he said. The turbolift dropped out from under them, sending the commander's stomach swirling.

To his relief, the doors opened onto a small lounge area that was little more than a few soft chairs, a game table, and a food slot. He could see a corridor leading off, presumabbly to the crew's quarters.

"Nobody here now," said Gimba. "Have a seat. Tell me what is on your mind."

"Just this," answered Sisko, improvising as he went along. "If we could arrange for you to get both the antimatter and the tanker, could you part with, say, four pods of antimatter? In our little craft, that would be enough for a year or two."

Gimba smiled. *"Three* pods. I can't give you any more."

Sisko shrugged. "All right. I haven't thought this plan through all the way, so if you have any suggestions, please let me know. Jade and I will work out an agreement that is very beneficial to the Bajorans. For example, you get the antimatter, and they get the tanker and a few bars of gold-pressed latinum."

"What?" growled Gimba. "That's too good!"

Sisko shook his head. "Don't worry, the deal will never happen. But it must be good enough for them to agree to it unconditionally. The whole point of this is to get one of us, probably Jade, aboard the tanker. We can say it's on the pretext of inspecting the antimatter pods before they're transferred over to you."

Sisko snapped his fingers. "Even better—to avoid any dishonesty on anyone's part, we'll say that only three people can be present when the storage pods are moved from the tanker to your ship—yourself, Rizo, and Jade. Everyone else will have to wait on the surface of the planet."

Gimba chuckled and massaged a massive earlobe. "I like that idea. Then we can just leave the Bajorans on the planet and let the insects deal with them."

After a moment's thought, the Ferengi frowned. "But how can just the three of us move all those heavy pods, even if we really aren't going to move them?"

"Don't worry," answered Sisko, "a Starfleet tanker is totally automated. The docking, the robotic conveyor belt—to do any of it you just have to press a few buttons."

Gimba narrowed his eyes. "How do you know that?"

Sisko smiled, while thinking quickly. "I worked on a Federation starbase for a while—as a chef—and I learned a great many things that have proven useful. If you have a better way to pry the antimatter away from the Bajorans, I would like to hear it."

Gimba scowled. "No, go ahead. So there will just be the three of us—me, Jade, and Rizo. Since I suppose I will have to stay on my ship, that means that Jade will have to overpower Rizo by herself. Can she do that?"

Sisko nodded. "Jade has hidden talents."

"Oooh," moaned Gimba, stroking his ear, "I would like to discover her hidden talents." He shook himself out of his reverie. "All right, then our plans are made. For three pods of antimatter, you will propose this simply terrible deal to the Bajorans. One of the conditions is that Jade and Rizo alone will be on the tanker when the pods are transferred. And we will trust Jade to do the rest."

His frown suddenly deepened as he leaned across the table toward Sisko. "You know what Ferengi do to those who cheat them, don't you? We have a sort of whip that can remove small pieces of skin, almost surgically. But without anesthesia. Those who experience this weapon always end up begging us to kill them. Of course, we might reserve other types of punishment for Jade."

"You don't have either the tanker or the antimatter now, and you don't have to give up anything. So you're not risking very much."

"I hope not," snarled the Ferengi.

An hour later, Odo listened impassively to the reports of Commander Sisko and Lieutenant Dax, as they related their adventures on the planet of Eco. Sisko's account wasn't surprising in the least—it entailed the usual obnoxious behavior of Ferengi, who would rather pursue a dishonest deal than an honest one. Odo could, however, enjoy the fact that the Ferengi had been double-crossed by their hired muscle, the Bajorans, and now they had to pursue their ill-gotten gains through the efforts of a dishonest intermediary.

Despite any illusions the others might have held, the security officer knew that he, Sisko, and Dax were little better than their quarry. Through dishonest means, they were attempting to steal back the antimatter. It bothered him, but there was no acceptable alternative. There was no law in this part of the Gamma Quadrant, at least none that recognized the Federation and its rights.

Dax's account was more troubling, because she actually seemed to enjoy the company of the terrorist, Rizo. Odo wouldn't go so far as to say that she was infatuated with him, but she could sympathize with his motives, if not his methods. As he studied the attractive Trill in her shimmering dress, he wondered if the role she was playing had affected her judgment. Perhaps, he decided, it was impossible to play the role of a femme fatale without losing a portion of common sense.

Odo had often assumed the guise of inanimate objects, small animals, and species other than his own, and he often developed an odd sort of kinship with his subject, even if it was a rat or a painting. He decided not to judge Dax too harshly until he saw how this game played out.

More chilling was their description of Elaka, a person he judged to be seriously deranged. That she was only one of a force of similar Bajorans was very troubling. He hoped that, perhaps, they could be left on the planet of Eco, never to endanger the Alpha Quadrant again.

"There you have it," Sisko concluded. He turned to Dax. "Do you think you can get Rizo and the Bajorans to accept our proposal? Essentially, we'll tell them they get to keep the tanker and a little cash, in exchange for the antimatter. But the transfer must take place with just you and Rizo aboard the tanker." He smiled at Odo. "Of course, you'll bring a handbag or a jacket with you."

The spots along Dax's hairline stretched as she frowned. "I don't know, Benjamin. They will probably accept the deal, but they're going to be very cautious. Rizo is going to expect some sort of trick."

Odo held up a slim finger. "May I make a suggestion?"

"Of course, Constable," said Sisko, leaning back in his chair at the conn station of the runabout.

"As long as we are being disgustingly dishonest," said Odo, "why should we be dishonest only on one side? Why can't the lieutenant tell the Bajorans that she is going to rig the deal for them?"

Odo continued, "The Ferengi vessel will also have only one person on board, and all the others will be on the planet. So, she could promise Rizo a chance to overpower this Gimba person and hijack their ship. They would leave the planet with two ships instead of one, all the antimatter, and whatever loot is on the Ferengi ship, which is probably considerable."

Dax asked, "What do we say we're getting out of it?"

"The same deal," answered Odo. "A few pods of antimatter to go on our merry way."

Sisko shook his head. "It's really dangerous."

The shapeshifter gazed at the ceiling. "Commander, it's debatable whether it's more dangerous to double-cross a pack of terrorists than a pack of Ferengi. Everything we are considering is dangerous, even if I disguise myself as a purse or a jacket. All it would take is either Rizo or Gimba getting to the transporter controls, and they wouldn't be alone anymore."

"Yes," mused Sisko, running his hand over his short-cropped hair, "the whole thing requires split-second timing. Maybe what we're trying to do is impossible. But what choice do we have?"

Dax took a deep breath and let it out slowly. "It's up to me," she said. "I have to convince Rizo to get me alone on that tanker."

Odo and Sisko exchanged a glance, and Odo knew they were both thinking the same thing. The way Lieutenant Dax looked in that dress, it shouldn't be difficult to get a man to want to be alone with her. Neither one was going to tell her what she could do, or ask her to do it. But she undoubtedly knew. There was also the problem of Elaka, who wouldn't take kindly to Dax making overtures to her mate, if she found out.

Sisko smiled and sounded upbeat. "But if we do this right, we'll have two people on the tanker and one here on the runabout, to cover the getaway. I don't see what can go wrong."

Suddenly, Dax leaned forward. "What was that?" she asked, peering toward the rear of the cabin.

Both Odo and Sisko swiveled their heads in the direction she was looking, but the shapeshifter couldn't see anything. "What did it look like?" he asked.

"Just something moved . . . along the floor." Dax slumped back in her chair and rubbed her eyes. "Never mind. I'm tired, and I drank a couple of ales. I'm sure it was just a shadow."

"Yes, we all need some sleep," said Sisko, rising to his feet and stretching his long arms.

"With your permission, Commander," said Odo, "I would like to go below to the planet. I haven't been there yet, and nobody has seen me. If the Ferengi or Bajorans are still there, perhaps I can overhear their conversation."

Sisko smiled. "Go ahead, Constable. If you meet anybody who's like you, I hope you have a nice reunion."

Odo would have blushed, if he were capable of doing so. He wished it weren't such an open secret that he was constantly on the lookout for others of his own species, whatever that was.

He took off his comm badge and other insignia and

put them in his pocket—at least he didn't have a Starfleet uniform to camouflage. The shapeshifter strode to the transporter platform, as Sisko leaned over the controls.

"Ready," said Odo.

"Energizing," Sisko replied.

CHAPTER
7

MAJOR KIRA sat in the conn seat of the runabout *Rio Grande* and monitored their progress. They would be reaching orbit around Bajor in about half an hour, she estimated. She glanced beside her at Amkot Groell, who was behaving exactly as she would expect a starship builder to behave—he was scrutinizing every blinking light and panel readout. He gazed up at the viewscreen to see a far-off globe that was getting larger with every passing second.

"That viewscreen is too small," he remarked.

Kira smiled. "I know. But we don't have unlimited energy in these runabouts. They're only supposed to be for short trips, you know."

"Weaponry?" he asked.

"Six small phaser emitters," she replied. "Two microtorpedoes."

"Only two?"

"Listen, Director Amkot, I didn't design these

runabouts, but I would have a hard time designing better craft for our use on the station. They have better range and speed than shuttlecraft, but they don't take up much docking space. That's important, since they're docked most of the time."

Director Amkot nodded. "Yes, I can see the utility in that. I have been very impressed with the design of the *Hannibal*. At first, I thought they were giving us a castoff when they asked us to build an Ambassador-class ship, but it's a very flexible design, very modern. The compact size of the space-time driver coil is quite amazing."

"I'm glad," said Kira wearily.

"You're not having an easy time of it, are you, Major? Tell me, has there been any word from Commander Sisko?"

Kira shook her short-bobbed head of reddish hair. "No. It's like they vanished from the universe. I sure wish they would come back."

Amkot gave her a sidelong glance. "Do you?"

"What's that supposed to mean?" Kira asked slowly.

"Nothing," replied the administrator. "I'm sure it's a shock to suddenly be without your commanding officer, but you're qualified to run the station, aren't you."

"I suppose," Kira answered doubtfully. "Don't forget, we're also missing our security chief and our science officer, and they're about as good as you can get."

The director smiled grimly. "But they are replaceable. Everybody is, including me."

Kira had been wondering how to bring up the subject of the explosions at the shipyard that had nearly killed her and Commander Sisko. Amkot's sudden burst of philosophy and personal prying gave her an opening. She seized it.

"What happened down at your shipyards?" she asked. "Who tried to kill us? And don't tell me it was aimless sabotage, that we were just standing in the wrong place at the wrong time. After what happened to the convoy, I know it was more than that. If both Commander Sisko and I had been killed, *Deep Space Nine* would have been in trouble, and the hijacking would have gone even better than it did."

Amkot brushed back his shock of white hair with a trembling hand. "You know. You recently dealt with them. They resent the Federation, even though they saved us from the Cardassians. They resent the fact that we *needed* the Federation, and they resent the fact that we need them now. They don't want peace—they want to keep fighting."

"The Circle?" asked Kira with amazement. "We stopped them cold. They're history."

The engineer shook his head. "Did you expose every sympathizer? Did you arrest every person who wants to see the Federation leave Bajor? No. They no longer have a name, but they remain—some in high places."

Kira slapped her console with frustration. "Who? Give me names!"

"If I give you names," rasped Amkot, "they will kill me. They came to me after Bajor was liberated and said, 'Amkot Groell, we know you served the Cardassians, but we are going to let you live. You kept the shipyards ready, and now we need them to build ships for Bajor.' They allowed me to build the *Hannibal* only to sharpen the skills of the workers. They told me who to hire, who to fire. They are always present."

Kira shook her head in disbelief. "Are you telling

me that you're being threatened? That someone is coercing you?"

Amkot lowered his head, and his voice was barely a whisper. "I had to agree in order to build the *Hannibal*. I had to build at least one ship before I died."

The major stared at him. "What did you agree to? You knew they were going to kill us, didn't you? You set us up! I ought to turn back to DS9 and throw you into a cell!"

The little man nodded. "You could do that, Major. At least I would be safe, but the *Hannibal* would never be finished. I'm not proud of what I've done—for thirty years I have not been proud of what I've done. I had to convince the Cardassians I was running a museum, a relic of the past. Now I have to convince the Federation I'm operating on their behalf, the government on their behalf, the underground on their behalf. I've been pulled in so many different directions, I don't know what I believe in anymore!"

His chin quivered, but he said forcefully, "I am proud of one thing—the *Hannibal*. That's *my* ship. My only wish is to live to see it fly."

Kira chewed at her lower lip, but she could think of only one thing to say. "After the *Hannibal* is launched, will you tell me who threatened you?"

The little white-haired man nodded; then he went back to studying the instruments. They spoke no more during the last leg of the trip to Bajor.

Odo stepped out of the receiving room, still marveling at the efficiency of the hive mind of the Ecocids. Of course, he had no weapons to surrender—he never carried a phaser. To him, life was too precious to risk ending it so abruptly, and he didn't trust electronic devices all that much. He looked at the array of brightly colored stripes lining the wall. From the accounts of Sisko and Dax, he knew that blue led to a restaurant, cyan to the Redemption Center, and yellow to the conference rooms. He chose to follow the red stripe, even though red signified danger in most cultures.

Odo spotted several Ecocids scurrying along the vents over his head, and he slowed his stride to walk beside them. Picking a few specimens from the black stream, he studied the small creatures. How did they communicate? he wondered. Pheromones? Low-level electric current? Sound? Touch? Or all of the above? When he rounded a corner, he noticed that the Ecocids were headed in the same direction he was, following the red line. Odo cocked his head and strode along beside them.

He passed another of the ubiquitous interface terminals, and he almost stopped to talk to the hive mind. He knew exactly what he would ask it—were there any other shapeshifters like him in Hive Three? But something in Odo's nature—a desire for privacy, an innate distrust—prevented him from revealing himself to the collective consciousness. Odo might not have known anything about his race or his origins, but he knew himself and his outlook on the universe: He was honest, and everyone else wasn't. Even his closest associates were never free from suspicion.

The black insects looked benign, but according to Commander Sisko, the hive mind was capable of lying. That was enough in his book to justify further observation.

After several twists and turns and considerable walking, he noticed that the corridor was getting narrower. The red stripe was now the only one on the

wall, and the number of Ecocids had increased expo-
nentially with each corridor that emptied into this
one. They now swarmed all over the walls and floor,
and Odo had to tread carefully to avoid stepping on
them. He wasn't sure why he was following the
Ecocids except that, subconsciously, he had chosen
this route, and he wanted to see where the red stripe
led.

Before he and the Ecocids reached their destination, a small hairy humanoid came ambling toward
him from the other direction, carrying a pail and a
mop. He looked suspiciously at Odo as they passed
each other, but he said nothing. The shapeshifter
assumed that this was one of the servants that Sisko
and Dax had reported seeing. His presence explained
why the red stripe extended down a corridor that was
apparently used only by Ecocids.

After another tributary emptied its six-legged traffic
into the main corridor, the insects were swarming
over the floor, walls, and ceiling. Odo inched along
without picking up his feet. A pungent odor rose all
around him, and he could hear the scurrying of a
billion little legs, and the flapping of a million tiny
wings. Thus far, the Ecocids hadn't seemed to mind
his presence, but he wondered what would happen if
he stepped on a few of them. He only wondered—he
wasn't about to find out.

He had to crouch down as the corridor lowered in
height as well as narrowed in width, but he could
finally see the end. Unfortunately, he had to stop
before he got there for fear of killing dozens of
Ecocids with each step. Ahead of him, a monstrous
hump of insects were swarming over something, and
he thought about the servant with the mop and pail.

At the end of the corridor, he saw a number of unevenly spaced holes, each about as big as his fist. They were black with insects crawling in and out.

The screeching of their tiny legs was becoming annoying. Then he heard the synthesized voice, which seemed to come from the vents over his head. The vents, too, were clogged with Ecocids.

"Warning," said the voice, "visitors are not permitted in the inner hive. Warning, please turn back. Warning, we cannot be responsible for your safety if you continue."

Odo didn't need to be told twice. He turned slowly, taking one last look over his shoulder at the mysterious lump of something at the end of the red-lined corridor.

Major Kira surveyed the room and swallowed hard. From their accusatory expressions, the gathering of Bajoran dignitaries looked more like a lynch mob than a casual fact-finding committee. Plus, she couldn't get the troubling words of Amkot Groell out of her mind. How many of these people were plotting to overthrow the provisional government, which was already shaky enough?

She recognized Roser Issa, Minister of Public Works, to whom Amkot Groell reported; Minister of Commerce Tanar Maya; Minister of the Interior Wistod Emen; council members Kawa Lerdo and Tagen Nico; and two members of the assembly, whom she didn't know by name but recognized by their robes. There was even a red-robed vedek, one of the Bajoran religious leaders. The only thing missing was a judge and a rope with a noose in it.

Minister Roser sighed contemptuously. "When I

last saw you, Major, you and your commander assured me that the antimatter would be transferred to the shipyards without incident."

"We thought it would," agreed Kira.

"Yet it was stolen right from under your noses."

"Not exactly," answered Kira. "It was stolen at a distance from the station of almost twenty thousand kilometers, too great for us to do anything about it. We sent out runabouts as quickly as we could. In fact, one of them is still out, pursuing the hijacked tanker."

Minister Wistod frowned. "I thought the Federation was supposed to be prepared for eventualities like this."

Kira replied. "The cruiser escorts were attacked at point-blank range by two Klingon warships, which entered the area cloaked. We tried to warn the convoy, but our communications were jammed. Under the circumstances, the best the cruisers could do was to drive off the Klingons."

"You mean, they let the Klingons escape," said Tagen Nico. "And they let the tanker be boarded. From your report, I understand that the tanker lowered her shields, knowing she would be boarded."

"If she hadn't," said Kira, "I probably wouldn't be standing here, and Bajor would have a new moon—of space rubble. They were firing on the tanker, and she had no choice. At least that's what the Federation captain decided."

"Do you agree with that decision?" asked Tagen.

"I . . ." Kira hesitated. "I'm second-in-command of *Deep Space Nine,* not the captain of a Starfleet tanker. I don't think it does us any good to second-guess what has already happened."

Tagen turned to his fellow council member. "I

warned you that we couldn't depend upon the Federation. We need our own capability for making antimatter, and we need to be building our own starships!"

There was mumbled agreement with that sentiment, and Roser Issa declared, "I told Commander Sisko as much when I last saw him."

Kira took a deep breath and had to shout over the officials to be heard. "Listen to me!" They blinked at her and fell silent. "You sit around in your soft chairs and decide this and that and the other, but it's people like me, Amkot Groell, and, yes, Commander Sisko who have to make things happen. Commander Sisko, my own security chief, and another Starfleet officer are in the Gamma Quadrant right now, risking their lives to retrieve that antimatter."

She bowed her head and lowered her voice. "If Bajor had the capability to build her own ships and generate her own antimatter, we would be doing so, instead of just talking about it. But we don't. Bajor is a poor cripple at the moment, and we've got to depend on somebody else to pick us up and get us back on our feet. I don't like it any better than any of you. So, if you can make antimatter and starships, go ahead and make them. If you can't, let the people who can do it."

Tagen Nico narrowed his eyes at the young major. "You are very impertinent."

Kira nodded. "Yes, I am. Every day, I deal with hundreds of races from all over the galaxy, all making demands on me. I was probably impertinent before I took this job, and now I'm worse. If you want to replace me, go ahead." She glanced at Amkot Groell, who was sitting in the far corner of the room. He smiled encouragingly.

"So," Kira continued, "we screwed up this time. The Federation also screwed up, and I'm sorry that some of you thought they were perfect." There were chuckles, and Tagen Nico cleared his throat. "But the Federation is giving us a chance to build something, something of value. No, we won't be able to keep the ship we're building, but we'll sell it for badly needed credits. We aren't taking charity on this job—we're earning it."

One of the assembly members suddenly lifted a robed arm and pointed it in Kira's direction. "That ship is an abomination, nothing more and nothing less! We should not be building weapons of destruction for the Federation, which they could use against us. That ship is a symbol of our oppression."

Kira bowed slightly. "I'm sorry you feel that way, sir. I respect your opinion, but I don't happen to agree."

The din of another argument ensued, and it didn't end until the Minister of Commerce, Tanar Maya, declared in no uncertain terms, "The government has chosen this course, and we all know it! If we don't fulfill our obligation to build this ship, no one—not the Federation or our own people—will trust us. We must see it through, no matter what doubts we have."

The older man turned to Kira and granted her a warm smile. "I want to thank Major Kira for coming here. I'm afraid we didn't make it very easy for her. I just have one more question for the major."

"Yes?" she asked.

"Assuming the first shipment of antimatter is not recovered, when can we expect another one?"

Kira shook her head. "I don't know. My next duty is to contact Starfleet Command. I've sent them a brief report, but I haven't talked to them face-to-face. I'm not looking forward to it either."

She half-expected one of the gathered dignitaries to

offer to smooth the way with Starfleet, to offer to contact them first. But most of them looked away and began murmured conversations with each other. Nope, she thought, these people were not going to do anything but talk. Even the ones who wanted her dead weren't worth worrying about. In this life, there were people who demanded that things be done and people who actually did them, and they were seldom the same people. Kira turned on her heel and marched out.

Miles O'Brien wrinkled his ruddy face into a frown and lowered his computer padd. Dr. Bashir had warned him about Captain Jon Rachman, but he couldn't imagine that a young Starfleet officer could be so obtuse and annoying. Well, he could imagine it—Bashir was sometimes annoying—but not as bad as this pup, who kept peering over his shoulder, complaining.

"Chief O'Brien," snapped the young captain, "when can the *Regal* return to service? I must demand that you give me a timetable."

"A timetable?" growled O'Brien. "Your flux generators are fried, the inertial dampers are destroyed, and the driver coil assembly is smashed! If you want to take a leisurely cruise around this solar system at half-impulse power, you can take her out now. And I'll see you in a few years."

Captain Rachman stiffened to angry attention. "Chief O'Brien, your attitude is not acceptable. All of these are simple repairs."

O'Brien clenched his fists, trying to control his Irish temper. "None of these are simple repairs, Captain, but they would be possible—if this were a starbase.

This is a Bajoran space station built by Cardassians. We don't have the parts we need, and we don't have the plans to build them. As far as qualified engineers —you're lookin' at him."

"What about replicators?"

O'Brien chuckled. "Cardassian replicators? They won't even make a decent hot-fudge sundae."

When he saw the crestfallen look on the young captain's face, O'Brien tried to hit a conciliatory tone. "Listen, Captain, I know you want to get after those crooks, and I would love to send you off with a hearty 'Hail Mary.' But I can't. This cruiser is in bad shape, and the *Valor* is worse. You put up quite a fight out there against bigger ships, after an ambush, but you have to accept reality. You're in dry-dock, and you're going to stay that way until we get the right parts from Starfleet."

Captain Jon Rachman slammed a fist into his palm. The handsome dark-haired officer looked as if he was about to take O'Brien's head off again. Or cry. The chief couldn't tell which.

"When will you request the parts?" Rachman asked.

"That's what I'm doing," answered O'Brien, "trying to find out what we need."

Their attention was diverted by a short woman with reddish hair who strode through the bridge of the *Regal* as if she owned it. Captain Rachman saw her distinctive tan-and-rust uniform and instantly got huffy.

"Excuse me," he said, "only Starfleet personnel are allowed on board."

"Is that right?" asked Major Kira. She turned to O'Brien. "I've got to talk to you, Chief."

"You must leave now," insisted Rachman.

"Belay that, Captain," snapped O'Brien. "This is the acting commander of the station, Major Kira."

"I don't care who she is," said Rachman. "She's Bajoran, she's not part of Starfleet, and she has to leave."

Kira whirled around to face the young captain. "I have had enough problems for one day. Maybe you would like it if I pulled Chief O'Brien off this detail and sent him to fix the airlocks on level six."

O'Brien grinned. "Sounds good to me." He shut off his padd. "I'll get right on it, Major."

"Wait, wait," said Rachman. "She can do that? She's your commanding officer?"

O'Brien nodded. "She's second-in-command normally, and she's in charge when Commander Sisko is away. This station is under joint administration."

Kira smiled pleasantly at the young man. "Where are you from?"

"Uh, Kansas."

"I believe there's an old Terran saying—you're not in Kansas anymore."

Rachman swallowed. "I'm beginning to realize that." He came to attention. "I am Captain Jon Rachman of the cruiser *Regal.*"

"Okay, Captain Rachman," said the major, "if you'd like to be useful, I've got a report to make to Starfleet, and you and Chief O'Brien can help me. I've got an Admiral Nichea waiting on subspace."

"Admiral Nicheyev," said the officer with awe.

"Do you know her?" asked Kira.

"Only by reputation."

O'Brien cleared his throat and added, "Admiral Nicheyev has a reputation for being rather tough."

Kira smiled. "So do I." She tapped her comm badge. "Kira to Ops."

"Yes, sir?" came a voice.

"Wait one moment," said Kira. She turned to O'Brien. "Is their viewscreen working?"

"That's about the only thing that is," the chief muttered.

"Ops," said Kira, "patch my communication with Admiral Nicheyev down to the *Regal* in docking bay four."

"Yes, sir. Routing communication."

The image of a spare middle-aged woman appeared overhead on the viewscreen. She did not appear happy.

"I am not accustomed to being kept waiting," said Admiral Nicheyev.

"I apologize," answered Kira. "I thought you would also like to discuss this matter with two of your officers—our chief of operations, Miles O'Brien, and Captain Jon Rachman of the *Regal,* one of the cruisers in the convoy."

"Where is Commander Sisko?"

O'Brien glanced at Kira, wondering how she would answer that question. The major calmly replied, "He is in pursuit of the hijackers who stole the shipment of antimatter."

"Is he on the other cruiser?"

"Negative," answered Kira. "Both cruisers are badly damaged. He is pursuing them in a runabout." Before the rigid admiral could ask more questions, Kira gave her a concise recounting of the events: the cloaked Klingon ships, the jammed communications, the pitched battle, and the insane attack on the tanker that resulted in it being boarded and captured. She ended with the tanker and the runabout vanishing into the wormhole, which was undoubtedly not the end of the story, but it was all she knew.

Admiral Nicheyev looked even less pleased than before, and O'Brien was glad this wasn't a face-to-face meeting. A second later, he was glad he wasn't one of the cruiser captains either.

"Captain Rachman," spit the admiral, "I know it isn't mandatory to come out of warp drive with shields up, but you were briefed on the history of Bajor. You know this is the farthest extension of Federation influence in this sector. A bit of caution would have been prudent."

The young captain stood at attention and framed his response carefully. "Begging your pardon, Admiral, but we had been traveling at warp speed for eighteen hours. I admit, we were relieved to be ending our journey—with a tanker full of antimatter—and that might have made us careless. Although I do not believe we were unduly careless. Plus, our orders cautioned us to avoid the wormhole more than renegade Klingons."

Admiral Nicheyev didn't look convinced, and O'Brien found himself bailing the young man out. "Excuse me, Admiral," he said, "all of us were stunned by the attack. But Captain Rachman and Captain Perez on the *Valor* did everything they could do. Commander Sisko took off in the runabout as soon as the attack started. When the Klingons opened fire on the tanker, we were all holding our breath. If the tanker hadn't lowered her shields, we would've lost all three ships, plus Commander Sisko and the runabout. And quite possibly the station."

The admiral's pinched face pulled tighter. "And

what did Commander Sisko think he could do in a runabout against two Klingons warships?"

"Anything he could," answered O'Brien. "He took Lieutenant Dax and our security chief with him."

Admiral Nicheyev looked thoughtful for a moment; then her shoulders slumped a bit. "All right," she conceded, "we may have failed to consider the volatility of the situation near Bajor. Major Kira, what is the status of the *Hannibal?* Is she safe?"

"Yes, Admiral," answered Kira. "We could start test flights as soon as we have more antimatter. Nobody in the shakedown crew was injured. In fact, our government is very interested in finding out when another shipment will arrive."

The admiral shook her head. "After this, we can't send just two cruisers as escort with the next shipment. We'll need to pull in some larger ships, and that may take a couple of days."

"Pardon me, Admiral," said O'Brien, "we also need a lot of parts for the two cruisers. I can send you a requisition."

"Send it to my attention," answered the admiral. "I'll ship the parts with the antimatter. I estimate that all of this will take about five days."

"Five days?" said Captain Rachman, shocked. "Begging your pardon, Admiral, but we've already lost two days. We need to get our cruisers operational, so we can go into the wormhole and chase down those hijackers."

Admiral Nicheyev's pale eyes grew steely cold again. "Captain Rachman, under no circumstances are you to proceed into the wormhole to pursue anyone. We know almost nothing about the Gamma Quadrant, and we have no idea what happened to the runabout or the tanker. Do we?"

"No, sir," answered Rachman with a hard swallow.

"Then we must assume that both craft are lost," the admiral concluded. "That is a hard thing to accept, I know, but we can't sit around waiting for a miracle to occur. By the time a second shipment of antimatter reaches you, a week will have passed. To be on the safe side, we will also send along replacements for Commander Sisko and Lieutenant Dax. At the moment, I have no idea who they will be."

The admiral took a deep breath. "Chief O'Brien, I will be looking for the parts requisition. Captain Rachman, I will expect a full report from both you and Captain Perez. Major Kira, I can't issue you any orders, but I would hope that you wouldn't endanger anyone by sending them into the wormhole after Commander Sisko and his crew. Perhaps they will return, perhaps not. But their fate is out of our hands."

Her lips tightened. "Keep me informed. This is Admiral Nicheyev—out."

The admiral's stern visage blinked off the viewscreen to be replaced by the distinctive oval insignia of Starfleet outlined against a light blue background.

O'Brien flicked off the screen and scowled. "Well, that was a cheery conversation, wasn't it?"

"Yeah," muttered Kira. "I guess she has to think that way."

Seeing their downcast expressions, Captain Rachman said, "I'm sorry. Here I am, worrying about looking bad and getting my ship flying again, and you've lost your commanding officer and two people from your staff. I'm afraid I've been behaving like a total ass."

"Apologies accepted," replied O'Brien. "I know it's

not fun to get your ship shot up. I'll do what I can for you right now, but you'll have to wait five days for the major repairs."

"Understood," said Captain Rachman. "Is there anything *I* can do for *you?*" He looked from O'Brien to Kira.

Kira nodded, and O'Brien could tell that she was barely in control of her emotions. "You can come with me," she said, "and meet Commander Sisko's son. I have to tell him about his dad's replacement before I tell anybody else. If you come with me . . . I don't know, maybe he would enjoy seeing somebody from Kansas."

"I'll do what I can," Jon Rachman promised.

Major Kira had lost all track of time in the unpleasant events of the day. She hadn't realized until she asked the computer where Jake Sisko was that the boy would be in the quarters he shared with his father, getting ready for bed. She also wasn't surprised to find Nog there with him. In troubled times, a good friend was worth his weight in gold-pressed latinum, even if he was a Ferengi. She and Jon Rachman entered the small apartment, and she put on her bravest smile.

"Hello, Jake. Nog," she said to the boys. "I'd like to introduce a guest to you, Captain Jon Rachman of the Starfleet cruiser *Regal.* He's from Kansas."

"Hello," Jake said noncommittally.

"Hi, Captain," said Nog, jumping to his feet. "Wow, that was some battle you had out there! We watched the visual log."

Rachman blinked in surprise. "I didn't know it would be used for entertainment."

The Ferengi boy looked embarrassed. "Well, my uncle has, you know, access . . ."

"To just about anything he wants," Kira completed the sentence. "That's all right. It's not a secret what happened."

"Any word about my dad?" asked Jake.

Kira shook her head. "I'm afraid not. They could pop through the wormhole any minute. We're keeping an eye out for them."

Nog was still excited about the battle. "That was neat the way that one crusier pretended to be dead. Was that you?"

"No," answered Rachman, "we went into warp drive, hoping they would think we were running. Then we warped back in and got off a couple good volleys."

"You sure did!" gushed Nog. "It was neat, wasn't it, Jake?"

The boy nodded and hugged his robe around his scrawny body. Kira could tell that Jake was trying mightily to think of something else—and Nog was doing everything he could to distract his friend—but it wasn't working. His dad was missing, in pursuit of dangerous criminals. There wasn't anything that anybody could say that would change that. And now she had to give him the only news she had—bad news— that Starfleet was sending a replacement for his father.

"Nog," she said, "do you think we could talk to Jake alone for a moment? It's getting pretty late, and you should be getting to bed, too."

The Ferengi boy looked at his friend as if it would take the Grand Nagus to order him away.

"Go ahead," said Jake. "I'll be okay."

"I'll meet you for breakfast," Nog promised, as he headed for the door. "Nice to meet you, Captain Rachman!"

"You too," Rachman answered.

For his young age, Jake Sisko has been around a lot, thought Kira. He had watched his mother die in a Borg attack. He had been shunted with his father from one assignment to another, like an old suitcase, ending up in what might be the weirdest post in all of Starfleet. Yet he had made the best of things, forming at least one true friendship on DS9. Jake was young, but he was no fool.

"Something has happened," he said. "What is it?"

"Really nothing," answered Kira, sitting beside him. "We had to contact Starfleet to ask them for parts to repair the cruisers, plus more antimatter for the shipyard. They thought it would be a good idea, since they would be sending another convoy anyway, to send an acting commander for the station."

Jake's eyes widened with horror. "They're replacing my dad?"

"It's just a precaution," said Kira.

"That's crap!" shouted Jake, fighting back tears.

Kira looked helplessly at Jon Rachman, and the young captain knelt in front of the boy. "It is crap," he agreed. "But your dad has an important job, and Starfleet can't leave it vacant . . . while he's away. I don't know your dad, but I know he risked his life to save ours. And I know that wherever he is, whatever he's doing, he's trying to make a difference."

The captain shook his head. "Hey, I didn't realize until I got here what a tough job you people have on *Deep Space Nine.* I used to think escorting antimatter tankers was hard duty, but it's nothing compared to being out here."

Rachman held Jake's hands. "I'm too young to have a boy your age, but if I ever do, I hope he's as brave as you are. You've got to have faith in your dad, because you know he wants to get back here just as badly as you want him back. Say, what do you know about the Wild West?"

Jake rubbed the tears from his eyes. "Wild West?"

"Yeah, the cowboy period of Earth's history," said Rachman. "I had an ancestor who was a marshal in the Kansas territory days. He often had to go out and chase down outlaws for weeks, or months, at a time. I guess his family worried about him an awful lot, but he always came back. He died an old man at the age of seventy-nine. That was old back in the nineteenth century."

"They didn't know where he was?" asked Jake.

Rachman chuckled. "Naw, the prairie was nothing but wilderness back then, full of Indians and outlaws. You must have a library here—I bet we could read about it. I think it will remind you a lot of life on *Deep Space Nine*."

Jake nodded, and his face crept into a smile. "I'd like that."

Kira looked gratefully at the young captain, and she, too, wished that he would have a boy like Jake someday.

"Major Kira," said Captain Rachman, "I don't have any quarters assigned to me yet. Do you think I could bunk here with Jake?" He turned to the boy. "If that's all right with you?"

Jake nodded eagerly. "Sure."

Kira rose to her feet. "If it's okay with both of you, it's okay with me. Jake can show you around the station." She started toward the door and stopped, trying to think of something else to say.

Jake seemed to sense her discomfort. "Good night, Major Kira," he said. "Thanks for telling me in person."

The Bajoran nodded. "I'm looking forward to telling Starfleet not to bother sending anyone. Good night."

Kira strode out the door, and it clanged shut behind her. She gazed down a vast corridor, empty except for a few visitors, who shuffled along on their tentacles. This amazing amalgam known as *Deep Space Nine* was under her command, she mused, at least temporarily. It was odd how much it had changed since the oppressive reign of the Cardassians, all for the better. How much of that change was dependent upon the quiet leadership of Benjamin Sisko she didn't know, but she suspected it was considerable.

If only she could get some idea what was going on. Snooping around was a job usually performed by Odo, but he was also missing in action. Reluctantly, Kira decided that it was time to pay another visit to Quark's Place.

CHAPTER
8

BENJAMIN SISKO sat at the conn station of the runabout and watched white clouds creep across the lime green surface of the planet of Eco. He would have preferred to see the more familiar sphere of Bajor below him, even with its pretty chieftains and strange dichotomies. He would even have liked to see the cold grayness of *Deep Space Nine,* with its faulty circuitry and never-ending parade of life-forms. Most of all, he would like to see Jake, and he hoped the boy was holding up under the uncertainty of his absence.

Could it be that he was homesick? Sisko had never considered DS9 much more than a way station in his career, a place to hang his hat between more conventional assignments. Though, he had to admit, it had turned into much more than that. He supposed it was the challenge of the job that appealed to him—never knowing what the day would bring. Unfortunately, with challenge came frustration, and he bridled at all

134

the miracles he couldn't pull off, such as bringing rebels like Rizo back into the community and resolving questions about the mysterious beings who had constructed the wormhole. The job was fraught with peril, as his present circumstances demonstrated.

Thinking about his son and his unlikely home made the commander wonder if they could pull off this ridiculous heist. Because that's what they were doing, trying to outfox the foxes. He hadn't seen much of the Ferengi Marauder in his mercifully short visit there, but he had seen enough to know that it could blow the runabout to pieces without working up a sweat. It could also chase the runabout down in the blink of an eyelash. He would like to think that help was on its way, but he doubted it. Antimatter was rare, but it wasn't rare enough for Starfleet to risk any more ships. They were on their own, and the slightest slipup would mean that they would never see DS9 again. Or Jake either.

"Are you all right?" asked a concerned voice, and he looked up to see Dax. He was relieved to see that she had changed back into her uniform, although it was still stripped of Starfleet insignia.

"Oh, just thinking," he said. "I didn't hear Odo come back. Is he still resting?"

Dax slipped into the Ops seat beside him. "I beamed him aboard a few hours ago. He should be getting up soon."

Sisko smiled, thinking that "resting" and "getting up" were interesting euphemisms for what Odo did when he reverted to and from a liquid state.

He sighed. "Old man, are we crazy? Do we have a chance of pulling this off? Or should we just get the hell out of here?"

Dax paused in thought, then chuckled. "It's funny. I

was going to say, 'When we were younger, we wouldn't have thought twice about stealing back the tanker.' Then I realized that I *am* younger than when we used to do a lot of crazy things. But we're both still here. The question is, Benjamin, do you feel lucky? The only thing we have on our side is their greed."

"It's up to you," answered Sisko. "You have the hardest job—convincing the terrorists to let you aboard the tanker. If you think there's any danger, you have my permission to call it off."

Dax shrugged. "We knew there was danger forty-eight hours ago, when we came after them. That hasn't changed. But what they did hasn't changed either. If they had done this to Klingons or Cardassians, they'd have a death sentence on their heads. I don't know, but I think they ought to be punished, even if it's just making sure they don't get anything out of it."

"All right," said Sisko, "you've answered my question. But you're the one who has to spend time with Rizo and his playmates—you tell us when to cut our losses and run."

Dax nodded somberly. "I will."

They heard soft footsteps behind them, and a chipper-looking Odo walked into the cockpit area. "Good morning," he said with a polite bow of his head.

"Good morning," answered Sisko. "What did you think about the planet of Eco?"

Odo sniffed. "If Quark ever asks me where he should go on vacation, I now know what to tell him."

"Did you find out anything we should know?" asked Dax.

"I found the Ecocids' entrance to the inner hive," answered the shapeshifter. "But I don't think it's a place a humanoid would want to venture. Then I stationed myself in a public place and observed the patrons for some time. They are engaged in buying and selling commodities at a rapid pace, but since they never actually see or possess the commodities, it's little more than a glorified game of chance. I'll be happy when we leave here."

"Won't we all," said Dax. She checked the ship's chronometer. "It's time to be going, Benjamin. I told the Bajorans we would meet them at eight hundred hours. Hopefully, the Ferengi won't be awake at such an early hour."

The commander stood and stretched his long arms. "At least we can get some coffee in the conference room. Hold down the fort, Constable."

"Don't I always?" asked Odo, taking a vacated chair.

"And keep the shields up," Sisko added as he strode to the transporter platform, with Dax close behind.

Odo swiveled in his chair to face the commander. "Be careful," he cautioned. "When I left, the price of antimatter was going up."

Sisko nodded and tried to smile, but he didn't feel very cheerful this morning. He had a bad feeling about something, but he couldn't tell what it was. Thus far, both sides had believed his and Dax's story and trusted them, as far as they trusted anyone. Their plan was indeed risky, but it entailed only one crucial element—getting Dax and a large Odo/handbag alone with Rizo aboard the hijacked tanker. The Ferengi would cooperate—they were in no position not to.

Nevertheless, Sisko couldn't help but to feel that he was overlooking something. A detail, an unnecessary risk. Probably, he decided, it was just his impatience and frustration that was spooking him. If they focused on what they had to do, they would soon get out of here.

"Energize," he told Odo.

Dax and Sisko materialized inside the now familiar conference room, and Dax wasn't surprised to find they were the first to arrive. While she walked to the door and peered out into an empty lounge, Sisko strode immediately toward the food slot.

"The usual," he ordered. At once, the alien food slot produced a steaming cup of java, and Sisko looked very satisfied as he picked up the cup and sniffed its aroma.

After his initial sip, he remarked, "I wonder how many bilbok one of these food replicators costs? It sure makes better coffee than anything we've got . . . you know where."

"I'll take your word for it," Dax replied. "Benjamin, I think we should have a code phrase for when there's trouble but we can't come out and say it. Something innocuous."

"All right," agreed Sisko, pausing thoughtfully between sips. "Just say, 'I drank too much coffee.'"

Dax nodded and began to pace. The Trill prided herself on remaining calm in any situation, but the next step of their con game was like playing a game of Dabo in Quark's Place. Every roll of the dice brought a new set of probabilities, unrelated to the probabilities of the previous roll. Just because you had won once didn't mean you would continue winning. Likewise, every lie they told the terrorists resulted in a new set of probabilities; just because they had believed the last lie didn't mean they would believe the new one. As Benjamin had said, it was up to her to know when to quit and head for the exit, and she would have to make that decision in a split second.

The door slid open, and Rizo filled it. She was amazed to see that the big Bajoran had cleaned himself up and had even shaved. She wouldn't say the clothes he was wearing were exactly clean, but they weren't stained with grease and blood. They weren't leather either, but a coarse handwoven fabric. He smiled at her and swaggered into the room. There was only one companion with him, and Dax was very relieved to see that it wasn't Elaka. It was the other female she had met, Petra.

"Good morning," Sisko said cheerfully. "Coffee?"

"Still no ale?" grumbled Rizo. At once, the food slot produced a mug of brownish ale. "Ah, that's more like it," the Bajoran said, grinning.

"Hello," said Petra, standing meekly by the door. She was carrying one of the computer padds from the tanker. Another piece of loot, thought Dax. They had grown accustomed to having that tanker and the wonders it contained, and they might be receptive to an idea that would let them keep it.

"You're keeping notes," she said to Petra. "Very wise. But some of what we're going to say shouldn't leave this room."

"Oh, yeah?" said Rizo, slamming his glass of ale on the table. "Why not?"

Dax looked at Sisko, wondering if he wanted to take the lead. He nodded to her in encouragement and stepped toward the door. "I want to keep an eye out for our Ferengi friends," he explained.

Rizo yanked back a chair and dropped his muscular body into it. "What's going on?" he asked. "Have the Ferengi made an offer?"

"Yes," said Dax, "and a very good one." She smiled

slyly and sat on the edge of the table, draping her long legs in Rizo's direction. "But you can do better yet."

"Oh, yeah? Tell me about it." He leaned forward, his dark eyes making a leisurely excursion up Dax's legs and torso to her lovely face.

Dax began, "They've offered to let you keep the tanker if you turn over the antimatter pods. Plus, they'll give you ten bars of gold-pressed latinum."

Rizo nodded, clearly impressed. "That will keep us in food and drink for a while, plus we'll have a place to call home. But this is too good—there's got to be some kind of catch."

"There is," Dax conceded. "They don't trust you."

The Bajoran roared with laughter. "Of course they don't! They've been dealing with too many other Ferengi—they don't trust anybody."

"They want some safeguards to guarantee the transfer of the antimatter," Dax continued. "They know the tanker operations are entirely automated, so they want to make sure there's only one of you aboard the tanker when the transfer takes place."

Rizo took a swig of ale and slammed down his mug. "Unacceptable."

"However," said Dax, "there will also be only one Ferengi aboard their vessel. And I'll be there, as an impartial observer, to keep you both honest."

The Bajoran looked thoughtful. "You mean, their whole crew will beam down here?"

"That's right," said the Trill with a sly smile. She turned to Petra. "Will you please stop recording what I say now?"

The young Bajoran looked at Rizo, and he nodded his approval. "Then what?"

Dax whispered, "Then you can take over their ship.

You can leave this planet with a fleet—a tanker full of antimatter and a Ferengi Marauder. There isn't much you can't bring down with that Marauder."

Rizo leaned back in his chair, a smile spreading across his face. He finally asked, "Why would you help us do this?"

Dax stood and walked slowly around the table, being sure to jiggle everything she had to jiggle. "We actually want more out of this than just a couple bars of gold-pressed latinum, but we know the Ferengi won't give it to us. We want enough antimatter to stay on this side of the wormhole for a good long time. We're in no hurry to go back."

"Ah," said Rizo with dawning comprehension. "You're crooked, too."

This was the crucial moment, Dax felt. Maybe they had been wrong to forsake the pretense of being honest arbitrators. But her mouth had no tractor beam that could take back words once spoken. What could she possibly say that would clinch this unholy deal? What would turn the probabilities of him believing her in her favor?

"You didn't think we were space cadets, did you?" she scoffed. "We have a chance of robbing a bunch of bloodsucking Ferengi of a whole ship and everything it contains. I can't tell you how many times they've cheated Marcus and me. Let's just say, we want to come out on the winning end this time."

Rizo nodded and scratched his clean-shaven chin, as if he hadn't felt bare skin there in many Bajoran moons. He looked at Sisko, apparently judging the human; then his gaze returned to Dax. His heavy-browed eyes roamed down her slim body, and she felt both his distrust and his lust.

He turned to Petra and said, "Go back to the ship. You can read them the terms offered by the Ferengi, but don't tell anyone about this other part. Let's keep that secret for the time being."

The young woman looked frightened at the prospect of keeping a secret from her comrades. "But why?" she asked with alarm.

"Because I say so!" he roared. Then Rizo took a deep breath and relaxed. "There are two reasons. One, I haven't decided to do it yet. And two, the fewer people who know about it, the better." He smiled at Dax. "I think Jade understands that."

Sisko asked pleasantly, "Why wouldn't you want to do it?"

Rizo gave the human an annoyed glance. "It's awfully hard to hide a Ferengi Marauder. And if I know the Ferengi, they'll have every bounty hunter in the quadrant after us. That includes our Klingon friends and probably the Cardassians as well. Still, it might be worth it."

He looked pointedly at Dax. "Mainly, I still don't know if I can trust you."

The Trill shrugged. "We're not the ones you should worry about. If you don't capture the Ferengi ship, or at least disable it, they can come after you any time they feel like it. Remember, once the antimatter is off that tanker, it becomes just another target."

The ridges on the bridge of the Bajoran's nose compressed in thought, until Petra came up and put her arms around him.

"Don't worry, Father, you'll make the right decision," she assured him.

Dax and Sisko exchanged a glance, and Dax found herself horrified at the thought that Petra could be

Rizo's daughter. How could somebody turn an impressionable child into a criminal, living hand-to-mouth, hunted by half the galaxy? The young woman's age had been troubling before, and now it was doubly so. Dax wondered whether Elaka could be Petra's mother, but she decided that was impossible. At the most, Elaka was only ten years older than Petra.

Rizo patted his daughter's arm. "Go on back. Just tell them what the Ferengi have offered us, and take a poll to see if we should accept it. I'll be along soon."

Petra nodded and stole a worried look at Dax before she touched her comm badge. "One to beam back," she said.

The young Bajoran disappeared in the swirl of a transporter beam. What was next? wondered Dax.

Rizo drained his mug of ale and banged the glass on the amber table. "I don't much like humans," he remarked, wiping the suds from his upper lip, "but they have a saying which I have to agree with: 'There is no honor among thieves.'"

"But you're not a thief," said Sisko.

"Don't flatter me," snarled Rizo. "You know damn well what I am, and now I know what you are. You, me, the Ferengi—we're all the same." He took a deep breath. "Maybe I should just take that tanker and fly the hell away from here."

He looked thoughtfully at Dax, and for the first time she spotted some concern—and fear—in his hooded eyes. "I'd like to do what you two are doing," he said, "just escape from it all and explore a quadrant where nobody knows me and I don't know anybody. But I've got too many people who still believe in me. Too many people who still have some honor."

Then he snorted a laugh. "I used to have honor, but

after some of the things I've had to do—" He swallowed hard and barked at the food slot, "Give me another ale!"

After the food slot had produced a second mug of brown suds, Sisko fetched it for Rizo and set it in front of him. The Bajoran smiled lazily at him. "Marcus, haven't you got someplace to go?"

Sisko looked at Dax, and his eyes bespoke his fears. But the Trill was a few hundred years old, and she knew what she was doing—she hoped.

"It's okay, Marcus," she said. "Why don't you find our Ferengi friends and tell them that the Bajorans are considering their offer."

"All right," answered Sisko without much enthusiasm. "Just let me get another cup of coffee." He did so, then walked slowly to the door and left.

It shut behind him with a resounding thud.

"At last," said Rizo in a husky voice, "we're alone."

Dax didn't run to the other side of the table, but she felt like doing so. She tried to keep her voice calm and sultry as she asked, "Aren't you afraid Elaka or somebody else in your band will beam down here?"

"They'd better not," answered Rizo, rising slowly to his feet.

He crossed the space between them in two long strides and grabbed her with powerful arms. His actions were so quick that she had no time to resist, even if she had thought resistance was a possible course. He pulled her roughly to his thick chest and squeezed her until she thought her rib cage might burst, while his hungry lips sought hers. It was only a kiss, she told herself, and she let his tongue push her mouth open. Perhaps, without the ale on his breath, it might have been more pleasurable; as it was, she forced herself to return the slobbery kiss, feeling more alarm than arousal.

The kiss satisfied him for a few moments. Then he backed her against the table and pushed his groin into hers, and she knew she had to do something fast. Dax feared she would be able to slip out of his grasp only once before he grew more forceful. After that, words would be her only defense.

She twisted and finally ducked under his arms. This time, she did run for the other side of the table.

"I don't want it like this," she panted.

"How the hell *do* you want it?" he growled.

"I've never shared a man," said Dax forcefully. "And I don't intend to start now. You belong to Elaka."

He snorted. "What if I don't care about Elaka?"

"Then I think you'd better have a long talk with her."

"Are you afraid of Elaka?" he asked.

"Damn right. I think you should be, too."

Rizo scowled and slammed his fist on the table. Then he grabbed his mug of ale and took a long swig. Dax took a deep breath, hoping the worst was over.

"What about Petra's mother?" she asked.

"What about her?" snarled Rizo. "Cardassians got her. I suppose they raped her to death—that's what they usually do. I never really did try to find out. I was a farmer until that point in my life. Can you believe it? Trying to scrape a few vegetables out of a chunk of barren earth they left us. But taking our land wasn't enough. If they saw women they liked in the village, those women would just never come home."

His face said the memory of the incident was still impossible to fathom, even after what must have been years. "So one day you've got a family and a chunk of soil, and you think it's yours, and then even that is gone. I asked around the village, but nobody would tell me what had happened. They didn't have to."

He stared past her and swallowed hard. "So I grabbed Petra—she was four years old—and we ran into the hills. Either we were going to die, the Cardassians were going to get us, or we were going to find the resistance. We found the resistance, and I killed my first Cardassian two days later." His smile looked demented. "It felt good."

Dax opened her mouth and started to say how sorry she was, but she held her tongue. This man was still a murderer, even after the Cardassians were gone. He didn't need pity—he needed treatment. Unfortunately, he would probably find death before he found any other kind of sanctuary.

He slumped heavily into the chair and began to drain his ale. "Go on!" he growled. "Get outta here! You're right, I'm an animal. I deserve Elaka, and she deserves me. The only fine thing I ever had in my life was taken away from me, and now I don't deserve anyone as fine as you."

His face contorted as he fought back tears. "Go on, I said! Get outta here!"

Dax didn't wait to be told again. She slipped out the door of the conference room and never looked back.

She walked the maze of corridors for what might have been hours, not paying any attention to the colored stripes on the walls or the various business and recreational areas she passed. It was impossible to imagine, but the symbiont part of her had lived for three hundred years and had never encountered one-tenth of the horror that poor man had faced. When she had volunteered for this mission, she had been seeking experiences that would be unique to Jadzia Dax and no one else. Now her outlook on experience had changed. Experience not only built character, it destroyed it.

All the while that Curzon Dax had been having what had seemed like grand adventures in life-threatening situations, the real lives of many people had been more than threatened. In an instant, their lives had been torn apart. Dax had never really understood what Benjamin Sisko had gone through when he lost his mate in the Borg attack at Wolf 359. For a Trill, no relationship could be greater than the one between symbiont and host, and it was expected to end, the way a journey in a starship was expected to end when it reached its destination.

Beings of normal life span, who mated for life, felt differently. Ironically, they never expected their blending with another being to end. When it ended prematurely, with so much of life left, it was a tragedy she could never hope to appreciate. Some people, like Benjamin, were only temporarily unhinged. Others, like Rizo, were permanently damaged, turned into monsters their former selves wouldn't have recognized. Three hundred years of experience, she thought glumly, and that experience was beyond her. She felt grateful but also sobered by the fact that longevity didn't guarantee a wealth of experience.

Without knowing where she was going, she found herself in the Redemption Center. A new golden gown exactly like the one she had purchased was revolving slowly in the showcase. *Sic transit gloria.* She checked to see that no Ferengi or Bajorans were in the vicinity; then she took her comm badge from her pocket and pressed it.

"Dax to Sisko," she said, surprised at the raspy quality of her own voice.

"Sisko here," came the answer. "I've been looking all over for you."

"I'm in the Redemption Center. I think it's better you come to me. Out."

He must have been nearby, because he showed up in a few minutes. Without giving it much thought, she rushed to him and gave him a desperate hug.

With alarm, he asked, "Are you all right?"

"Yes," she said, rubbing under her eyes.

"You look like you've been crying."

"Was I?" she asked in amazement. "That's unusual for me, isn't it?"

"What did he do to you?"

"I'm fine," she answered. "It's not what you think, really." She debated whether to tell the commander that she finally understood what he had gone through, but this wasn't the time to bring up painful memories. They already had enough ghosts from the past to contend with.

"Rizo is mentally unstable," Dax said finally. "How he got that way is a very sad story, and I'm sure you could figure it out if you tried. The question is, how far can we trust somebody who's unstable? I mean, even though both the Ferengi and Bajorans are double-crossing each other, we have to count on them to play straight with us."

Sisko sighed. "I know. I found Gimba in the gaming room. He was losing, so he wasn't very cheerful. He insisted that his Marauder is such a large ship that he could keep some people on it without the Bajorans knowing it. Since we're acting like we're rigging the deal in his favor, I couldn't argue strongly against it."

"Well," said Dax, "he'll still have to transport

several hundred of his crew down to the planet, if he wants to make it look good. Our main concern is still Rizo and the Bajorans."

Sisko nodded and glanced around the room. "Will they let you on the tanker? Alone with him?"

She shook her head. "I don't know. We didn't part on such good terms. Being alone with him can be quite an adventure."

Sisko's jaw tightened, and he said decisively, "This whole thing is too dangerous. I'm calling Odo to tell him we're getting out of here."

"Human!" barked a voice.

Despite the fact that it was a female voice, the cold timbre of the syllables sent a chill down Dax's spotted spine. She turned to see Elaka, staring at them from the doorway of the Redemption Center. The hatred in her eyes burned brighter than any of the colored lights marching across the ceiling. She strode toward them, jiggling nothing on her hard, compact body.

"We agree to the terms," she sneered. "Tell the bloodsuckers that we will make the exchange tomorrow at nine hundred hours. We will beam down our crew, and the Ferengi must do likewise. All shields must be lowered, so that both sides can make a sensor sweep. Gimba is to remain alone on the Marauder, and Rizo will pilot the tanker to it and commence docking."

Elaka gazed at Dax with pure spite, and the Trill made it a point not to look away. "Of course, you'll be there, my dear. We'll beam you up from here. We'll do a weapons scan on you before you're allowed on board." She smiled. "And maybe a strip search."

Dax smiled. "Will Rizo do that personally?"

Elaka shoved a grimy finger in Dax's face. "Don't press your luck."

"This is indeed good news!" Sisko chirped brightly. "Please relay to your captain our heartfelt gratitude that this has worked out to everyone's mutual benefit."

"And you tell that fat Ferengi to have the latinum." Elaka scowled. "There won't be any more communication between us."

Sisko nodded, and Dax tried to maintain a pleasant smile. Elaka gave her one last unbridled glare before she marched off.

The commander let his breath out. "What does that mean?" he asked. "Are they expecting to take over the Ferengi ship, or not?"

Dax shook her head. "I don't know. But we're apparently getting our wish—I'm going aboard the tanker."

"We'd better let Gimba know," said Sisko, heading for the doorway. Dax followed close behind.

"Marcus Garvey! Jade Dixon!" called another voice, causing them to halt in their tracks. This voice was very familiar and friendly, even if it was synthesized.

They looked down at the interface terminal in the alcove by the door. "What do you want?" asked Dax.

The hive mind replied, "We are pleased that your negotiations have proven successful. We know they weren't easy negotiations."

"Thank you," muttered Sisko, walking away.

"One moment, Marcus Garvey," said the voice. "Or should I call you Commander Sisko?"

That caused both of them to whirl around and cautiously approach the device.

"Who?" asked the commander, trying to sound confused.

"Let's not be coy," said the collective consciousness

of a billion insects. "You know who you are, and we know who you are, even if your negotiating partners do not. There is one negotiation which is still unresolved."

"What is that?" asked Dax warily.

"Our piece of the action," answered the interface.

CHAPTER
9

THE MIDDLE-AGED CARDASSIAN was short but wiry, like a coiled eelbird. His splotchy gray complexion and the bony protuberances around his eyes and forehead gave him the appearance of a rotting corpse. The moment Major Kira saw him on the Promenade, she felt the bile rise up her throat like a volcanic eruption. A rush of adrenaline made her want to charge after him, but she reminded herself that the Cardassian hadn't broken any laws. He was alone, walking briskly, but he waited patiently when a group of Bajoran schoolchildren crossed in front of him. Not shoving them out of the way made him exceptionally well mannered for a Cardassian.

As part of the treaty that had seen their withdrawal from Bajor, Cardassians had demanded access to *Deep Space Nine.* They came to the station in such small numbers that no one seemed to mind. Well, no one but Kira and every Bajoran she knew. Every time she saw a Cardassian, she wanted to squash it like a bug. Their civilized veneer hid a culture steeped in the pleasures of torture and warfare. Their disastrous handling of the Bajoran economy made it clear, at least to Kira, that Cardassians conquered mostly for fun.

The old hatreds bubbled and boiled inside her until she felt queasy. Kira forced herself to slow down and follow the Cardassian from a discreet distance. After all, he was headed the same way she was—to Quark's.

The major wasn't surprised to find two more Cardassians waiting in Quark's casino, nor was she surprised to find them chatting with the jovial proprietor. She knew she shouldn't blame the Ferengi— customers were customers—but she hated Quark for his collusion with them. He had functioned as well under the Cardassian reign of terror as he had under the Federation's benign but bumbling rule. Of course, his sleazy mixture of gambling, libations, and holosuite fantasies would always be a draw, and it did bring needed hard currency into the station. But it also brought the wrong kind of customers, like these arrogant, stiff-necked Cardassians. They were hoisting glasses of ale like the victors in an escaped refugee hunt.

Kira knew she couldn't be circumspect, like Odo, or diplomatic, like Sisko—she could only be direct. She recollected hearing about the arrival of a Cardassian trade delegation, and she assumed this must be them. No matter what they called themselves, all they ever wanted to trade was their horrific brand of oppression for your sorrow and blood.

"Welcome to *Deep Space Nine,*" she said curtly as she strode into their midst.

Her arrival was so sudden that the Cardassians jumped, and one of them spilled his ale down his gray tailored suit. The other two glared at her, as one might look at a person who had just relieved herself in public. Her very existence was an affront to them.

Quark didn't look too happy to see her either. "Major Kira," he hissed, "what a pleasure it would be to serve you *at some other time.*"

"I don't need service," she said bluntly. "I need information. And I would prefer to talk to you, privately." She glanced at the Cardassians and swallowed the bad taste from her mouth. "You can tell your customers that you'll only be a moment."

The older Cardassian raised his hand. "Don't disobey your keeper," he smiled. "The Bajorans always insisted to us how peaceful and pleasant they were, but we always found them simply rude."

"Look," she told the Cardassians, "I haven't got time for you today. Just steer clear of me, and we'll get along fine."

The shorter one snorted a laugh. "Yes, we heard about you losing a shipment of antimatter to a ragtag band of your own people. Must be quite embarrassing." His fellows chuckled.

"And none of your concern," snapped Kira. "I need to talk to you, Quark."

"By all means," said the elder Cardassian with a good-humored chuckle. "Don't let us detain you, Quark. We have to get back to our ship, anyway. A pleasure, as always."

The Cardassians marched off, and the Ferengi waved after them with desperation. "Come back, if you have time! She never stays long!" Quark turned and glared at the Bajoran. "Don't you have anything better to do than to chase off customers?"

Kira's lips thinned. "Why were you talking to them? What did you tell them?"

"Exactly what Odo told me to tell them," he answered. "To leave me out of it. To keep me uninvolved. I wouldn't trade information to them, even if I had any."

"You really don't know what's happening on the other side of the wormhole?" asked Kira in disbelief.

"I didn't say that, exactly," answered Quark, picking up a glass and inspecting it. "Listen, Major, if you promise to leave, I'll tell you the one piece of information I know that not everyone else does."

"All right," answered Kira, leaning on the bar.

Quark whispered, "The cartel was involved in the hijacking—as the liquidators of the merchandise. But they're not at all happy with the way things are going. They sent one of their best operatives over to the Gamma Quadrant a couple of weeks ago, and he was supposed to return with the antimatter by now. Nobody on this side of the wormhole knows what the delay is, and the cartel is getting nervous."

"Who is this operative?" asked Kira.

"I didn't promise to tell you that," said Quark. Then he smiled with fond remembrance. "But he has a wonderful harem."

The major nodded. "So we know the Ferengi are involved in a big way. What about the Cardassians? Why were you talking to them?"

"They're dignitaries," answered Quark with indignation. "Trade representatives."

"And I'm a royal princess," sneered Kira. "What did they want?"

"Like you—information. Help. But I'm steering clear of this antimatter business. Contrary to what you think, Major, I don't want to see DS9 blown up. I *like* it here, and that wormhole gives us a great tourist attraction. As far as I'm concerned, the antimatter can just stay over there."

"You sound like Odo," sniffed Kira. "This one time, I'm almost inclined to agree with you. I'd be content just to have Commander Sisko, Odo, and Dax come back—without the antimatter."

Quark frowned. "It's not a foregone conclusion that they will come back. In fact, if you really believe the *Mekong* will come back in one piece with all aboard, I can get you a wager at three-to-one odds."

Kira bolted upright and snarled, "You're disgusting." She beeped her comm badge. "Kira to Ops. I want all transmissions to and from the Cardassian ship monitored. And keep me apprised of their status."

"Funny you should ask that, Major," O'Brien's voice cut in. "They just sent a message—short but encrypted. Then they asked for permission to shove off."

"Keep them here," said Kira. "Make up some excuse for a delay. Can you decode their message?"

"Given enough time," answered O'Brien. "I'll get to work on it. O'Brien out."

The Ferengi was collecting more glasses and appeared not to be listening, but Kira knew how much his gargantuan ears picked up. "So what are the Cardassians going to do?" she asked.

"They're scavengers," growled Quark. "They can smell the deal falling through, the rodent about to die in the desert. If the antimatter is up for grabs, they will be grabbing. You know, I hadn't realized how highly prized Federation-made antimatter is. By all accounts, it is the most pure, and they have the best storage pods. Do you suppose they would consider selling me a franchise?"

Kira muttered, "We already asked them, and they said no."

"Pity," shrugged Quark. "They are losing so much profit. Cardassians, I can understand; these do-gooders, I cannot."

Kira's comm badge sounded, and she straightened to attention before tapping it. "Major Kira."

It was O'Brien, and he sounded excited. "Four—yes, I think it's four—small cruisers headed our way. They may be no more than one-man craft, but they can do warp speed."

"What is their destination?"

"They're just slowing down," said O'Brien. "Their impulse speed is impressive, too."

"Where are they going, Chief?" Kira demanded, trying to keep her voice calm and level. She knew that Quark and several of his customers had stopped to listen.

"The wormhole," he answered. "I hope they slow down long enough to get through it. We could fire on them, but that's about all we could do to stop them. They're spreading out—if their engines are tuned properly, they should make it through all right."

"Where are they from?" asked Kira, the bile rising in her throat again.

"I've never seen anything like them," answered O'Brien, "but maybe this Cardassian computer has. Let me try to get a match." Kira heard silence, but she could sense the rumble growing beneath it, like the prelude to thunder. O'Brien finally exploded, "Yeah, this computer knows them all right! Cardassian registry, and they came straight out of Cardassian space!"

Kira sighed. One thing she could count on with

O'Brien was that he hated Cardassians as much as she did. "No need to decode that message now, Chief. Exactly how many went in?"

"Four ships. I don't know how much range they have, probably not as much as the runabout, but they're small and fast." O'Brien's voice grew hoarse. "Major, you just give me the word, and I'll go after them. We'll find the *Mekong* and bring 'er home."

Tempting it was, so tempting, to send O'Brien to rescue Sisko, Dax, and Odo. But Sisko had been right—the station needed O'Brien where he was. And Admiral Nicheyev had been right—there was no sense endangering more ships to save two that could already be lost.

"No, Chief," she said, "I'm sorry, but two runabouts would be almost as badly outnumbered as one. I want you to send the Cardassians a very stern message that if they send ships through the hole again, without going through the proper procedures, we'll fire on them. And we're holding the ship that's docked here for investigation."

"Aye, sir," answered O'Brien, not hiding the disappointment in his voice.

Didn't he know, thought Kira, that she would like to do more? But decimating the command staff of *Deep Space Nine* wasn't going to help matters much.

She remembered the gleam in Sisko's eye when he had asked for volunteers to go with him on the runabout. It was a roguish quality he had exhibited only a few times, but it gave her confidence that he could succeed. The commander knew the dangers, and he knew that his opportunities would be limited. Either things were breaking their way or not, and only he could make that decision. Kira certainly hoped that fortune had been with the *Mekong* so far, because it had just turned against them.

Quark looked glum, too. "Zot," he muttered, "at this rate, I'll never get anyone to bet on Sisko coming back."

Kira scowled, *"You* bet on him. Jack up the odds, and you'll win big." She turned and stalked out of the casino.

"Hmmm," mused the Ferengi, giving it serious thought.

Benjamin Sisko just stared at the nondescript terminal, rage seething inside of him. Unless he was having an unpleasant dream, several billion bugs were trying to extort money from him. He hadn't asked for the Ecocids' help, even if their timely lie—saying that he and Dax had been on the planet for days—had paved the way for their acceptance by Gimba and Rizo. He knew that once you started lying, and enlisted others to lie for you, things often went haywire, but he hadn't expected to be shaken down by a hiveful of bugs.

"Your . . . your piece of the action?" he asked incredulously.

"Of course, Commander Sisko," answered the synthesized voice of the interface. "That is your real name and rank, isn't it? You have many secrets, Commander, and this would not be a good time for them to reach the surface."

"But . . . but we haven't . . . we don't have anything!"

"Marcus, you're sputtering," Dax observed. "Please allow me."

Sisko threw his hands in the air and stepped back.

The attractive Trill smiled pleasantly at the interface, which was undoubtedly a wasted gesture.

"If you know so much about us," she began, "you must know that we pursued these criminals here from the Alpha Quadrant. All of our actions have been intended to recover stolen property, namely, a tanker full of antimatter. Even if we're successful, we're not going to make any profit."

"We have no such restrictions," answered the hive mind. "We *are* going to make a profit, and we can make it from you or one of the other groups involved."

Dax shook her head. "That's unlikely. If you tell the Bajorans, they'll probably become wary and just take off with the tanker. And the Ferengi are already out a sizable amount—they won't want to share anything with you."

"That remains to be seen," answered the hive mind. "We believe that you owe us something. If you don't cooperate, we can make your stay here very unpleasant."

Sisko growled, "This is pointless. The Ecocids are demanding something from us that we don't have!" He grabbed Dax's arm and started off. "Let's go."

The Trill followed, but her spots stretched worriedly along her hairline. "Was that wise, Benjamin?"

"I don't know," he admitted. "But I refuse to talk to that thing any longer. If it tells them the truth, then it has to admit that it lied to them. All that matters is that we get you and Odo aboard that tanker tomorrow morning. If we can't do that, we've failed, anyway."

Sisko's peripheral vision caught a wriggling stream of blackness just over his head, and he sank back. He wished he weren't prejudiced against the Ecocids, but he couldn't repress his repulsion at their sheer number and formidable presence. As a kid, he loved bees and ants, but giant burrowing insects were beyond his capacity for love. Especially when they were greedy and dishonest. Dax seemed to have no trouble empathizing with the Ecocids and treating them as an equal, but she had merged with an alien species. That's what Sisko had to admit—despite the fact that he had lived with insects all his life, they were still an alien species.

"You need some rest," Dax suggested. "We all do. I hadn't realized how exhausting it is to be dishonest. Plus, tomorrow looks to be an eventful day."

"Yeah," sighed the commander. "It'll be great to get home."

Jon Rachman dangled his toes in the cool stream and looked around at the idyllic setting of Sabino Canyon, with its gentle currents and drooping cottonwood trees. Like alien soldiers frozen by a sudden cold wave, saguaro cactus lined the rugged hillside. Multicolored clouds lay smeared across the big sky behind them, reminding him of a giant's finger painting. A little farther up the stream, Jake and Nog howled with laughter and splashed with abandon as they tried to catch crayfish.

"There's just one drawback about commanding a cruiser." Jon Rachman grinned. "No room for a holodeck. Boy, I'd like to be able to do this more often!"

"Is this what Kansas looks like?" called Nog. "Sorta weird?"

"No, no," said Rachman. "When we asked for something from the Wild West, your uncle did the best he could. By the looks of these stovepipe cacti, we must be someplace in Arizona. What do you think, Jake?"

"This is great!" he shouted. "I'm going to save up my allowance to come back here. Wait till Dad sees it." His voice trailed off in sudden remembrance.

His buddy, Nog, didn't let the moment linger. He scooped up a double handful of cold stream water and doused his friend. Sputtering and laughing, Jake gave chase.

Rachman breathed a sigh of relief. Jake had finally come out of his funk over his dad's absence—and his imminent replacement. The captain had regaled both boys with tales of dangerous missions in Starfleet, all of which had turned out happily. Of course, Jake had been there at Wolf 359, so he knew that not all missions turned out happily. But plenty had. Then when Chief O'Brien piped in with a couple of the incredible scrapes the *Enterprise* had survived, everybody believed that the runabout could make it back. They believed it until they were reminded of the alternative.

The persistence of his friend Nog had also gone a long way toward elevating Jake's mood, and Rachman found himself liking a Ferengi for the first time. He certainly didn't know why anybody would complain about Nog's uncle Quark, the owner of this remarkable holosuite. The Ferengi proprietor had been the height of hospitality to the young captain, giving him the run of the holosuites plus treats from the replicators—anything he needed to keep Jake Sisko's mind off his dad. Rachman thought *Deep Space Nine* was the kind of place where he might settle down one day, if he got tired of roaming the space lanes. After all, the Bajoran women were quite attractive, and he found himself visualizing Major Kira. Maybe a swim in this very spot—

His communicator beeped, startling him with its intrusion. Rachman shook off his pleasant reverie and tapped his badge.

"Captain Rachman here," he announced.

"It's Chief O'Brien," came the Irish drawl. "Sorry to interrupt you, but there's been a development."

"A development?" asked Rachman. He was trying to keep his voice down, but Jake and Nog had stopped their play with the second sense children have when an adult doesn't want them to hear something. They were sloshing their way toward him through the stream, and he finally decided that Jake deserved to hear whatever it was.

"Go ahead," he said.

"Four small Cardassian fighters have entered the wormhole. We think this happened not long after they found out about the missing antimatter. Anyway, we assume that whoever comes out of there with the tanker might have a very unfriendly escort. Major Kira thinks we should mount a show of force, and the *Regal* is about all we have. At least you have impulse power and a few weapons. The *Valor* isn't going anywhere, and our runabouts aren't going to frighten anybody."

"What about the *Regal*'s shields?" asked her captain.

"We can give you about fifty percent," said O'Brien, "if you take a skeleton crew. That will let us steal some energy from the life-support systems. You understand, Captain, you're not really going to be able to do very much, you just have to look like you could in a pinch."

"Understood," said Rachman grimly. He glanced at

the two boys. "But no actual word yet on Commander Sisko and the others?"

"No," answered O'Brien. "But it's a cinch that somebody is going to come out of that wormhole. We'd like to have you at the dock to tell us what you absolutely need, and what you can do without."

"I'm on my way," said Rachman. "Out."

The young captain looked plaintively at the boys and shrugged. "I guess playtime's over, at least for me."

"Thanks," said Jake, extending his hand. "You know, you didn't have to spend so much time with us."

"Believe me, I enjoyed it," said Rachman. He jumped to his naked feet and shook the young man's hand. Then he began looking around for his socks and boots. "You're good kids, both of you. And, Nog, your uncle is a terrific guy, too."

"Yeah, he is, isn't he?" The small Ferengi grinned. "You should see some of the programs *he* wrote for this holosuite."

"I'd like to," said Rachman innocently. "You fellas take care. I'll see you back at your apartment, Jake."

"Thanks, Captain."

"Bye, Captain!" crowed Nog.

After Rachman had been absorbed into the holosuite scenery, Nog looked at his friend and shook his rubbery ears in incomprehension. "They're *too* brave. You have to be too brave to be in Starfleet. I respect Captain Rachman a lot, but I'm going into business when I get older. No offense, Jake, but I'm not the Starfleet type."

"Not everyone is," the boy remarked.

Nog seized upon this new topic of conversation.

"What did you say you were going to be when you got older?"

Jake gave his friend a lopsided grin. "A professional baseball player."

"Oh, yeah," said Nog. "Sounds neat. Let's catch some crayfish."

The two friends waded back into the gurgling water, as the desert brooms swished gently in the breeze.

Kira looked right in the eyes of the Cardassian seated in the investigation room.

"We don't know what you're talking about," he sneered. It was the third time that he had delivered that answer, and Kira was getting annoyed, despite her best intentions to remain calm.

"What do you mean, you don't know what I'm talking about?" she asked in amazement. "That squad of fighters went through immediately after you sent your message."

"Coincidence." The trade representative shrugged. His short stature was countered by massive shoulders, Kira noted, and old scar tissue that rimmed his bony eye sockets. He was a soldier of some sort, that was evident. Like most Cardassians, he was also an accomplished liar.

Chief O'Brien cut in. "We could decode that message, you know. Find out exactly what you said."

The Cardassian smiled pleasantly. "You would find it very innocuous. A birthday greeting to someone's spouse, if I recall."

Kira let out a sharp breath. "That probably is all it says. They would code the message, too. This is useless, because we know he'll never admit to anything. None of them will."

"Too bad we're not Cardassians," O'Brien muttered, "or we could torture it out of them."

Jukal laughed with what seemed like honest amusement. "That is why we are clearly superior to both humans and Bajorans. A culture which doesn't use the means at its disposal—any means necessary—will always be at hampered in its development."

Kira put her fists on her hips and glared at her subject. "All right," she said, "you won't tell me anything about those four small craft you sent through. I'm not surprised. But do you have any information about the tanker itself, or is this just a scavenger hunt on your part?"

The Cardassian glowered at her. "Are you insulting me by calling me a scavenger?" he bridled. "We had nothing to do with the disappearance of your tanker. That was due entirely to your own ineptitude, and the treachery of your own foolish people."

Kira's body tensed, and she felt like strangling the arrogant popinjay. Instead, she backed away from the interrogation table and prowled around the security room, her hands clasped behind her back.

O'Brien asked pleasantly, "So what *are* your scavengers doing over there?"

The Cardassian jerked forward with a sudden display of anger, and his eyes grew black in their sunken hollows. Quickly, he regained his composure and sank back into his chair. "As I told you before, I don't know who those ships represent. However, it would certainly be within the interests of the Cardassian Empire to prevent a massive detonation of antimatter, in either the wormhole or the Gamma Quadrant. Since *you* don't seem to be able to control the situation, why should we sit idly by?"

O'Brien smiled sourly. "Just trying to be good citizens, eh?"

"Precisely," answered Jukal. "Now, may we leave the station?"

Kira looked at O'Brien, and the Irishman scowled, but he didn't give her any good reason for detaining the Cardassian ship. This was the third dignitary they had talked to, and their story hadn't changed one syllable. "We don't know what you're talking about" was the answer to every substantive question.

"Make sure you really leave," said Kira. "Put some distance between yourselves and this station. I don't want your ship hanging around—I don't want it to be anywhere on our sensors. Or I'll treat it as an act of war and start shooting at any Cardassian vessel I see."

Jukal forced a chuckle. "That would be over-reacting."

"Maybe." Kira smiled. "But Starfleet is sending a new commander and several ships, so I don't have much more time to be in command of DS9. Until they get here, I'm going to do whatever I damn well please, and firing on Cardassians is something I enjoy doing. Do I make myself clear?"

Jukal's laughter sounded nervous. "Oh, you warlike Bajorans. Just let us go, that's all we want."

"Go," Kira ordered, waving at the door. "But do remember that the antimatter belongs to Starfleet, until they hand it over to Bajor."

The Cardassian chuckled. "They already handed it over to Bajor. Farewell."

Kira ran her hand over the security panel, and the door slid open. Just as quickly, the Cardassian slid out.

O'Brien muttered, "Lying sons of . . ."

Kira held up a hand. "I know. But when things go wrong, you have to expect the jackals to get the scent."

"Please let me go after them," begged the chief. "I'll be careful."

Kira considered O'Brien's offer for a moment, but only for a moment. She shook her head glumly. "No, Chief, going after them is not being careful. And the Gamma Quadrant is more dangerous now than it was a few hours ago. I'm sorry, but I need you here. How are repairs going on the *Regal?*"

O'Brien shrugged. "It'll look ready for action, and I hope that will be enough. Taking the station's grapevine into account, we're spreading the rumor that the *Regal* is going to be fully functional in twelve hours."

"Good," said Kira. "I don't want to see Commander Sisko replaced, but I wouldn't mind if Starfleet showed up with a couple of warships right about now."

O'Brien nodded and managed a smile. "You're doing a good job, even if you won't let me risk my neck. If it were up to me, I'd leave you in charge. If worse came to worse, that is."

"Thanks for the vote of confidence, Chief." She touched her comm badge. "Kira to Ops. Let the Cardassian ship go, but monitor their course."

"Yes, sir," came a crisp reply.

O'Brien shook his head, and Kira knew exactly what he was thinking. Worry was carved all over his ruddy face. If worse came to worse, what would any of them do?

It was a peculiar sort of dream, one that was sensory more than visual, but Benjamin Sisko found himself only vaguely troubled by it. For one thing, the soft prickling on his skin was caused by sand blowing off gigantic dunes. As far as the eye could see, dunes undulated in every direction—a dry sea of salmon waves that flowed ever so slowly with the wind.

The prickling was only part of it, as the desert had a distinct odor, like burnt charcoal that had been left out in the rain. Like an old house that had been long neglected. It couldn't be the sun that drew this strange odor from the sand, because the sun was only just rising, like a vague halo, over the tallest dune. Or was it setting? All Sisko knew for certain was that he was asleep and dreaming of an alien vista.

Did he know this place? What was he doing here? What was his reason to be here? A dream can't go on long with nothing happening, thought Sisko, because dreams are very plot-heavy. With the realization that he knew he was dreaming, the dreamer willed something to happen, and sure enough, the dunes began to shift rapidly. The wind had picked up, and the sand was pummeling him with itchy ferocity. Yet he strode knee-deep through the dunes, because the erosion was revealing something underneath—something dark and massive.

It was black sand, he thought, like the kind in Hawaii. It was writhing under the fierce wind, and it bit his skin and assaulted his nostrils with that pungent smell. Nevertheless, he didn't cover his eyes and run away—he drew closer, stumbling down the shifting dune. He could see the black sand churning, as if it were caught in a giant blender, and curiosity drew him closer yet. By the time he saw the true nature of the blackness underneath the sand, it was too late. He grasped for the dune to halt his descent, but the sand oozed through his fingers. In slow motion, he slid toward the mass of writhing Ecocids.

He plunged into them, gasping and flailing his arms.

With desperation, he willed himself to wake up—to stop this horrible dream. But consciousness brought no relief, because the black bugs were still swarming all over him! They were in his hair and mouth, under the waistband of his underwear, creeping and crawling along his naked chest. He screamed with terror as he tried to scrape them off. But they were tenacious creatures, and they nipped his flesh with their pincers.

"Ahhh-aaagh!" wailed Sisko, certain he was being eaten alive.

CHAPTER
10

THE DOOR TO Sisko's tiny cabin jerked open, and Odo loomed in the doorway, followed by Dax, who peered over his shoulder. They were two of the most stoic creatures in the galaxy, but they shuddered at the sight that greeted them, and their mouths twisted with revulsion. Seeing their expressions, Sisko knew that it must be serious, that he wasn't hallucinating—he really was covered by squirming Ecocids.

"Get them off!" he yelled. "Get them off!"

Odo instantly stepped forward and began batting the creatures away. But they either scurried out of sight or began leaping onto the shapeshifter. Dax pitched in, too, but the sheer number of the creatures made the job impossible. Sisko tried to help them, but he was seconds away from giving up any attempt at control and screaming.

Finally, Odo's hands metamorphed into giant scoops, which shoveled the insects off the commander and threw them against the bulkhead with odd cracking sounds. Sisko began to rip off his clothes to let Odo reach the bugs underneath. When he was completely naked and almost rid of the Ecocids, he rushed to the high-speed shower in the back of the runabout and doused himself with as much pressure as he could stand. Even that wasn't enough to help him feel clean.

He stepped out, looking for a towel, and Dax handed him one. He quickly wrapped it around his waist.

"Sorry," he breathed. "Forgot you were here."

Dax smiled. "That's all right. It's nothing I haven't seen before. Where the hell did those things come from?"

"I don't know," answered Sisko, looking around warily. All the Ecocids had taken flight and burrowed out of sight; it was as if they had never been there. He shuddered. "If that's what they meant about making my life unpleasant, they succeeded."

Odo lifted his arm, and he was still holding one of the intruders in the slim fingers of a hand returned to normal. "They're really quite fascinating," he remarked. "I believe they are capable of generating small amounts of electricity, like insects which can illuminate themselves. Each one is like a tiny processor, and together they form a computer."

"Damn them!" cursed Sisko. "There must be hundreds of them. How did they get here?"

"They might have been breeding here," suggested Dax. "Or perhaps they brought some eggs aboard. But how?"

Odo cocked his head thoughtfully. "The biofilter's been malfunctioning lately. We could have gotten a handful with every transporter trip."

Sisko scowled. "And we probably transported some back down with us—that's how they knew about the coffee and our real identities. We have to look at this attack as a warning shot across our bow. Well, I got the message."

The commander began pacing. "First, I want a sweep of this entire ship, and I want every one of them off. That'll be the easy part. But how do we make sure they don't screw everything up? The hive mind is the key. Does anybody have any idea how to distract it, give it something else to do besides tormenting *us*?"

"A diversion," said Dax. "But what would work? They can successfully screen out weapons, and the individuals are so widespread it would be hard to imagine that one single incident could distract all of them."

Sisko gazed at the Ecocid in Odo's grasp. "I wonder how much like Terran insects they really are?"

"What do you mean?" asked the morph.

"Well," said the commander, "a hive on Earth would have one queen, no matter what size it was. It's the queen's job to lay the eggs, and if she's threatened, the whole hive goes berserk. It goes into chaos."

Odo observed, "I would think the queen would be well protected."

"Not necessarily," said Dax. "I think the commander has something here. The queen has to be accessible to the drones and the helpers. The first step is to catch the Ecocids on board and examine them. If they're all the same sex, or no sex, that may mean they have a single queen."

"And she's somewhere in the inner hive," added Odo with a sigh. "I had the feeling I would be going back down there."

"Let me ask you something," said the commander. "You've had plenty of time to do scans of the planet. What are those salmon-colored areas down there?"

"Vast sand dunes," answered Odo. "Oceans of sand."

Sisko shivered. "That's what I thought."

Using tricorders to locate them and phasers to stun them, it had proven surprisingly easy to round up the stowaway insects. Pressing a medical tricorder into service, Dax had managed to make a detailed examination of one hundred Ecocids before she reached the conclusion that they were all sexless soldiers. They had even found a cache of egg sacs that had been secreted aboard, which accounted for the number of stowaways. Both of these discoveries made it likely that the hive had a single queen to handle its reproductive needs.

Six hours before the antimatter exchange was scheduled to take place, Odo found himself strolling along one of the meandering corridors of Hive Three. He was following the red stripe, but he wasn't in much hurry to reach the teeming entrance to the inner hive. He had to meet somebody first. Finally, he spotted him—one of the hirsute servants who did the grunt work in Hive Three. Were these humanoids natives of the planet, he wondered, or had they been imported for this work? Quite possibly, they performed similar work on other planets in the Gamma Quadrant.

"Excuse me!" he called to the creature, who stopped and gazed at him with polite disinterest. The servant was carrying a silver tray piled high with brightly colored packages. "Could you give me directions, please?"

Odo came as close to the being as he thought his sense of personal space would allow, and he studied him intently, imprinting every shank of hair and pool of sweat into his memory. It wasn't so much memory as a mold, a vessel he filled with impressions of a thing he was about to become.

"What, sir?" growled the creature, as if he didn't like to talk. Perhaps, thought Odo, he didn't like the new language he'd had to learn since visitors had shown up from the Alpha Quadrant.

"Is it this way?" asked Odo, pointing in both directions at once like a confused tourist. "Which color is it to get to the laundry?"

"Purple," snarled the creature through uneven teeth.

Odo looked at him, absorbing a few final details, such as his musty breath and the length of his bare toenails. He stepped back to get a sense of height and proportion. "Thank you," he said.

The thing grunted and scurried away, and Odo turned to pick up the red stripe on the wall in earnest. He soon found himself in the final corridor, the one the others emptied into on their way to the inner hive. Without losing a step, his body started to mutate.

Odo's skin went as sleek as the surface of a pond for just a moment before it hardened and grew swaths of coarse brown hair. His face melted, then wizened into a hairy simian countenance. He had to take quicker steps as his legs shortened, and he stepped cautiously for a few meters, learning how to move in this unfamiliar form. Finally, he mastered the shape and moved forward cautiously, encumbered by his own fatigue and the surging influx of black insects.

They swarmed all over the walls, floor, and ceiling, and Odo studied them. Aboard the *Mekong,* he had stared for an hour at the stunned Ecocids, and he knew their dimensions. Now he wanted to know the way they moved.

As the flow of insects became dense and noisy with

the scraping of billions of legs, Odo slowed to a deliberate shuffle. Thus far, he felt, his disguise was working. He remembered the lump he had seen in the corridor his first trip down here, and he assumed that an intruder wouldn't last long if the Ecocids attacked him en masse. Getting in, he thought, wouldn't be a problem, but he was concerned about how he would get out, if he had to revert to his normal size.

Even in the smaller humanoid shape, Odo had to bend over as the corridor constricted around him, the walls black with rippling waves of insects. He could see the mass of fist-size holes along the final wall, each teeming with chaotic traffic. He shuffled slowly toward it, passing the place where he had heard the audio warning, then past the place where he had seen the lump on the ground. The chirping/scraping sound of the insects was almost overwhelming, and he could sense their disturbing smells. Holding his breath, he reached out to touch the highest opening in the wall.

Where Odo's finger lit on the fist-sized entrance, the rest of his hand began to pool. His entire body stretched like taffy as it glommed onto the wall and sucked his mass off the floor. Soon, he was a pulsating mass of jelly at the edge of the hole, and the surrounding insects gave him a wide berth. Odo's only thought was to make the transition as swiftly as possible, before they decided he was an intruder.

Suddenly, he had arms and legs again. Lots of them. And he ducked into the hole before the other Ecocids could scrutinize him. He couldn't move very quickly, but neither could any of the others, so closely packed were they in the tiny opening. Beyond the entrance, he found himself in a chute, one that curled downward at a remarkable angle, and he was thankful for the sticky surface of his spindly legs. The chute meandered downward into the inner hive, into utter darkness. This wasn't a complete surprise for Odo, but he wasn't looking forward to using touch and smell as his only means of navigation. He had to figure out quickly what clues to use to find the queen.

Pressed as he was against a mass of insects in the tunnel, he soon sensed the differences among them. The majority were stalwart soldiers, like those who had sneaked aboard the *Mekong*. Others were smaller and less numerous, and he categorized them as the helpers, or nursemaids. Their place was with the maggots, and he didn't really want to go there.

Members of the third class were rare, at least in this part of the hive. They were slow in their movements and somewhat imperious, and Odo probed his mind for the information given him by Sisko and Dax. He decided that these were the drones, the queen's consorts, and he snuck up behind the legs of one of them, prodding him with his pincers. Perhaps, Odo hoped, he was headed for a little tryst with the queen.

As he crawled along, Odo decided that he could see his surroundings a bit. It wasn't sight in the normal sense—the winding passageway was still pitch black —but radar or some sixth sense gave him a feeling of the dimensions of the passageway and the occasional openings. With six tactile instruments at his disposal, Odo probed the walls of the passageway, trying to determine what it was made from.

The tunnel was an amalgam of materials: it was mostly packed sand, hardened by some type of excretion, but there were also slivers of metal beneath his tiny claws. And he could feel the metal imparting a mild sort of charge, a sensory flow of information. Of course! The metal slivers in the passageway were the contacts to the hive mind's interface, the means by which it became a sentient being that communicated with others. Every single Ecocid within the inner hive was a component of this biological computer. When the insects ventured into the outer hive to mingle with their customers, they became scouts, bringing back information. Whenever there was an exchange over the interface, each of them shared the information as well. This was a natural form of distributed computing and parallel processing.

This information was crucial, felt Odo, because it meant that no single Ecocid—not even the queen— was sentient by itself. Only together, flowing like electrons through these charged passageways, did the Ecocids achieve consciousness. Of course, each individual still had its basic instincts and its unique function within the hive, and that included protecting the queen. At his present size, each one of them was dangerous.

Odo continued to stick close to the drone in front of him, aware of time running out and the effort it required to maintain this shape. He was encouraged when the drone he was following turned off onto a side passage that was inhabited mostly by drones and nursemaids.

Odo had assumed the soldier shape, and he tried to bustle along so as not to call attention to himself. He left his sluggish drone to catch up with a faster one. They passed a major intersection, where most of the nursemaids branched off, leaving the passageway relatively uncrowded. With great relief, Odo allowed his segmented body to expand a bit and his legs to stretch. Now the darkness worked in his favor, because he knew he no longer looked much like an Ecocid. But he was doing the best he could.

Two things happened simultaneously. His radar

sense told him that he was entering a much large cavity; at the same moment, two nursemaids latched onto his legs with their heavy pincers.

Odo came as close to screaming in pain as an insect could, and he knew he had been found out. He could sense the other Ecocids in the vicinity converging upon him, and he realized that if he didn't act fast, they would tear him apart. An image flashed through Odo's mind—that of a daugu, a phosphorescent reptile native to Bajor. It was a cave dweller and provided its own light, which was exactly what the shapeshifter needed at that moment.

He morphed into a snakelike creature with stubby appendages and skin that glowed milky white, especially near its upturned snout. He dragged the attached Ecocids with him as he lumbered through the cavity in search of the queen. A gathering of cowering drones gave her away, and the glowing reptile galloped toward her, flicking his tongue at the threatening insects.

The queen was impressive—she had a regal golden color and was three times the size of the biggest drone. Plus, she stood her ground to meet his attack head-on and protect the egg sacs that were awaiting transport. She snapped at him with immense pincers, and he could imagine her using them to grip her helpless suitors until she was through with them. But Odo was already changing into something else—he needed the dexterity of his human hand. As the hand stretched toward the queen, he assumed the humanoid form he presented to denizens of *Deep Space Nine*.

His delicate fingers engulfed the queen while his expanding shoulders pressed against the sand that enclosed the hive. He had no idea whether it would crumble at his touch or entomb him, or how deep he was. So he ducked when the sand and metal caved in all around him. It was stifling, but it didn't crush him. Likewise, he kept his grip on the queen light, so as not to crush her, ignoring the way she nipped and clawed at his palm. At least he couldn't feel the gnawing of the Ecocids at his extremities anymore.

With his free hand, Odo clawed through the sand until he had loosened an area around his face. The sand was just too heavy to allow him to claw his way to the surface, no matter how far away that was. Besides, he was terribly weakened from his various transformations, and it was all he could do to keep his customary form together. He turned his collar outward, revealing his Bajoran communicator badge. He squeezed it with what little strength he had left.

"Odo . . ." he breathed. A moment later, his body transported from its premature burial plot.

The queen was not of that genus, but she was as mad as a hornet inside the laboratory jar. She kept trying to claw her way up the smooth sides of the jar. When that didn't work, she thudded around on her heavy wings until she dropped, exhausted, to the bottom. Dax didn't think it was possible for insects to pant, but that's what it looked like this one was doing.

She shut off her tricorder. "We can't keep her long," the Trill announced solemnly. "She's weakening, she won't eat, and she'll die soon."

"Terrible," said Sisko, not sounding like he meant it. "They must have other females."

"Not like this one," said Dax. "A proven producer. Females may be born spontaneously, but they're probably killed or driven from the hive as long as this one is healthy. More likely, they have to produce a queen by feeding royal jelly to the larva—a process that could be very uncertain. I don't mind what we did for expediency, but we have to return her fairly soon. If another one isn't born to replace her, the hive could die."

The commander straightened up and put his hands behind his back. "All right, Dax, go down and talk to the interface. I'd go with you, but Odo is resting and one of us should stay on alert. Tell the hive mind that we'll return their queen as soon as they stop interfering."

"They'll probably want to know exactly when that will be," said Dax.

Sisko frowned in thought. "In four hours, just before we pull out of here. I'll beam all of the Ecocids back then. If they've cooperated, that is."

Dax went to the storage closet to fetch her unmarked jacket. "There will be no negotiating," she promised. "I'll tell the Ecocids they'll get their queen back in four hours if they keep quiet and don't interfere."

"Exactly," answered Sisko.

Dax slipped into her jacket and heard something jingle in the pocket. She reached in and smiled at what she found. "I've got two bilbok left," she announced. "Anything you want me to buy before we leave here?"

"Bug spray," said Sisko.

Dax transported to the Redemption Center, which had become their unofficial headquarters on the planet of Eco. She glanced at the display cases, wondering what two bilbok would buy. Of course, she already had a dramatic souvenir from this mission—the golden gown—and it was unlikely she could top that.

Unfortunately, Benjamin would probably court-martial her if she tried to wear it again.

She saw a bulky creature standing by the terminal, shaking both his heads. As she drew closer she saw what he was unhappy about—the interface screen was blank. One of the heads swiveled to look at her, and the other one looked at the ceiling, rolling its three eyes. The other row of eyes regarded her with pity; then the being shrugged his mighty shoulders and shuffled off, muttering in two voices.

Dax stood at the interface, waiting for it to greet her in its familiar synthesized voice. But it said nothing. It did indeed appear to be turned off. She glanced behind her and was relieved to see that the familiar scrawl of figures was still lighting up the ceiling.

"What's the matter?" she asked. "Lost your queen?"

At once, the terminal blinked on. "Jade Dixon," said the voice. "Famous abductress. We were wondering when you would come crawling around."

"You began this," said Dax. "We came here for the sake of justice, not profit. You helped us once, and now all we ask you to do is to stay out of the way. Stay neutral in our affairs."

"Our queen—have you killed her?"

"Of course not. You had information about us, and we needed something equally important to bargain with you. This is *your* game we're playing. We would like to finish it in approximately four hours."

"And you will," said the cold synth voice. "We will remain neutral from this point onward, saying nothing to anyone about this matter. We will even wipe out your bill and make your stay complimentary. When can we expect to have our queen back?"

"In four hours."

The interface said nothing. What could it say? Dax felt bad about using such desperate tactics, but they had been left little choice. She turned to go. "Thank you."

"One moment," said the somber hive mind. "I was instructed to leave a message for you. A representative from the Bajorans is waiting in your conference room to discuss some of the arrangements."

"Was this message for me or Marcus Garvey?" asked Dax.

"It doesn't matter," answered the machine. "Farewell." The screen went blank.

Dax shook her head, thinking that someday she wanted to make amends for this visit. She wanted to come back to Eco as what she was, a representative of the Federation, not just another con artist. But that visit would have to wait.

She set off following the yellow stripe, even though she barely had to glance at it, she had been there so often. The Trill decided that she should take a cup of coffee back to the commander. Benjamin would be appreciative, because the replicator in the conference room was the only thing he had liked about Eco.

She strode across the lounge, and the door whooshed open at her approach. Without pause, she stepped inside the familiar room. The lights were lower in brightness than normal, but she attributed that to the late hour.

"Hello!" Dax called, squinting into the dimness. She heard the food slot slowly filling a cup of coffee.

The door banged shut behind her with a finality that made her jump, and she turned around to see somebody rising from behind the table.

"Hello," yawned Elaka. "Excuse me, I had just dozed off. I wondered when you would be getting down here."

Involuntarily, Dax backed up. "I didn't think we were supposed to meet for four hours."

"But we have to decide where to meet," said Elaka, circling the table. "We forgot to decide that. Rizo said you should be beamed aboard as soon as all the rest of us are beamed down here."

The Bajoran motioned around the room. "We're going to bring all of our people right here—I think we'll all fit. I hope the Ferengi weren't planning to use this area."

"No," said Dax, relaxing a little. "They've got hundreds of people, so they've taken a banquet room. And some of them are going to the gaming room. When everybody is down—except for the three of us—we'll run the scans."

Elaka nodded. "Good. Then you should meet us here. I'll be glad to get this over with."

"Me too," agreed Dax.

Elaka stopped in front of the food slot and looked inside. "Oh, you probably would like this cup of coffee." She reached in and pulled it out. "Here you are."

Dax took a few steps forward to retrieve the cup from Elaka's outstretched hands. As her hand was about to grasp the cup, Elaka heaved it forward, and the scalding liquid struck her in the face. When Dax shrieked and staggered backward, the stocky Bajoran leaped like a mugato and went for her throat. Snarling like a beast, she wrestled Dax to the ground and tried to strangle her with her bare hands.

Dax's face was searing with pain, and her breathing had stopped—but the Trill's self-preservation was just kicking in. One didn't live to be three hundred years old without having quite a bit of it. Even though the host's brain might short out after a few seconds without oxygen, the symbiont deep in her torso had its own brain, one that was quite capable of commanding this youthful body in a ruthless fashion. Dax formed two fists and brought them together on Elaka's head like a cymbal player doing the *1812* Overture.

The Bajoran screamed with pain and loosened her grip just a little. Dax beat on her forearms mercilessly and kicked her long legs upward like a bucking bronco. All of this finally worked, and Elaka lost her grip on Dax's throat and was tossed off. Unfortunately, the air assaulting her throat made the Trill gasp for breath, and Dax could barely roll over and get to her knees before Elaka buried her head in her chest.

Dax groaned and fell onto her back again. The wind she had struggled so hard to get was knocked out of her, but the symbiont still commanded her hands. Those hands gripped Elaka by the close-cropped sides of her head and pulled with all their might. Elaka whimpered but kept on trying to get another grip around the Trill's neck.

Dax's eyes burned bright as all rational thought left her brain and the self-preservation instincts of the symbiont took over. She plunged her thumbs into Elaka's eyes, and the Bajoran screamed with terror and was forced to go on the defensive. Squealing, Elaka peeled Dax's fingers off her eyes, but it took her several seconds to regain her vision. Before she did, the Trill snapped her right hand back, formed a fist, and smashed the Bajoran in the nose.

Blood spattered over both of them as the women struggled to their feet, grunting with the effort. Elaka kicked viciously, trying to smash Dax's kneecap, and the Trill jumped back just in time. Elaka kept coming, like a boa constrictor. Without thinking, the Trill grabbed the terrorist's collar and pulled their heads together in a crunching blow. When Elaka battered Dax's hands away and staggered backward, her entire face was awash in blood.

Elaka spit out a tooth and snarled, "Bitch!" She wiped a sleeve across her oozing face, then pulled a gleaming cord from her pocket. Slowly she wrapped the ends around her hands and smiled. "I'm going to hang your head on the bridge of that tanker."

CHAPTER
11

DAX REACHED FOR her comm badge, but it was inside her jacket pocket. That moment of forgetfulness nearly cost her her life when Elaka lunged across the room and wrapped the cord around her neck.

At the last microsecond, Dax got her hand to her throat, and the thin muscles of one hand had to battle the brawny forearms of the Bajoran woman. Elaka yanked for all she was worth, trying to tighten the cord; Dax staggered, just trying to stay on her feet. This bizarre dance continued around the table until Dax got enough wits about her to remember her legs. In a fundamental judo move, she wrapped her leg behind Elaka's and punched her in the chest with her free hand.

The maneuver worked better than expected, because Elaka not only lost her balance but fell against the wall and struck her head. Dax was instantly in her face with another right cross that snapped her head around and sent her sinking to the carpeted floor.

Dax staggered backward, massaging a hand that felt as if it had been mangled by farm machinery. Her neck was raw and swollen from all the abuse, and she could only swallow with great pain. With her better hand, she reached into the pocket of her jacket for her comm badge; then she thought better of it. If she didn't somehow make peace with Elaka, she would be at her throat again the next time she saw her, and the entire caper would be too risky.

So Dax grabbed a chair and threw it on top of the Bajoran. She threw her weight across the chair, leaned over the edge, and peered into the terrorist's face, waiting for her to revive.

She did a second later, sputtering and squirming. "Why don't you just kill me? You beat me—you deserve it. Or let me go!"

Dax's voice was hoarse when she replied, "No. You tried to kill *me,* and I want to know why."

Elaka snarled, "You mated with Rizo!"

"No!" shouted Dax. "Whoever told you that is a liar." She shook her head and began to cough; then she paused to catch her breath. "I know who told you that . . . those blasted bugs!"

"Then it's not true?" asked Elaka in amazement. "You flirted with him enough."

"I flirt with everyone," muttered Dax. Actually it was Jade Dixon who answered that one.

"Why would the Ecocids lie?" asked the Bajoran.

"Because they want a piece of this deal, and we won't give it to them. That's the whole thing. They don't mind lying if it's to their gain."

"Are *you* lying?" snapped Elaka. "If you are, I will find a way to kill you."

"There's nothing between me and Rizo, except

business," answered Dax, being specific in her denial. "Look, in a few hours, you will never see Marcus and me again. I promise."

Elaka pouted, but Dax could see the fight drain out of her, along with a lot of blood. "I never thought you would defend yourself like that. You're a fighter."

"Thanks," said Dax. "But I don't enjoy it, like you do."

"Something in you enjoys it," said Elaka. "Let me go. I'll leave you alone, I swear by the revolution."

Every muscle in her body aching, Dax staggered to her feet and pulled off the chair. She certainly hoped that Elaka wouldn't renew the fight, because she felt unable to defend herself against a stiff breeze. Elaka looked worse than she did, but the Bajoran sprang to her feet with a reserve of energy. Warily, she studied the Trill.

"Remember," she said, "there had better be no lies."

At this point, Dax was too weary to tell another lie, so she merely shrugged. Elaka cast her a final glare, unmindful of the blood drooling down her face; then she marched out the door.

Jadzia Dax sank into a chair and lifted her right hand to pull her comm badge out of her pocket. It was the hand that had stopped Elaka's cord, and it was shaking so badly that she doubted if she had any control over it. She had to use her left hand to fish out the badge and beep it.

"Dax to *Mekong*," she said. "Beam me up. Better get out the medkit."

"Medkit?" said Sisko with alarm. "What happened?"

The Trill rubbed her bruised neck. "Another interesting experience."

* * *

Commander Sisko was seething. "That woman needs to be taught a lesson!"

"I think she learned a few things," said Dax. She grimaced in pain as Odo flattened out her hand on the treatment table.

"Supposedly, this machine will speed up the healing of your ligaments," he said, gazing doubtfully at a silver tubelike device. "But I would be careful with that hand, if I were you."

Dax smiled gratefully. "Just do the best you can."

"Look at that neck," muttered Sisko with alarm. He shook his head miserably. "I shouldn't have let you go down there alone."

"It turned out okay," Dax assured him. "I accomplished my mission, and the hive mind will stay out of it. We just have to hope that Elaka was the only one they told."

"But what if she tries it again, or somebody else goes crazy?" asked Sisko.

Dax shrugged. "We'll deal with it when the time comes, like I did with Elaka. I think I made my peace with her. But these are unstable people, and that includes the hive mind."

"There," said Odo, lifting the instrument and turning off its vibrant green beam. He craned his long neck to study the Trill from stem to stern. "I don't think there's anything we can do about the bruises on her neck, except some cold packs and a hypo for pain. You need to rest, Lieutenant."

"I will, Odo. Thanks." She craned her neck to check the time, then groaned slightly with the pain. "What time is it?"

"We have less than three hours," said Sisko. He turned to Odo. "You'd better rest, too, Constable."

"And what will you do?" asked the morph.

"Worry." He patted Dax on the shoulder and smiled. "When things start popping, I hope I have time to beam those insects back."

"You've got to," Dax insisted. "We can't deprive them of their queen."

"I'd have to lower my shields to do it," said Sisko. "This whole thing will require split-second timing."

Odo growled, "And a lot of luck."

"That, too," agreed the human.

"Then if luck is the deciding factor," said Dax, "a few seconds won't make any difference. I gave them my word we would return their queen to them."

"You're awfully forgiving," said Sisko, "considering how they set you up."

Dax coughed. "I think the hive mind is another one who has learned a lesson."

Odo cut in, "Commander, she has to rest. If you insist, I will, too."

"I insist," said the commander. "Leave the worrying to me."

Captain Jon Rachman manned the conn of the Starfleet cruiser *Regal* as she disengaged from the docking ring of DS9 and eased into space. Chief O'Brien sat right beside him at the Ops console, monitoring ship's systems. The crew was extremely skeletal—rounding out the bridge crew were an engineer and two lieutenants, one on weapons and the other on communications. Life-support was cut off everywhere except for the bridge and Engineering, which had a crew of two.

"Half impulse," ordered Rachman.

O'Brien punched in the command and nodded with satisfaction. "Half impulse is totally stable. You can always fall back to that."

"Setting a course for Bajor," said the captain, entering the coordinates himself. "Let's try full impulse."

O'Brien gave him a hopeful smile. "Nothing ventured, nothing gained."

A few seconds later, the chief was satisfied, but the engineer at his station called out, "Twenty-percent drop in fusion rate. I wouldn't want to keep this up more than a minute or two."

"Blast it," muttered the chief. "I thought it would hold better than that."

"That's okay, Chief," said Rachman. "Drop to half impulse. Shields up."

Everyone held their breath for a few seconds, until O'Brien announced, "The shields are holding steady at seventy percent. Any power loss?"

"None," said the ship's engineer. "We could keep this up all day."

"That's better than I expected," said the captain. "Congratulations to you, Chief."

"Oh, it's a pretty good craft," O'Brien responded modestly. "Don't get me started with the things I wasn't able to do."

"Weapons status?" Captain Rachman called out.

"All systems functioning," answered the lieutenant on the weapons console. "Photon torpedoes loaded, phasers powered."

"But the phasers could be erratic," said O'Brien, "and a real power drain."

"That's okay," answered Rachman with a smile. "As long as we're in this sector, we're not lowering the shields except to dock. Maybe not then," he joked. "I'll stick with the torpedoes."

"But if you get into a toe-to-toe—" O'Brien started to say. He didn't need to finish.

"I understand," the captain said grimly. "We'll just look tough. No slugging it out." He turned toward the communications station. "Open a channel to *Deep Space Nine*. Tell them we're coming home."

"Yeah, home," mused O'Brien. "Who would think you could call a place like that home?"

"I'd like to spend some time on *Deep Space Nine*," said Rachman. "Maybe I'll request a transfer. I like being on the frontier."

O'Brien wrinkled his face. "Do it while you're single. I'm not so sure if this is the place to raise a family."

Rachman scratched his dimpled chin. "Speaking of which, does Major Kira have a steady, er, arrangement?"

O'Brien laughed out loud. "Now you *are* getting ambitious. Why don't you stick to something easy, like making admiral before you're thirty."

"A challenge never discouraged me," said the young captain. "Computer, what are my chances with Major Kira?"

"I do not understand the question," said the computer bluntly.

"Okay," said Rachman with a deep intake of breath. "We're ready."

The transporters worked overtime, especially those on the Ferengi Marauder. If anyone on Eco thought it was odd for an entire ship's complement of several hundred people to beam down all at once, they didn't say so. Dax watched with awe as a banquet room on Hive Three filled with Ferengi of every description, including young children, grizzled crew members, aged retainers, and several cadres of naked women. Dax didn't want to think of them as harems, but that's what they had to be. Food and drink were being served by the ubiquitous servants of Hive Three, but several of the Ferengi snuck off to explore the underground metropolis.

Dax set her heavy handbag on the floor and hoped, for Odo's sake, that he wouldn't have to maintain that shape for a lengthy time. As far as the Ferengi were concerned, the evacuation was going as efficiently as possible, and they had twenty times more people than the tanker. Dax didn't want to see the Bajorans again, but she couldn't avoid it if she was going aboard their ship. She left the Ferengi fiesta to head to the conference room and check on the Bajorans.

Minus their leader, the rest of the terrorist band sat around the conference table or slumped against the walls. A few were quietly sampling treats from the food slots. She had met only a handful of the hijackers, and the impoverished condition of the other dozen or so troubled her. For the last two days, they had been eating regularly, but she doubted if many of them had before that. Several of the terrorists were sick or nursing wounds. One woman was in a litter and had to be carried from place to place. About half of them were wearing captured Starfleet uniforms, and she kept her jacket zipped up so as not to reveal her own.

The age of the terrorists also troubled her—Rizo had to be one of the older ones, and they ranged down to the early teens, mere children. Petra was a typical age, and she probably wasn't even twenty. Dax supposed that rebellion was an activity for the young, and she wondered how many of their parents had died trying to cast off the Cardassians. She wanted to tell them that it was time to rebuild, not tear down, but that would be the same as admitting who she really was.

It dawned on her that—if they were successful—they were abandoning these lost souls on the planet of Eco. What would their fate be at the whims of the hive mind? She didn't want to think about what might happen to them, but then Eco was a large planet and there were undoubtedly other cultures and other hives, perhaps more scrupulous. They might end up working for a hive, as did the hirsute creatures; or perhaps the Ferengi would find some use for them. At any rate, the punishment for their crime was exile from their homeworld to a world ruled by insects.

It was hard to feel pity for these murderous thieves, but she only had to look at Elaka and Petra to see the two extremes. One psychologically damaged and possibly beyond redemption, and another who simply knew no other life. In Petra's case, Dax hoped, the exposure to the Ecocid culture would be positive. Whatever happened, it could scarcely be worse than the way they were living now.

"Jade!" said an angry voice.

Dax whirled around to see Elaka, and she instantly tensed for an attack, even though they were surrounded by people.

"I kept calling your name," said Elaka. "Are you all right?"

Dax pulled her collar up around her throat, to hide the bruises. "Thanks to you," she muttered, "I didn't get a lot of sleep last night."

"So sorry," said Elaka. "A little fight is good for you—keeps your battle skills honed. We're both still walking today, aren't we? Say, why are you bringing that purse aboard?"

Dax was ready for this question. "We're picking up a little gold-pressed latinum, too." She still didn't know whether Rizo or Petra had taken Elaka into their confidence about hijacking the Marauder. The absurdity of the idea made Dax cringe, and she wondered whether anybody was really believing their crazy stories. The hijackers were supposed to fall into their trap, but what if it was the other way around?

"I don't know about that bag," Elaka was saying.

"You can scan it, search it manually—anything you want," Dax responded. "Look, I'm a little tired this morning, but everything will go okay."

"It had better," warned Elaka. "We're all down, except for Rizo, of course. How are the bloodsuckers doing?"

"They were doing quite well a few minutes ago," said Dax, relieved to be headed toward the door. "Let me check on them again."

The Ferengi captain assured her that the entire ship's complement was on the ground, except for Gimba. Dax knew this wasn't the truth, but it would have to do. She could see in the captain's eyes that he knew the fix was in. Just going through the motions in order to dupe someone—nothing out of the ordinary for him. She could only hope that the Bajorans weren't trying similar tactics. Dax hefted the heavy bag, thankful to have a secret weapon.

The Trill returned to the conference room and the motley collection of Bajoran terrorists. Petra smiled at her trustingly as she entered.

"The revolution will remember you," said the young woman.

Dax wanted to tell her to get a shower and get away from these people, not necessarily in that order, but she held her tongue. She sought out Elaka, who was overseeing medical treatment of the wounded woman.

"They have medical facilities here," she said, handing Elaka her two leftover bilbok. "See if that will get her some treatment."

The Bajoran women stared at her, as if her act of charity was both a miracle and an affront. Elaka said, "You act like you're not coming back."

"I've had enough of this place," said the Trill. "As soon as Marcus and I get a little antimatter for our reactor, we're leaving here."

"We'll soon have our own latinum," said Elaka proudly.

"But you have this now," insisted Dax, wrapping the other woman's fingers around the rectangular coins. "On Eco, gold-pressed latinum may not buy a bucket of warm spit."

That argument struck home, and Elaka pocketed the bilbok. "Fare thee well, fighter," said the Bajoran. "If you ever care to fight for more than your life, come find us."

"I will," Dax promised, thinking she would bring an army of counselors with her when she came to look for them. "The Ferengi are in the hive, so I think we can proceed."

"All right," said Elaka. "Hand me the bag."

Dax hesitated. "You can scan it. Besides, the Ecocids wouldn't let me carry a weapon down here."

"I want to look inside," the Bajoran insisted. "If it's empty, I'll give it back."

So as not to reveal the bag's unusual weight, Dax opened it and held it open for Elaka's inspection. The Bajoran reached inside and felt around for hidden objects, but she never removed the bag from Dax's grasp.

"Nice bag," Elaka said. "Supple leather." She slapped her stolen Federation comm badge and announced, "It's me. Jade Dixon says the Ferengi are all down, and she's ready to go up."

Rizo answered, "Tell her to go outside the door of the conference room, and I'll lock on."

Elaka quickly added, "She's clean, Rizo, no need to search her."

Rizo grumbled something and signed off. Elaka pointed to the door and said in a whisper, "Remember, Jade, he's my man."

"I know," said Dax. "Take care of your people."

Elaka gave her another strange look, but Dax wasn't about to explain her comment. She strode out the door, trying to look comfortable carrying the heavy bag. As soon as she reached the deserted lounge area, she felt her body tingle in the distinctive way a transporter beam affected it.

Dax materialized, along with her handbag, in the transporter room of the Starfleet tanker *Phoenix*. It was very cramped and utilitarian, mostly for personnel, because antimatter cannot be transported. The docking bay of the *Phoenix* was probably much more impressive, thought Dax.

She wasn't surprised that Rizo wasn't there to meet her, because he was alone on the Starfleet tanker. Or at least, he was supposed to be. The knowledge that the Ferengi Marauder was somehow keeping people back didn't sit well with Dax either. This was like a convention of snakes with no one to be trusted or predicted.

She found a turbolift and entered it, saying merely, "Bridge." The hijackers must have rigged it by now to accept commands from virtually anyone, she thought. Sure enough, the turbolift rose swiftly.

As the door opened, she hoisted the bag, trying to make it look light. Dax smiled as she strode onto the compact bridge of the tanker, and she saw the broad back of the hijacker as he sat hunched over the navigation readouts.

"Take Ops," Rizo ordered. "I can't do every damn thing by myself."

Dax almost set the bag on the floor where she stood, but she decided she had better keep it close. She hauled it to the Ops station and carefully set it on the floor beside her. Then she slipped into the seat and looked at an array of familiar instruments.

"Docking is almost automatic," she said. "At least that's what Marcus told me. Just select the ship you wish to refuel, and the computer and gyrostabilizers will take over."

"Yeah?" scowled Rizo. "All right, then. Let's start that scan of the Marauder, and I'll be looking over your shoulder."

Efficiently, Dax responded, "Both ships are supposed to contact each other first. That's what we agreed to."

Rizo stopped for the first time to look at her, and he gave her a lopsided grin. "Well, we wouldn't want to break an agreement, would we? Contact them."

Dax hoped that Rizo wasn't watching her too closely, because she couldn't entirely hide her proficiency at the Ops station. She hoped he wouldn't notice that she was routing most of the command functions of the ship, including communications and weaponry, into her console.

But Rizo was busy pacing, staring at the viewscreen. "What are those bastards up to?" he muttered. "Are they really off the ship?"

"You never told us," said Dax, as her fingers sped

across the colored panels. "Are you going to try to take the Marauder?"

"No, I'm not," rasped Rizo. "I can't put my people through any more of this. We already have a Starfleet tanker, and what good does that do us? We need to go someplace and hide out, rest, get our bearings. We'll probably end up selling the tanker for a little peace and quiet. I don't want to have to worry about a Ferengi Marauder, too."

Dax shifted in her seat, uncomfortable with the way she was cheating Rizo. He deserved punishment, but he deserved honesty, too. He deserved to have someone treat him fairly, and she was upset that it couldn't be her. She was also sorry that he wasn't going to be one of the terrorists who got a fresh start here in the Gamma Quadrant. He was a casualty of the Cardassian invasion, and he would remain so.

"Jade Dixon to Ferengi vessel," she said in a sultry voice. "Do you read me, Gimba?"

The viewscreen lit up, and a chubby Ferengi grinned lasciviously. "Read you, Jade Dixon? I'd like to smother you with . . . Oh, hello, Rizo. I was hoping I could talk to Jade privately for a moment."

"On your own time," scowled the Bajoran, "not mine. Let's start these scans, and they had better come out clean."

"Yes, they had better," Gimba agreed pleasantly.

Rizo strode behind Dax's back. "You seem to know how to operate that thing. I won't ask you where you learned it. Start the scan."

Dax bit her lip to keep from saying too much. If she was found out now, at least she was aboard, and her secret weapon was only a few centimeters away.

"Starting scan," she said, directing the tanker's

impressive array of sensors at the Marauder. This step was actually necessary, because the tanker's computer needed to know what type of vessel it was dealing with.

On the viewscreen, Gimba leaned over and prodded his panel with stubby fingers. "I'm starting mine," he announced.

Rizo leaned directly over Dax's shoulder, so close she could feel the heat of his breath and the hardness of his chest. "What have you got?" he said hoarsely.

"Scanning all decks," answered Dax. "Looking for life-forms. None registering, except for Gimba on the bridge."

Rizo was smarter than he looked. "What's that blinking area?" he asked, pointing to an abnormal section of the readout.

She swallowed. "An area inside their engine room cannot be scanned. Some sort of interference."

"What the hell kind of interference?" growled Rizo. He glared at the viewscreen. "Gimba, why are you interfering with our scan? What have you got in your engine room?"

But the Ferengi was barely listening. His eyes kept widening as he punched his console and scanned through the screens. "What are *you* braying about? *You* are trying to cheat *us!* I make a number of possible life-form readings in cargo bay two."

Rizo shrugged. "Those are dead bodies you're reading. We never had time to dispose of them."

Dax's lips thinned, knowing whose bodies they were. Former crew members, people she had met in a hundred Starfleet installations, part of her family. She said nothing, because the deal was already teetering enough.

"Well, yes," conceded Gimba, "there is something wrong with them. But a living person could be hiding in that mass of tissue."

"Not likely," answered Rizo. "There's no atmosphere in cargo bay two. Jade can tell you."

The hijacker looked at her expectantly, and Dax had to admit by her actions that she knew the controls well enough to run a status report on cargo bay two.

"It has no atmosphere," she reported.

"What about that spot in your engine room?" countered Rizo. "What's in there?"

Gimba shook his floppy ears. "I have no idea what you're talking about. Now that we have all the crew off the ship, we *are* running some low-level tests for radiation leaks, and that might be affecting your instruments. That's all I can think it would be."

Dax held her breath, waiting to see what effect this lie would have. When no one spoke, she told Rizo, "Their engine room is eight decks away from their main cargo bay. I don't think this should be a deal-breaker."

Rizo cocked his head and smiled. "Expert opinion? Go ahead, Jade—you're in command. Start up the docking procedure."

That had been what Dax was waiting for. As the tanker drifted toward the Marauder to dock, Gimba would be off his guard, and a phaser blast might cripple the Ferengi warship long enough for them to get away. If they didn't delay the Ferengi, they would hunt them down in the wink of an eye. She entered the docking sequence and turned over control of the *Phoenix* to the computer. The ship began to move out of orbit, setting its course automatically.

"I need to go down to our cargo bay," said Gimba. "How long before we dock?"

"Hold on a minute," said Rizo, circling behind Dax. "Gimba, there's somebody I want you to meet."

"Who?" said the Ferengi, showing his anger. "You're supposed to be alone!"

"Except for Jade Dixon," said the terrorist. Brutally, he gripped her ponytail and snapped her head back. "You've met her—now meet Jadzia Dax. A Starfleet lieutenant!"

Dax started to protest, but the pain and the threat of more pain quieted her. She glanced at her handbag. It was as still as she was.

Gimba laughed. "A Starfleet officer? Believe me, I've met Starfleet officers, and they don't look like Jade."

Abruptly, Rizo let go of her hair, and Dax slumped forward. When she swiveled in her seat to look at the Bajoran, he was aiming a phaser at her.

"Tell him," Rizo ordered. He moved the weapon slowly up and down her body. "I wouldn't want to burn any holes in that pretty body. Tell him."

Dax managed a sneer. "You don't believe that stupid hive mind, do you? It's been causing trouble for me since the beginning. What does it matter who I once was—you're getting what you want, aren't you?"

The rugged terrorist shook his head. "Not good enough."

A blue beam stretched between the phaser and Dax's chest, and she bolted backward in her chair. With a moan, the Trill toppled to the floor.

CHAPTER
12

Odo remained perfectly still. As much as he wanted to leap up and throttle the hulking Bajoran, he didn't. With Rizo holding a phaser and Gimba looking on from his warship, it was wiser to be a handbag than a hero. The mission was in jeopardy, but as long as Odo kept his true nature hidden, there was still a chance for success. He hoped Dax wasn't dead or badly injured, but what could he do about it if she was? After he revealed himself, the element of surprise would be gone forever.

Odo sat still and waited. Gimba, in shock, was the first to speak. "By Zot, you haven't killed her, have you?"

"No," said Rizo, lowering the phaser. "It was set on light stun—she'll be out only a few minutes. That should give me enough time to tie her up. Believe me, what I told you is true. The hive mind showed me proof."

"This shouldn't change our arrangement," Gimba said pleasantly. "We're still going to make the exchange, correct?"

Rizo scratched his stubbled cheek with the tip of his phaser. "That depends. You weren't in league with her, were you?"

Gimba chuckled. "With the Federation? Please, we're not that desperate. In fact, we could make a side deal for . . . whatever her name is. I'll give you another ten bars of gold-pressed latinum for her."

Now Rizo laughed. "She's worth a lot more than that just in ransom from the Federation. And for what you want to do with her—twenty bars."

"Fifteen."

Rizo looked down at the unconscious figure and grinned. "Maybe I'll keep her for myself. You don't find one like this every day."

"Sixteen! Not a credit more."

Rizo held up his arms. "Okay, Gimba. I'm in a generous mood. That means you will have twenty-six bars of gold-pressed latinum waiting for me. Nothing funny, all right? I'm not in the mood. And I know all the other settings on this phaser, too."

"Agreed," said Gimba. "I'll get the latinum and go to the cargo bay. I'll route my communications down there."

Rizo glanced at Dax's screen and reported, "Estimated docking in four-point-four minutes."

Gimba nodded, and the viewscreen went blank. Rizo scrounged around in the pockets of his leather vest for a length of cord, and Odo wondered whether this was the moment to make his move. He was about to do so when he heard a moan coming from the floor.

Rizo sneered and leveled the phaser at her. "Hello, Lieutenant Dax. You must have the constitution of a pugabeast. This phaser is still set on stun, but the instructions say it's not good to stun someone repeatedly."

Dax groaned and lifted herself up. "I'll behave myself. But if I don't check in with my ship in a minute or so, Marcus is going to start firing."

Rizo smiled. "You mean Commander Sisko."

She shrugged and lifted herself back into her chair. "If you think he's a Starfleet commander, then you know he can aim a torpedo."

"He won't blow up the tanker," said Rizo confidently.

"If I don't check in soon, he's going to think I'm dead," said Dax. "Then he won't give a damn what happens. He's funny like that."

Rizo waved the phaser nervously. "What are you going to tell him?"

"That the docking is proceeding as planned. No matter what you think, we just want to get out of here with a chunk of antimatter and our lives."

Rizo held the phaser at the back of Dax's head, where it would be unseen by the viewscreen angle. He clicked up the phaser setting several notches. "Say the wrong thing," he warned, "and it'll take a month to clean you off this bridge."

Dax swallowed and rubbed her head. "I understand." A few seconds later, she announced, "This is the *Phoenix* calling the *Mekong*. Marcus, this is Jade."

The face of Benjamin Sisko came on the viewscreen, and he gave them his chipper Marcus Garvey smile. "How good to see you," he chirped. "Is everything proceeding as planned?"

Dax took a breath and rubbed her hands together. "It seems to be going well. I'm a little nervous, that's all."

"Why are you nervous?" asked Sisko pleasantly.

"Yes, why?" echoed Rizo.

Dax smiled. "I don't know—guess I drank too much coffee. But we have started docking procedures with the Marauder, and that's going well."

"Understood," said Sisko calmly. "If you cannot pick up our fee at this time, I'll understand. Do you still have your bag to bring back the latinum?"

"Yes," she answered.

"Just keep me posted," said Sisko. The viewscreen went blank.

This was the time to act, thought Odo. They had to do it while they were out of contact with the Ferengi vessel, and Sisko had just been notified. If there were only some way he could communicate with Dax—

The Trill sensed the same urgency. "May I stand up and walk off this headache?" she asked.

"I'm keeping my eye on you," Rizo warned her. "And this phaser is still set to do some damage."

When Dax stood up, she did the best thing possible by walking away from Rizo and forcing him to turn his back on the handbag. "Was that true," she asked, "about you wanting to get away from the fight to rest and evaluate your life?"

"It's a nice idea," said the terrorist wistfully. "But somehow the fight always comes after me."

At that moment, a slender figure was looming behind the Bajoran. Dax tried to show no reaction, except to stare at the phaser that was leveled at her. When she saw the shapeshifter's hands rise above Rizo's head and form a large mallet, Dax poised to dodge. The mallet came crashing down, and she leaped out of the way—just as a phaser beam ripped through the air. The science console burned and sizzled until Rizo lost his grip on the phaser, followed by his grip on consciousness. He slumped to the floor.

At once, Odo grabbed the cord from his outstretched hand and began to tie him up. Dax rushed to the Ops console and punched the panel that put the Ferengi Marauder on the screen. The distinctive crab-shaped vessel almost filled the viewscreen.

"We're too close," said Dax, "to fire on the Ferengi ourselves. We'll have to get the commander to do it."

Odo continued to wind cord around Rizo's hands and feet. "I heard his explanation about the dead bodies in the hold. Do you really think they're all dead?"

"I don't know," admitted Dax, plying the controls. "I can't get the internal sensors to work—a lot of the circuitry was destroyed. The best I can do is to seal off the cargo bays. Just in case, you had better keep an eye on the turbolift."

Odo nodded and finished tying up Rizo. With distaste, he picked up the discarded phaser and handed it to Dax. Then he stood at attention, swiveling his head slowly from the Trill to the unconscious prisoner to the turbolift door.

"Are we taking him back with us?" asked Odo.

"We should, shouldn't we?" said Dax.

"Yes. Murder, hijacking, terrorism, kidnapping—I believe we have enough charges to hold him."

"We've got to get home first," added Dax. She gazed from her instruments to the viewscreen, but the information was the same. Under computer control, the tanker was making a cautious but inexorable approach to the Ferengi Marauder.

Thinking out loud, she muttered, "If Gimba is alone, or nearly alone, maybe he won't have time to monitor our transmissions. We have to hope so, because we've got to contact the commander. If Gimba hits us with a tractor beam, we belong to them."

With determination, she plied the controls. "Jade to Marcus. Come in, *Mekong.*"

Sisko's grave face burst upon the viewscreen. "Marcus here. What is your status?"

"Better," said Jade, "since our last message. Our captain is indisposed at the moment, and we are right on top of the Marauder. It should happen soon."

"I understand," answered Sisko. "I took us out of orbit and headed your way after our last conversation. I suppose it will be up to me to say our final good-byes."

"I'm afraid so," Dax answered calmly. "Did you send our visitors back?"

The commander scowled. "Yes, right after I talked to you. I was relieved to see them go."

"Then we can get on with our business," said Dax.

Sisko's jaw clenched. "Whenever you wish."

Dax stroked the panel, and the tanker stopped dead in front of the foreboding Ferengi Marauder. She punched in a rough course toward the wormhole and sent the ship into impulse power. The boxy craft couldn't make an elegant maneuver, but it did a slow about-face and lumbered toward the stars.

Sisko's face was immediately replaced on the viewscreen by an angry Ferengi, standing in an empty cargo bay. "What do you think you're doing?" raged Gimba, shaking his fists. "Where's Rizo?"

Dax just stared at the Ferengi, counting the seconds until the runabout showed up. As Gimba was about to demand an answer, the Marauder was rocked by phaser blasts. Gimba staggered from the impact, and she could see other Ferengi rushing from their hiding places—crew members who weren't supposed to be there.

"Weapons!" he yelled. "Shields up! Get to the transporter room! Get our bridge crew back!"

His ship was rocked again, and the screen degenerated into a mass of crackling interference. There wasn't much Dax could say to Gimba, anyway, and she knew the runabout couldn't permanently cripple the big ship. If they'd had a full crew and people manning the bridge, the runabout would probably have been blown to space junk by now.

"Going to warp four," said the Trill.

Odo nodded and slipped into the chair beside her, but his attention was riveted on the unconscious Bajoran and the turbolift door beyond.

Commander Sisko saw the *Phoenix* elongate slightly and streak out of sight, and he knew it was time for him to make *his* getaway. He had been firing his small phaser emitters so rapidly that he hoped he had enough power left to reach warp drive. The Marauder had put her shields up by now, so he cut off his attack and cruised away. He realized that the lack of a crew was the main reason the Ferengi ship wasn't coming after him immediately.

His viewscreen blinked on, and a truly disgusted-looking Ferengi glared at him.

"I congratulate you," muttered Gimba. "You fooled us completely, you and your lovely accomplice. But business comes before revenge, we Ferengi always say, and I am just as willing to negotiate with you for the antimatter as I was with the Bajorans. In fact, I'm not terribly disappointed to see them replaced in this deal."

"I don't own the antimatter," said Sisko. "It belongs to the Federation, and I'm just returning it."

"By Zot!" snapped Gimba. "You *are* a Federation sympathizer! You can never trust humans. Listen, human, you have a long way to go to get back to the Federation, and our bridge crew has just beamed aboard."

"Then I had better get going," answered Sisko. He saluted and broke off communications.

Warp four was close to the limit for the runabout, but they couldn't chance getting away at a slower speed. The Marauder was capable of warp nine and would be on them in a thrice. He plied the controls and forced the tiny ship into warp drive, hoping his attack had bought them enough time.

Rizo howled in anger, and the big Bajoran strained and twisted against his bonds like a shark thrashing about on the floor of a boat.

"I'll kill you!" he screamed. "I'll kill you!"

"If he doesn't shut up," said Dax, "we'll have to stun him."

Odo gazed sternly at Rizo. "I'll leave that pleasure to you, Lieutenant. You know, after he stunned you, he tried to sell you to the Ferengi."

Dax smiled. "For how much?"

"Sixteen bars of gold-pressed latinum. To his credit, the Ferengi originally offered ten."

"I'm flattered," said Dax.

Rizo muttered, "I was just toying with them. I wouldn't have sold you to the Ferengi. You're too valuable as a hostage."

"Am I?" asked Dax, never taking her eyes off her instruments. "I'm afraid I'm not your prisoner. It's the other way around."

"For now," said Rizo. "But you're running, just like we were. And you'll never make it back."

"Perhaps you should stun him," suggested Odo. "He hasn't exactly shut up."

"No," said Dax. "We have several hours before we reach the wormhole, so we might as well make the best of it. Besides, I'm interested to know who will stop us."

Rizo laughed. "The Ferengi, for one. And you don't know who else might be out there. The resistance has a lot of friends, you know."

"Do your friends have a ship?" asked Dax.

"Why not?" snarled Rizo. "Until a few minutes ago, *I* had a ship. Plus, we have friends who have ships."

That thought gave Dax pause, because she remembered the ruthless tendencies of the Klingon renegades. They had gladly allied themselves with the Bajoran terrorists in the past.

"It doesn't matter," she said. "We've gotten this far, and we can't turn back. You should be more concerned about yourself."

"Me?" scoffed Rizo. "I'm a dead man. But I've been dead for years. I'll kill myself before I let you put me in a cell for the rest of my life."

"I would think you could get treatment," Dax suggested.

"Treatment? Is that the new punishment for murder and hijacking?"

"Not on Bajor, it isn't," said Odo. "We have several interesting penal colonies, most of them built by the

Cardassians. They're fairly empty, so you'll have lots of room to relax."

Rizo growled, "That's great. The Federation can give me treatment, and the puppet government can lock me up for the rest of my life. I'll be the most well-adjusted prisoner you ever saw!"

Despite being tied up on his stomach, Rizo shook his head angrily. "Kill me now, because I'm not going to rot in a cell. Kill me! Kill me!" he screamed, and continued screaming until it grated on Dax's nerves.

She shook her head sadly and picked up the phaser. "We'll see you in a few minutes, Rizo."

Commander Sisko looked at his sensors and grunted with alarm. No, it wasn't a phantom—a photon torpedo was right on his tail, launched by a Ferengi Marauder that wasn't far behind. He braced himself as the torpedo overtook him and shook the small craft with a near miss. At once, his power began to drop, and the runabout shuddered as it came out of warp drive.

He banged on his comm panel. *"Mekong* to *Phoenix!* I'm under attack!"

Dax's concerned face appeared on his viewscreen, but her image wavered when he put up the runabout's shields. "Benjamin, we have a fix on you—we can double back. Is it the Marauder?"

"Yes. But keep on going! Don't come back."

"Interference in that last part," said Dax, cutting off communications.

Sisko didn't have time to scold her or worry about the tanker, as he could see the Ferengi Marauder glide out of warp drive, not ten thousand kilometers away. He threw the runabout into full impulse and began evasive maneuvers. Such a stratagem had saved his life at Wolf 359, and Sisko was in complete charge of the small craft. The Ferengi vessel opened with phasers, but Sisko dodged out of range and took only a peripheral hit. They were forced to give chase through an expansive solar system, with only three small planets as guideposts.

After a few tense maneuvers, the commander took the time to wipe the sweat from his lofty brow and short-cropped hair. As quickly as they had come after him, he figured the Ferengi still had only a minimal crew, and the Marauder wasn't designed to be flown solo like the runabout. The *Mekong* was small but it was responsive—he could zig while they were still zagging. At full impulse, he was gradually pulling away from them.

That was the good news. The bad news was that he would run out of fuel, or fall asleep, long before they did. And warp drive was a death trap, not a means of escape. Time was on their side.

The Marauder soon lagged far enough behind him that he wondered if he could turn and get off a shot of his own. As long as Dax had insisted on joining the fight, he might as well give her a stationary target. He had only two microtorpedoes, but they wouldn't do him much good if a Ferengi torpedo caught him first. Then he would be a cosmic cinder.

The Ferengi captain tried to hail him, but Sisko ignored his angry pleadings. There was nothing left to negotiate. He turned swiftly while checking to make sure torpedo bay one was ready, and he caught the Ferengi vessel making a slow turn to reach his last position. He locked in on his target and launched the torpedo without hesitation. It streaked toward the sluggish starship.

The explosion lit the starscape like a nova, and Sisko leaned forward eagerly. His joy was short-lived, however, when it became evident that the Marauder had its shields at full effectiveness and had sustained minor damage at best. The Ferengi were not known for being great warriors, but they were known for having excellent shields.

Sisko braced himself to be obliterated, and he was surprised when there wasn't an answering torpedo. Maybe the Marauder was more damaged than it looked, he thought hopefully. His hope was dashed a moment later when the Ferengi began hailing him again.

He put the smiling image of Gimba, who was still stationed in the empty cargo bay, on the viewscreen. "If that's the best you can do, Marcus Garvey, then you had better surrender yourself. We have no desire to destroy you—just to reclaim what is ours."

Sisko answered calmly, stalling for time. "If your wish is to see the tanker returned to its rightful owners, then let us go."

"We *are* the rightful owners," snarled Gimba. He quickly replaced his anger with his usual superior air. "Why do you insist upon making this difficult? Tell Jade to return with the tanker, and we'll conclude our business, as planned. You can receive the latinum we promised the Bajorans, and we'll leave you with the ship you have. What more could you possibly ask?"

"You won't try to hold us?" asked Sisko.

The Ferengi chuckled. "What do I look like, an Orion slaver? Trust me, it is the antimatter and the tanker we have always wanted. This entire deal has been more trouble than it's worth, I can tell you, and we'll be lucky to turn even a minuscule profit."

"Poor thing," said Sisko with mock sympathy. He

suddenly had an idea. "Put down your shields, and I'll beam over to talk about it."

Gimba smiled pleasantly. "You put down *your* shields, and we'll transport you over."

Despite his bravado, Sisko was worried. He had no options, and he had no idea what good Dax could do in the tanker once she showed up. The tanker probably wasn't armed much better than the runabout, and neither one of them could outrun the Marauder. It appeared, at best, that only one of them could get back to the Alpha Quadrant.

The commander resolved to make sure it was the tanker that got back. He readied the self-destruct sequence for the runabout and plotted a suicide course straight into the Marauder. Then he aimed his second—and last—torpedo at the Marauder's main cargo bay.

"We are waiting," said Gimba. "Put down your shields, disarm your weapons, and we'll behave as partners again."

Sisko thought about the whip Gimba had described at one of their meetings, and the way it was used on people who double-crossed them. He scanned his sensors for the arrival of the tanker, and he saw it at the same time that somebody came running forward to alert Gimba. Sisko launched his torpedo just as Gimba's eyes widened at the news.

The Ferengi vessel shuddered at the impact, and sparks burst from a flaming control panel behind Gimba. The crew ran for cover, and Sisko wondered if the cumulative effect of his attacks had been greater than he had imagined. He put a wide view of the starscape on his screen, and he saw the tanker lumber over his head and get off a phaser array of its own. The

Marauder teetered in space and lit up like a crab-shaped Christmas-tree ornament.

There was no time to gloat, however, because the Marauder would soon be getting off shots of its own. One misplaced hit on the tanker could end it all rather quickly. Sisko hit his communications panel. *"Mekong* to *Phoenix.* Bypass our first rendezvous point and go straight to the second."

"Acknowledged," answered Dax.

Sisko waited to leave until he saw the tanker streak into warp drive; then he took off on its tail. He realized the rear of the convoy was the more dangerous position, especially since he had used up all his microtorpedoes; but Sisko had brought them here to save the tanker, and save it they would. The goal of self-preservation was also on his mind, and that was another reason to keep the tanker from being the first one hit.

Without torpedoes, he still had his phaser emitters. But he had already emptied them into the Marauder without much effect, so he didn't hold much hope for the phasers as a deterrent. With a sigh, the commander canceled the self-destruct sequence on the runabout. He knew that Gimba would be happy to perform that service, free of charge.

For her part, Dax was also deep in thought, wondering how they could extricate themselves from this race they couldn't win. She had no illusions that the Marauder was out of it. In fact, her long-range scanners picked up the fact that the starship had moved from its last position. If it could manage even half of the warp drive it was capable of, it would easily catch them again before they reached the wormhole.

Something thudded beyond the turbolift. "What was that?" asked Odo, rising to his feet.

They heard wheezing laughter coming from the ground. "Ghosts," answered Rizo. "Coming to get us, to make us atone for our sins."

"You're awake," said Odo with disappointment. "It might be harmful to stun you again so soon, but I am perfectly willing to put you in the hold with the dead bodies."

"Fine with me," answered Rizo. "I have more in common with them than with you. Besides, we all share the same future."

Dax ignored him and warned, "Somebody could be trying to climb down the turbolift shaft, to avoid the forcefields I put in the corridors."

"I can go look for them," offered Odo, "but I don't know the design of this craft very well."

Dax sighed. "Yes, and it's bigger than it looks. I'd better be the one to go."

"Look how brave you are!" crowed Rizo. "You really are a Starfleet lieutenant. That's amazing. I never thought we could trust you, but I didn't think that was the reason. You should feel very proud of yourself."

"I'm not proud of using subterfuge," answered Dax, rising to her feet. She picked up the phaser. "Call me if you see anything unusual on the readouts."

"I would prefer to go instead," said Odo. "Perhaps if I took a moment to study the schematics of the ship—"

Dax wasn't a coward, but it wasn't fair to make Odo take over the unfamiliar controls of the tanker under these conditions. At any moment, a Ferengi torpedo could catch up with them. She set the phaser back on the Ops console and returned to her seat.

"I'll bring up the schematics on your screen," offered the Trill, "with an emphasis on the cargo bays and the turbolifts leading to them. And I'll show you which corridors are sealed off. We ought to check on the antimatter pods as well. But for the moment, let's just keep an eye on our passenger."

"Absolutely," said the security chief, fixing his most dour gaze upon the Bajoran.

"Ghosts." Rizo grinned. "They're out there all right. All the ghosts of the crew we killed, and our own brave comrades as well. Most of them murdered on this very spot, right where you're sitting."

Against her will, Dax looked down, and she did see the smeared stains on the deck. Someone had tried to wipe them up, but there had been a lot of blood.

The bound prisoner wheezed a laugh. "They couldn't escape, and neither can you."

CHAPTER
13

BENJAMIN SISKO had a bad feeling, the same feeling he'd had just before the Ecocids revealed themselves as extortionists. By all rights, things were going better than they could expect. In a few minutes, they were due to rendezvous near a giant asteroid belt they had passed on their initial dash across the Gamma Quadrant. They had been able to skip their first rendezvous after the unscheduled stop with the Ferengi. Since then, the Ferengi vessel had remained out of scanner range, if it was behind them at all.

It was too early to say if the Marauder had broken off its pursuit, but there was at least a chance it had. Of course, the Ferengi knew the position of the wormhole as well as anyone, and they could be trying to do an end-around, to get there first. That prospect was real, yet it wasn't the cause of Sisko's apprehension.

Real, even likely, obstacles Sisko was used to handling. It was the unseen, the unreal, the unexpected that bothered him. By that token, the absence of the Marauder was troubling, because Sisko knew that the Ferengi never let go of money. The antimatter represented cold cash to them, including expenses uncollected. If the Marauder was able to fly at all, it should be right on their tail.

He pressed his communications panel. "Sisko to Dax. Do you see any sign of that Marauder?"

"No, Benjamin," answered Dax. "She was on the move last I got a reading. I thought she had gone into warp, but there's been no sign of her. The *Phoenix* has excellent scanners, but we're out of range from where we left her. Maybe we hit her harder than we thought."

"This may sound crazy," said Sisko, "but I'd like to go back and see what happened to them."

Odo had remained silent until that point, but he jumped up and filled Sisko's viewscreen. "That's very humanitarian of you, Commander, but we aren't on a rescue mission. To say that Gimba deserved what he got is putting it mildly. Their ship didn't look so badly damaged that they couldn't make it to Eco or some other port of call."

"That's the point," said Sisko. "If they're not badly damaged, why aren't they after us? Look, Constable, I don't have to go all the way back, just far enough to get them in sensor range. Maybe they're still where we left them. They might also be trying to go around us, trying to reach the wormhole first."

"Odo," said Dax, "the commander is right. Either they are too damaged to come after us, they have broken off, or they are planning an ambush. Whichever it is, we need to know." She smiled. "Besides, it *is* the humanitarian thing to do."

Odo bowed his head and said nothing more.

Sisko remarked, "You can keep going to the wormhole. Perhaps we don't need to rendezvous sooner."

The commander saw Dax glance at Odo; then he heard laughter coming from off the screen.

"The tanker is haunted, Commander!" called a voice from the floor. "There are bumps and thumps in the night. I say it's the ghosts of all those bodies in the hold—what do you think?"

The computer located the source of the voice and widened the angle to include the hog-tied Bajoran.

Sisko muttered, "I had almost forgotten about you, Rizo. Are you so desperate that you have to make up imaginary allies?"

"They may not be imaginary," said Dax. "We feel there could be someone else aboard. The internal security on the tanker has been destroyed, and we'll have to go out with tricorders to check the ship. We also need to check on the antimatter pods, so we would prefer to stop at the asteroid belt as planned. The computer says the pods are all right, but—"

"I understand," said Sisko, "you need to eyeball them. I don't blame you—we have gone to an awful lot of trouble to get them. I'm going to backtrack just enough to find out the status of the Marauder, while you continue on to the rendezvous. I don't suppose there are any detention cells on that tanker?"

"No," said Odo.

Rizo began to laugh. "Don't you understand, Commander?" yelled the Bajoran. "That stuff is cursed! Everybody who handles that antimatter is going to die. We're not going to make it back."

"Have you stunned him?" asked Sisko.

Odo sighed. "Yes, and cracked him on the head for good measure. That's another reason for stopping— to find a secure area to put him."

"Proceed," ordered Sisko. "I'll let you know as soon as I locate the Ferengi. Sisko out."

After the screen switched back to the slightly blurred starscape of warp drive, Odo looked with disgust at his prisoner. He expected even captured criminals to act somewhat dignified, which didn't include ranting about ghosts and haunted spaceships. Of course, the prisoner was the only one who knew if the tanker had any stowaways. Odo didn't imagine there could be more than one, but one more terrorist made the odds even—two against two.

Having taken the craft once by force, the Bajorans wouldn't be averse to trying it again. Plus, they would get desperate as they realized their only alternative was probably life in prison.

"Constable?" said Rizo, gazing up at him. "Is that really what they call you? That was a neat trick, coming aboard as a handbag. How do you do that?"

Odo cocked his head and looked annoyed. "I don't wish to hold a conversation with you, especially about matters that are none of your business."

"Oh, touchy," cooed Rizo. "But look at me, Constable—I'm not shouting and screaming now. I'm merely trying to pass the time. What kind of species are you?"

The shapeshifter shrugged. "Does it matter? Have you ever seen any like me?"

"No," admitted the Bajoran. "But you would be invaluable to us, if you decided to have a little excitement in your life."

Odo gazed around the unfamiliar bridge of the tanker, and his eyes came to rest with distaste upon his prisoner. "I've got quite enough excitement in my life, thank you. Besides, your days are going to be considerably less exciting from now on."

Rizo closed his eyes and struggled to find a comfortable position. "If you really find a room to put me in, are you going to take off these ropes?"

"Eventually," said Odo, "I'm sure they will come off."

"Maybe we can rig up something with forcefields," Dax suggested, "and monitor him on one of the viewscreens."

"Are you two really from *Deep Space Nine?*" asked Rizo, suddenly friendly. "I've only heard about the station—my life doesn't lend itself to taking vacations."

"I'm the science officer," said Dax, "and Odo is the chief of security. DS9 was built by Cardassians, so, in case you were wondering, it has plenty of detention cells."

Rizo scowled. "I liked you better as Jade Dixon. Both of you are being wasted in Starfleet."

"I'm not in Starfleet," Odo added. "I work for Bajor."

"So do I," snapped Rizo.

Odo shook his head. "I don't think so. The Bajor I work for is trying to build upon its hard-won freedom. It's trying to stop fighting and make peace with itself, and its neighbors."

The Bajoran muttered, "Does that include Cardassians?"

"I'm afraid so," said Odo.

"Then the puppet government is weaker than I thought," Rizo decided. "It's a wonder anyone supports them. You know, we only stole the antimatter to keep that new starship for Bajor."

"All you did was to delay its testing," countered Dax. "If you want to stop fighting and live peacefully, now would be a good time to start."

"Yeah," scoffed Rizo, "as we run from a starship fifty times our size. Save me your platitudes, Lieutenant. You did what had to be done to recapture this tanker. You opened fire on the Ferengi and left hundreds of innocent people down there on that bug-infested planet."

"We can go back for them," said Dax.

Rizo shook his head. "You won't. Nobody will. Because nobody will ever know where they are—after this tanker blows up, and we all die."

Dax flashed anger only briefly before she grit her teeth and announced. "Coming out of warp drive. Going into synchronous orbit with the largest asteroid, G-One, for lack of a better name."

Odo asked worriedly, "You're not going to orbit an asteroid in the middle of an asteroid belt, are you?"

"No," said Dax. "We're coasting along beside it, at a safe distance, orbiting whatever *it's* orbiting. I imagine it's taking a leisurely trip around that red giant in the corner of the screen. This position should be safe, and it has the advantage of shielding us from a casual scan."

The Trill entered some final commands on her console, grabbed the phaser, and stood up. She checked the setting, took a few steps back, and leveled the weapon at Rizo.

"Go ahead, untie him," she ordered.

"All right," said Odo, bending down to undo his handiwork.

"Hey, friend," said Rizo to the shapeshifter. "Don't you ever carry a phaser?"

"Never."

"How come?"

"For one thing," answered Odo, "if you don't carry a phaser, it's impossible for a prisoner to take yours away from you."

Odo finished untying the Bajoran and stepped back, unarmed but ready to react quickly.

Dax pointed to the turbolift with the phaser. "You go first."

Rizo grinned. "You want the ghosts to get me first?"

"Move it," ordered Dax. "How you act will determine the kind of holding cell we put you in. There may be some spare antimatter pods, and we could seal you up in one of those."

Rizo laughed nervously. "She's just joking, right, Constable?"

"I haven't known Lieutenant Dax to joke," answered Odo. "You had better follow instructions."

Humming loudly and off-key, Rizo swaggered toward the turbolift doors, which flew open at his approach. "It's just me—Rizo!" he announced. "Do your worst, ghosts. I know we're not going to make it back to Bajor."

Odo looked at Dax and shook his head in disgust. The more he thought about it, the better he liked the idea of sealing the terrorist inside an empty antimatter pod. But first, they had to make sure there weren't any more of his playmates around.

The shapeshifter entered the turbolift immediately after Rizo. When Dax entered, he stationed himself between her and the Bajoran, knowing that Rizo might try something in the confines of the turbolift.

"Deck three," said Dax. "We should check on the antimatter first."

"Are the forcefields still up?" asked Odo.

"I turned them off on deck three," answered Dax. "So we can move around. This ship has only three levels, and the bottom one is nothing but cargo bays. That's where they keep the antimatter."

"And the bodies," Rizo whispered.

The turbolift came to a stop, and the door whooshed open. Odo stepped out, dragging Rizo by the arm, and pushed him a safe distance away from Dax and her phaser.

The Bajoran ignored the rough treatment and kept his attention focused on Dax. "Which one are we going to see first, Lieutenant, the antimatter or the bodies?"

"First we have to find some tricorders," answered Dax. "You wouldn't happen to know where some are, would you? I couldn't find any on the bridge."

The Bajoran laughed. "I knew where some *were*, but we handed them out to everyone. I think some were traded to the Ecocids for bilbok."

While this conversation was going on, Odo stole a moment's attention from Dax and Rizo to look around the anteroom of the cargo bay. It was like a miniature bridge, with its own viewscreens and workstations, one for each of the three large doors that surrounded them. The doors were marked One, Two, and Three, and a thick-paned window on each did little to reveal their contents. He could see vague white shapes beyond door one, but cargo bays two and three looked dark and dismal.

It was very quiet in the hold of the deserted tanker, and Odo wondered if the earlier sound they heard was just an aural mirage. But, no, he thought. The Ferengi captain had also been suspicious, but he had been playing the same game and couldn't complain. Rizo had at least entertained the thought of taking the Marauder, and he certainly had no scruples to prevent him from keeping another killer on board.

The shapeshifter turned to see Rizo take a threatening step toward Dax. "Keep your distance," he warned.

"It's all right," answered Dax. "He was walking past me to show me where there might be a tricorder."

"I'll go," offered Odo. "Where is it?"

"A bit touchy, aren't we, Constable?" sneered Rizo. Nevertheless, he pointed. "In that panel under the console for bay one. There was some stuff in there before."

Odo opened the panel but could find nothing in it except for wads of bloody bandages. A human might not have been able to search through the soiled bandages, caked with bodily fluids, but Odo had no such compulsions. His only disappointment was that there were no tricorders in evidence.

"Anywhere else?" he asked.

Rizo shrugged. "What can I tell you, we're pirates, and we sacked the ship. I'm sorry we didn't treat it as nicely as you would, but we're not used to many nice things."

Dax frowned. "Rizo, if you can't be of any use to us, I'm going to find a place to put you. Any ideas, Constable?"

"Yes," replied the shapeshifter. "If cargo bay one holds the antimatter pods, and bay two holds the bodies, what's in bay three?"

"That would be the smallest of the cargo bays," answered Dax, moving behind its controls. She punched in some commands, gazed at the readouts, and frowned. "All the logs have been erased and disabled. We'll never know who came in and out of these cargo bays, or what they were carrying."

Rizo grinned. "Sorry, Lieutenant. We didn't know what we were doing."

"I think you knew exactly what you were doing," muttered Dax. "There's nothing left to do but fill them with atmosphere and go have a look. I'm filling bay three with atmosphere."

She moved to the center console. "Filling bay two." She glanced at the controls for the largest bay. "Bay one already has atmosphere. I hope you didn't disable the automated docking systems, too."

"No," said Rizo, sounding hurt. "The idea is to *get rid* of the antimatter, remember? We're simple people, and we trust each other. So we shut down a few security systems."

Dax moved back to the controls for cargo bay three and pressed the button that opened the door. It slid open with a gasp of fresh atmosphere, and the lights blinked on, illuminating the auxilary cargo hold. Odo strolled a few meters into the chamber. It was empty now, except for assorted robotic arms, belts, and bumpers that guided antimatter pods toward a freight turbolift. Odo imagined that the turbolift took the pods straight out the docking module in the nose, or perhaps to the other cargo bays. An efficient setup, he observed—also a means of escape from the ship.

Nevertheless, they couldn't drag Rizo around with them everywhere they went. It was simply too dangerous, considering the constant demands on their attention. Besides, outside the ship was nothing but cold space and asteroids.

Odo returned to the doorway. "I'm going to search

for an intruder, or weapons. If this bay is clean, I suggest we put our prisoner here. Can we disable the controls?"

Dax shrugged. "Why not? Everything else has been disabled."

Odo nodded and went back into the empty bay. The storage area struck him as small, but he reminded himself that this was the most auxiliary of the cargo bays on the *Phoenix*. The dull yellow walls bespoke a utilitarian existence for the room. The only features of interest were the robotic mechanisms that moved the storage pods in their inexorable journey to a matter/antimatter reactor. Without pods to move, they looked like frozen monuments to tasks uncompleted. He wandered between two big arms and a viselike pincer, and he was reminded uncomfortably of the Ecocids. This was a machine an insect might appreciate.

With no sensors or weapons at his disposal, Odo perused every centimeter of the silent chamber. He crouched down and looked into dark crevices, and he opened storage and equipment panels. He was on the lookout for tricorders as well, but everything of value had been stripped by the scavengers, replaced by bandages and soiled clothes. He wondered if they had slept in here, too, but then he decided that they would have taken over the crew's quarters on the second deck. That thought hiked Odo's threshold of anger for a moment, but he quickly shook it off and returned to his search.

The emptiness of the cargo bay made his investigation easier, and he was soon convinced that cargo bay three was empty.

"Come in, Rizo!" he called. "And go to the far corner, where the scale is."

The Bajoran did as he was told, shuffling into the empty room and taking a sullen position near a floor scale in a remote corner. Dax entered and went straight to the control panel, which duplicated the console outside the door, except for its lack of a chair and a viewscreen.

Rizo grinned and looked around the room. "So this is to be my grave? My tomb. You'll leave me here to die, just like you left my comrades on Eco, just like you left the Ferengi vessel."

"We won't be able to hear him in here, will we?" asked Odo.

"Not likely," said Dax with a smile. "They've disabled all the password protection, so I'm going to do what they did—destroy the circuitry."

She reached into a panel and pulled out an isolinear chip, which she set on the floor. She proceeded to reset her phaser, take aim at the chip, and strike it with a pinpoint blue beam. After a second, the chip was a wisp of smoke.

"We just ground them with our heels," said Rizo.

Odo backed slowly away from the terrorist, expecting him to make his move. But something within Rizo was beaten down—despite his bravado and crude energy, he seemed weary. He sat on the floor, testing the scale with his hand. A digital readout was a blur as it registered the changes in weight.

"Lieutenant," said the Bajoran. "I wish you well, truly I do. This isn't a fight you should be involved in. Bajor must be just for Bajorans. We don't know the Federation very well, but we know how a conqueror can start off with promises and aid, only to turn into an occupying army. We let ourselves be conquered once—it can't happen again."

"I have sympathy for your feelings," answered Dax.

"And the suffering you can't get over. There's been nothing in my life to compare to it, and I'm eight times your age. But many of your people have put the horror behind them in order to get on with their lives. I might remind you that the Federation also fought the Cardassians."

"It was the resistance!" insisted Rizo.

"Both," admitted Dax. "Nevertheless, we have earned your trust. The Federation could keep a much greater presence on Bajor, but we don't." She motioned around the empty cargo bay. "And sometimes it gets us into trouble."

The Bajoran shook his head. "I doubt if everyone in your Federation is as noble as you, Lieutenant." He glanced at Odo. "There are too many alien species on Bajor already."

Odo scoffed, "We're wasting time. We may have to search this entire ship."

Dax lowered her head and nodded. "I'm afraid you're right. Rizo, we'll bring you food and water later."

He waved at her. "Good-bye, Jadzia Dax. And Jade Dixon."

Dax hurried out, quickly followed by Odo, and the door clanged shut behind them. While Dax stopped at the controls to make sure the makeshift cell was secure, Odo strode to the massive door marked One and gazed through the thick window. He could see the storage pods—hexagonal cylinders each about the height of a man but much wider—stacked end to end in neat rows. Not only was this bay twice as large as bay three, but it had an intricate network of thick tubes crisscrossing its high ceiling.

"What are all those tubes for?" he asked.

"Under normal circumstances," said Dax, "the

storage pods wouldn't leave the cargo bay during refueling. Using those shielded conduits, the antimatter would be moved directly from the full storage pods into the empty pods on the starship. But the *Hannibal* is a new ship without any storage pods of its own, so the pods themselves are going on board."

She moved to the controls for bay one and announced, "I'm opening the door."

Odo stepped back as the door drew open. He braced himself for a possible attack, although he thought it unlikely that their stowaway, if they had one, would be hiding among the antimatter. It wasn't the kind of place a person would want to stay for hours on end. There was something distinctly foreboding about the large white canisters, emblazoned in red letters that issued severe warnings in several languages. They looked like rows of alien coffins.

He moved into the room in a crouch, glancing into the corners and low places. Bright overhead lighting dispelled most of the shadows and made his search easy. Like the other cargo bay, this was a big room, but it didn't offer many hiding places. Three-fourths of the space was taken up by the storage pods and their support mechanism. The rest was simply vacant, and he figured there was room for ten more pods.

Dax stopped at the closest pod and bent over to study the readouts on its tiny screen. Odo recalled from his research that each storage pod was a self-contained unit with its own computer and monitoring systems. The internal systems had to be good, because only the stability of the magnetic field stood between safety and total annihilation.

Odo heard a gentle chirping noise and whirled around to face an offending pod. "What is it doing?" he asked.

Dax smiled as she moved from pod to pod, inspecting their readouts. "They're quite remarkable, these pods. Each has its own diagnostic system set to start at a different time. The beeping means a pod has completed its diagnostic sweep. It will sleep for several hours and do it again."

"Is the tanker equipped to eject these pods?" asked Odo.

Dax shook her head. "Not in the way a starship can. Of course, we can shoot them out the space dock, but they're not plugged into an ejection system here, like they will be on the *Hannibal*."

She chuckled. "I think Benjamin once referred to a Starfleet tanker as a giant gas can. He's not far from wrong."

Pressing flat against the wall, Odo maneuvered his way around the storage pods and made a complete excursion of the cargo bay. He peered into the freight turbolift, under the conduits and pipework, and between the gigantic robot arms, but he didn't find anything amiss. Still, the somber storage pods made him uneasy, and he stood outside the door as Dax completed her inspection of each individual container.

She stepped out, and the door shut automatically behind her. "The pods appear in order," she announced. "At least Rizo and his friend didn't tamper with them."

Dax drew her phaser and motioned toward the middle door. "I'm afraid this next one will be a chambers of horrors."

"I don't have a weak stomach," said Odo, gazing through the window into the forbidding darkness of cargo bay two. "In fact, I don't have a stomach at all."

"You're lucky," Dax remarked. She went to bay

two's console and punched in some commands. Not even the lights came on.

"This bay is badly damaged," she said. "It now has an atmosphere, but I'm going to have to override the circuits to get the door open and the lights on. They didn't want anybody just wandering in here."

Odo watched the three cargo bay doors while Dax worked on the controls. The impatient part of him thought they should forgo this search in order to make it back to the Alpha Quadrant as quickly as possible, but the cautious part knew they had to be thorough. The middle of the wormhole was not the place for a sneak attack from within. Besides, Commander Sisko was off on an errand of mercy, or at least curiosity, and maybe this was a good time to take stock of their situation.

They had managed to wrest the tanker away from the criminals, and they had at least one prisoner to show for it. A couple of dozen prisoners would be more to his liking, but Odo was willing to settle for their success so far. Unfortunately, he had a feeling that this adventure was not finished yet.

The lights came on in cargo bay two, and the door whooshed open. Odo stepped inside to be greeted by a grisly sight, which brought home the full impact of what the terrorists had done. Twenty-one bodies of young Starfleet officers in their prime lay before him, mostly human, about evenly divided between male and female. Their bodies were bloodied and burned, but they had benefited from being stored in an airless cargo hold. He could detect no unpleasant odors or pools of blood, and their skin had started to mummify.

Neatly separated from the Starfleet bodies were the bodies of seven Bajoran terrorists, also bloodied, burned, and mummified. Except for their clothing, it would have been difficult to tell them apart from the larger group.

He heard Dax enter behind him, and he was glad he had a Trill with him instead of a human. Humans would have been uselessly emotional at this sight, although it was difficult for him to suppress his anger. He wanted to go next door and throttle Rizo.

Dax let out a heavy sigh. "Any sympathy I had for them just went away."

"Good," said Odo. He studied the rest of the cargo bay, looking for anything out of the ordinary. Like cargo bay one, bay two had a full complement of both magnetic conduits and robotic devices, to move the antimatter either alone or inside its pod. It wouldn't take much, he thought, to eject the bodies into space, and he marveled that the terrorists had the consideration not to do so while in orbit around Eco.

"Look there!" said Dax, pointing to one of the thickest pipes snaking across the ceiling.

Odo saw nothing out of the ordinary, except for a wadded bit of yellow cloth hanging over the conduit. But the cloth evidently meant more to Dax, because she stood under it, staring at it.

"Can you get it?" she asked.

"Certainly," said Odo. He reached up, and his arm stretched double its normal length to snag the yellow cloth. To his surprise, there was considerably more of it stashed behind the pipe than he had thought, and he ended up pulling an entire spacesuit from its hiding place. A helmet tumbled on the floor after it.

"With that," said Dax, "you could hide in here without atmosphere."

"We are not alone," breathed Odo.

They heard a rumbling sound, and they whirled around to see the heavy door shutting behind them.

Commander Sisko rubbed his eyes and stared at the sight before him. He was at a distance of tens of thousands of kilometers, but the small shapes on the viewscreen were unmistakable. So was the ferocity of the battle, with phaser blasts streaking silently across the blackness. The scanners confirmed his eyesight— four small craft had the Ferengi Marauder surrounded and were blasting the hell out of it.

The Marauder tried to escape, but it was like a bear cornered by a pack of dogs. Wherever it turned, a smaller craft zoomed to cut it off, while the other three nipped at its heels with phaser fire. When the Marauder turned to stand and fight, the four sleek craft broke off and fell back. They were trying to surround it, thought Sisko, to keep pounding away from four different directions. But the Ferengi captain didn't panic—he calmly picked one of the retreating ships and unleashed a torpedo at it. The smaller ship sputtered like a wet candle and went dark.

"Good for you!" Sisko found himself saying. He wished he hadn't done so much to cripple the Ferengi ship. They were greedy and dishonest, but they didn't deserve to be blasted out of the sky.

He racked his brain to think who the attackers could be. His first thought was that they were Ecocids, but he didn't recall seeing any ships like that while orbiting the planet. Who had small one- or two-person fighters? In the Gamma Quadrant, it could be anybody. Coming from the Alpha Quadrant, it could only be a handful of races. Who hated the Ferengi, or had a score to settle? That could also be anybody.

The Marauder changed course and was on the move again, this time headed toward Sisko. Had he been spotted by the larger craft's sensors? Would they think he was enemy or foe? As desperate as the Ferengi probably were at this point, they didn't care. They saw another ship, and they were going to try to get some help.

Could he help the Marauder? The answer, sad to say, was no. He had no torpedoes left, and his phasers weren't capable of stopping the sleek craft the way the Marauder's torpedo had. An unarmed runabout and a badly damaged warship just weren't going to defeat three fresh fighters, even if the fourth one was out of it.

Sisko's only question was: When should he run? If the mystery fighters caught him in their sensors, would they come after him, too? He really didn't want to find out.

The commander was about to reverse course and head back into warp drive when a distress signal blinked on his console. He thought about the delay it would cause if he listened to the Ferengi, but he couldn't ignore their plea. He put the transmission on the screen.

He saw a smoke-filled bridge and a dead body draped over the navigator's chair. The Ferengi captain rushed toward the screen, waving his arms frantically.

"You can't help us! Go away!" he howled. "These are Cardassians—"

A direct hit rocked the Marauder, and the captain screamed and tumbled out of sight. The image broke up, and Sisko reached for the controls. Before he could go to warp, a tremendous explosion lit up the cockpit like a strobe light, and he was forced to cover his eyes. He opened them to see the Marauder streaking across the starscape like a giant Roman candle, until it exploded into chunks that glimmered and grew dark, like the entrails of fireworks.

He also saw that the three fighters were changing course and picking up speed.

Damn, he thought, *they've seen me!* Sisko punched the runabout into warp drive and began to pray.

CHAPTER
14

LIEUTENANT DAX whipped out her phaser, adjusted the setting, and drilled the doorway that was shutting behind them. With pinpoint accuracy, she fried the seals and the sensors, then she swerved her fiery beam to the controls on the wall and reduced them to a shower of sparks. Odo was already running for the door, and he dove under it as it lurched to a stop.

Dax turned off her phaser and paused to assess the damage. Cargo bay two was even more disabled now, because the door wouldn't even shut. Perhaps, she thought, it was fitting that the door be left open and the bodies visible to all.

She crawled out from under the partially closed door into the anteroom, expecting to find Odo holding the culprit by the scruff of the neck. Instead, she found him hunched over the controls for cargo bay one.

"I think our visitor went back into bay one," he

said. "And unless I miss my guess, he's activated the freight turbolift."

Dax rushed to Odo's side. "Is there any atmosphere in there?" She gazed at the screen. "Yes, there is. They can move between the cargo bays."

"Rizo!" barked the shapeshifter.

In tandem, they rushed to the console for cargo bay three. Dax bent over the controls and was relieved to see that nothing else had been disabled. She keyed the command to open the doors and drew her phaser again.

Odo tensed beside her and began a slow approach to the auxiliary cargo bay. Dax didn't know if Rizo had joined with his confederate to fight or escape, but she was prepared for the worst. She set her phaser to heavy stun and waited to see what Odo encountered.

He was in a spidery crouch as he rounded the open door and gazed into the hold. Then he froze, and she started to rush to his side. Before she reached him she saw Odo relax and assume his usual stiff-backed posture, so Dax lowered her phaser and rounded the corner of the door.

Inside was Rizo with his arms wrapped around Petra, his nineteen-year-old daughter. He was trying to calm her, and Dax could only imagine from her wild eyes the kind of experience she had been through. Hiding in a spacesuit in a dark vacuum full of dead bodies, then dodging their determined pursuit, while trying to mount a final attack. The poor girl had a right to look exhausted and crazed.

"I told her it was no use," said Rizo hoarsely, as he cradled his daughter. "We have reached the end. When the Federation is this determined to stomp us out, they will do it. You're a different kind of foe to us, Lieutenant Dax, because you turn our own people against us. For all their ruthlessness, the Cardassians were never able to do that."

Dax didn't know what to say. She didn't want an innocent to be tarred with the same brush as the guilty, but how many of those Starfleet officers had Petra killed? Her fate had long ago been corrupted and sealed.

"You can stay here until we arrive at *Deep Space Nine,*" said Dax. "I'm going up to the crew quarters to fix some food and drink for you, and I'll beam it directly here. We don't want to harm you, but this shipment of antimatter has to be returned to the Federation."

"And us?" Petra asked meekly. "We only wanted to go someplace where there wasn't any war."

"I'll help you find that place," Dax promised. "But I can't help you avoid your rightful punishment, whatever that will be."

Dax nodded to Odo, who stood by the door and waited until she had left the cargo bay. When Odo came out, she rushed to the controls to shut the door and disable the freight turbolift.

"I think they'll stay where they are," she said. "The fight seems to have gone out of them."

"They're murderers," Odo reminded her.

"I know."

Commander Sisko cursed himself for his own stupidity, good-heartedness, or whatever foolishness had brought him back to search for the Ferengi Marauder. Her killers were on his tail, at a respectful distance, but nevertheless on his tail. The sleek fighters were faster than the runabout and could have caught him in a matter of minutes, but they seemed content to follow him. That was more frightening than if they had just come after him, because then he would be forced to fight and get it over with. If he was going to be blown to bits, he wanted it to happen *before* they found the tanker.

If they really were Cardassians, he thought glumly, the hijacking was public knowledge on the other side of the wormhole. Sisko shivered, thinking this could be only the beginning of the task of defending their hard-won prize.

He estimated his rendezvous time at the asteroid belt to be less than half an hour, and he hadn't decided what to do yet. If he kept going to the wormhole, they might follow him all the way through, and the tanker would be spared. At least temporarily. If the Cardassians were doing sensor sweeps, they might detect the tanker and go after it—no matter what he did. The Ferengi Marauder had probably been putting out a distress signal, and it had cost them their lives.

Sisko knew he couldn't leave his comrades in the dark about this new threat. He would have to tell them, and they would have to obey his orders. But first, he would have to make certain of the Cardassians' intentions.

He opened a standard hailing frequency and announced, "This is the runabout *Mekong* from the United Federation of Planets, hailing the ships that are following me. This is Commander Benjamin Sisko—please respond."

A young Cardassian female appeared on the viewscreen. She was surrounded by an impressive array of instruments in her cocoonlike cockpit. Her brown hair was pulled back severely, and she had an arrogant gleam in her sunken eyes.

"Commander Sisko, we assumed that was you," she remarked. "This is Gul Nerwat of the *Yaro,* an experimental vessel. Would you please stop so that we can come aboard and search your vessel?"

"What business do you have to search my vessel?" asked Sisko, getting huffy. "The Gamma Quadrant doesn't belong to you."

The Cardassian smiled, because she was in a position to do so. "We have learned that a rogue shipment of antimatter is endangering the Gamma Quadrant and the wormhole. We are pledged to find this shipment and safeguard it."

"Like you safeguarded the Ferengi ship?" asked Sisko.

The Cardassian's smile faded a little. "We don't believe that is any of your concern. The Ferengi were, shall we say, belligerent. We know they were in league with you, but we don't know where the tanker is. Can you tell us?"

"No," Sisko lied. "I don't know what you're talking about. I'm on a routine mission from *Deep Space Nine* to open trade with a planet called Eco. You can check all of this out. In fact, I think you should go to Eco—maybe you'll find what you're looking for."

"No, thank you," answered the fighter pilot. "You have ten seconds to stop and let us board you. One—"

Cursing under his breath, Sisko flicked the viewscreen off. He opened up an audio channel that was little used, except for Starfleet emergencies. "Sisko to Dax," he said. "Come in, *Phoenix.*"

"Dax here," came the reply. "Benjamin, I've got something to report—"

"Listen to mine first," he ordered. "There are three Cardassian ships on my tail—one-man, experimental craft. They've already destroyed the Ferengi Marauder, losing Gimba and all hands, and they want the antimatter."

He could hear Dax swallow. "What do you want to do?"

"Proceed to the wormhole. I'll hold them off."

"With what?" asked Dax. "You haven't got any weapons to speak of, so you couldn't delay them more than the time it takes to blow you up."

The commander's lips thinned. "I gave you an order."

"Lure them into an ambush here," answered Dax, "in the asteroid belt."

Sisko shook his head with frustration. "You haven't got enough weaponry to take out three ships either. Maybe one, if you got real lucky."

Suddenly, his short-range scanners began to flash, and Sisko nearly jumped out of his seat. "I can't believe it! They've launched a torpedo after me!"

For the third time that day, Sisko took evasive action. He dropped the ship out of warp, hoping the torpedo wouldn't be able to accomplish the same feat. The fighters were sophisticated but small, and they probably had simple torpedoes, he hoped, like the microtorpedoes on the runabout. Sure enough, his sensors tracked the torpedo as it whizzed by him. But the Cardassians had accomplished their objective—they had gotten him to slow down. He went to full impulse power and began more desperate maneuvers.

He checked his readouts and saw that the antimatter in his warp reactor was getting dangerously low. He didn't have time to appreciate the irony—running out of antimatter while guarding a full tanker of the stuff. Besides, the Cardassians would probably obliterate him before he had a chance to run out of fuel. He glanced over his shoulder, although there was nothing to see but the back of the cockpit area. But he could feel them breathing down his neck.

The three fighters came out of warp at a considerable distance, but they instantly hit top impulse and spread out to surround him. When he zigzagged, one kept on his tail, another tried to cut him off, and the third tried to anticipate his next maneuver and beat him to it. There was none of that leisurely pace that had saved his life when the Marauder was chasing him. He took to mixing vertical and horizontal course changes, but the third fighter began to anticipate those moves and gain on him at an alarming rate.

The Cardassians tried to hail him, to say, he supposed, that his ten seconds were up. Sisko began to wonder if perhaps he *should* let them board the runabout as a delaying tactic to let the tanker escape. A second later, a phaser blast rocked the runabout and reminded him that he was not the one making the decisions. The Cardassians had stopped hailing him.

Commander Sisko made his sharpest turn yet and came around hard. They had attacked him, and that made up his mind what he had to do. He wanted to contact Dax and order her to escape, but he didn't dare try another transmission with the Cardassians so close. Besides, there wasn't any time. He picked the center fighter and fired up all of his phaser emitters; then he leaned forward and punched a fist in the air as the phasers raked the target. It blinked and swerved off course, although Sisko knew that its shields deflected most of the damage.

The other two fighters swerved hard to meet him head-on, and he gripped his chair as their combined phaser fire pounded the runabout. The tiny ship bucked like an angry bull, and the lights in the cockpit ran through a spectrum of colors before the emergency reds came on. Behind him circuits were burning and raining sparks on the back of his neck, but Sisko remained at his post, staring at his instruments through acrid smoke.

He tried the helm and discovered that he had no control. This was it, thought Sisko—death in an unknown sector of the Gamma Quadrant. It might as well be the Gobi Desert.

Suddenly, a bulky vessel streaked out of warp drive, sending the two undamaged fighters scurrying. Sisko shook his head and tried not to blame Dax too much. Where old friendships were concerned, the Trill had always had more loyalty than sense. But she knew a sitting duck when she saw it—she picked out the crippled fighter and hit it with full phasers.

The small craft shuddered and fizzled like a wet firecracker. Then it went completely dark. Another fighter zoomed in and unleashed a phaser barrage upon the tanker.

Sisko punched his comm panel and opened hailing frequencies. "Gul Nerwat," he warned, "do not fire on that tanker—unless you want to blow us all to kingdom come!"

The Cardassian's face appeared on his viewscreen, and she scowled, "Our sister ship does not respond. Tell the tanker to drop her shields and prepare to be boarded. Or we will retreat to a safe distance and blow it up."

Sisko heaved a sigh. He could stall for time, but what good would it do? The normal running lights flickered on in the cockpit, and he was thankful that some of the runabout's systems were coming back on-line. However, a quick check of his instruments showed that both his shields and phasers were inoperative—the computer had assigned all available energy to the helm and life-support.

"Let me confer with the captain of the tanker," he

told the Cardassian. He didn't want to reveal the fact that her crew were all dead and she was being piloted by two of his staff.

"Five minutes," sneered the Cardassian. "Then we destroy you first, as an example."

Taking out the battered runabout shouldn't be too difficult, thought Sisko glumly. He went back to the emergency audio frequency. "Dax," he said, "I told you to make a run for it."

"You didn't order me," the Trill replied calmly. "Besides, we're in this together."

"We're deep in it," Sisko muttered. "The runabout has no weapons or shields left."

"Then you're out of it," answered Dax. "They don't want the runabout, anyway, so *you* should make a run for it."

"But you can't hold out," Sisko answered. "If you don't let them board you, they'll back off to a safe distance and just keep pounding away."

Odo's voice cut in. "Pardon me, sir, but we're sitting on more raw explosives than ten photon torpedoes combined. Isn't there anything we can do with it?"

The commander frowned mightily for several moments; then he snapped his fingers. "Depth charges!"

"Pardon me, sir?" asked Odo.

Dax answered, "It's an ancient Terran weapon used by seagoing vessels against submarine vessels."

"To great effect," added Sisko. "Dax, is there any way to eject a storage pod and set it to explode at a given distance?"

"Not at a given distance," answered Dax, "but at a given *time,* yes. You simply program the pod to shut down its magnetic field at a given moment. The antimatter is released and hits the pod—and kaboom!"

"I can't be any help," Sisko murmured. "For this to work, they'll have to be chasing *you.*"

"You should go now," said Dax. "Somebody has to get back to DS9 to let them know what happened. Tell the Cardassians to give us a few minutes, then we'll let them board us. I have to do some calculations and get set up. We can't eject a pod at warp speed, but we should be able to do it at full impulse."

Sisko said hoarsely, "I don't want to leave you out here, old man."

"You haven't got much choice," said Dax in her usual businesslike manner. "Besides, we've been through worse scrapes than this." She paused. "Although I really can't remember any."

He shook his head, thankful that they were on audio only. "I don't remember ever leaving you behind. I'm not going to do it."

"Yes, you are," answered Dax. "I hate to use clichés, but I've led a long, full life, and you've got a son who needs you. Please get going, Benjamin."

"Odo," said the commander, "I want to beam you over."

"I'm afraid not," answered the shapeshifter. "With the state of the controls over here, I'm sure it will require both of us to eject a pod. Rest assured, Commander, I will not volunteer for any more rescue missions."

"We'll be right along," Dax assured him.

Sisko gulped. "You'd better be. Out."

He cut off communications and stared at the Cardassian ships on his viewscreen with an overwhelming mixture of hatred, grief, and frustration. A shred of hope was somewhere in that muck, but he feared giving it too much credence. Best to act as if Dax, Odo, and the *Phoenix* were gone. At least he would get back to DS9 and try to prevent the Cardassians from bringing the antimatter back.

He opened a channel to Gul Nerwat and reported, "The tanker needs five minutes to prepare for boarding."

"Why?" snarled the Cardassian.

"There are safety precautions to disable," answered Sisko, hoping that sounded plausible. "My life-support systems are failing. Do you mind if I try to get back to the wormhole?"

The Cardassian woman paused in thought, and she finally asked, "This isn't a trick, is it?"

Sisko shrugged. "I have no shields and no weapons. Your own scanners probably tell you that. I couldn't do anything to you even if I wanted to. Plus, if you destroy me, the tanker will fight to the end, and you'll have to destroy it. You'll go back to Cardassia having lost two ships from your squadron, with nothing to show for it."

Sisko was quite content to talk all day and give Dax as much time as she needed, but the Cardassian captain was decisive. "Go," she ordered. "Tell your people that Cardassians are merciful."

No one would believe him if he said that, thought Sisko, but he smiled pleasantly. "You are indeed merciful. I bid you good-bye."

"May we meet again," answered the Cardassian woman with a smile that could only be called lascivious. "Under more pleasant circumstances."

Sisko hid his repulsion. "Perhaps," he answered. He cut off the transmission and slumped back in his chair.

It was all up to Dax now. With his fingers crossed, he put the battered runabout into low warp drive and headed for the wormhole.

When Dax entered cargo bay two, Rizo was just finishing a drumstick of fried chicken. Petra was asleep beside him on the barren cargo bay floor.

Rizo licked his lips appreciatively. "How did you know I liked this dish called 'fried chicken'?"

"Lucky guess," said Dax. "I notice it's popular among humans, and Bajorans are a lot like humans."

"I'm not sure if that's an insult, or not," muttered Rizo. He stood to his impressive height and wiped his hands on his shirt. "Have we gone through the wormhole? It didn't feel like we went very far."

"We haven't," answered Dax. "We're surrounded by three Cardassian ships. They've already destroyed the Ferengi ship, killing Gimba and all aboard, and now they're after us."

Rizo's face twisted into a frightening mask of hatred. "Cardassians," he hissed. "You must destroy them."

"We have a plan," answered Dax, "but it will take three of us. Odo doesn't want to trust you, but I don't see that we have any choice. Will you give me your word, by whatever philosophies you hold dear, that you won't turn on us?"

The Bajoran brushed back his hair and stared at her in amazement. "Do you think *I* want to be captured by Cardassians? What do you think they would do to me? Or you! They don't want to destroy us—they want to take us alive. Let me die fighting them, and I will die happy."

"You may be very happy," muttered Dax. "If what

we have planned doesn't work, we're out of options. Come." She started to the doorway.

"One moment," said the big Bajoran. He leaned down and stroked his daughter's rough-cut hair off her forehead; then he kissed her.

"Daughter," he said, "I don't wish to wake you, but I have to go with Lieutenant Dax."

The young woman sat up, confused and alarmed. "Where are they taking you?"

"Nowhere," he said. "I'm going to help them. You stay here and sleep. Eat."

"Yes," agreed Dax. "We may need your help, too. For now, you should try to get some rest."

"It will be over soon," Rizo promised her.

Dax strode out the doorway, motioning Rizo after her. He was rubbing his eyes as he came out. "I've been no fit parent," he admitted, "but we are no better than the mold which forms us. If we die killing Cardassians, it will be worth it."

Dax shook her head and walked to the turbolift. "Remember, our mission is to recover the antimatter. Not kill Cardassians."

"My mission is always to kill Cardassians," answered the terrorist.

She explained the plan briefly to Rizo on the way up the turbolift. When they reached the bridge of the tanker, Odo gave them a dour expression and leaped to his feet, assuming a defensive posture. Rizo tightened his fists and glared at the security chief.

"At ease," ordered Dax. "You'll have to trust each other for the next few minutes, or you'll die as comrades, no matter what. Odo, you will take over the conn. I've set the course, but you'll have to relay to me the exact distance and speed of our pursuers. Rizo, I'll need you below on the controls for cargo bay one. I'll be inside the cargo bay, adjusting the program on the pod we're going to eject."

A beep sounded, and Odo glanced at the controls. "They're hailing us," he reported.

"Put down our shields," answered Dax, "and tell them to start making their approach. When I give you the word, go to full impulse. Our shields have to be down, anyway, so we might as well do it now. Any questions?"

"Will you let Petra go?" asked Rizo.

Dax shook her head. "That's a question for a tribunal, not me. If you don't help us, she'll be dead, or a Cardassian prisoner."

Rizo nodded grimly. "Lead on."

Dax could hear Odo speaking to the Cardassians as the turbolift doors shut between them. She tried to relax, but the idea of turning antimatter storage pods into deep-space depth charges was not a relaxing notion. Suicidal was more like it.

When they reached the cargo bay anteroom, Rizo rushed directly to his post like an eager Starfleet cadet. He smiled at her. "I'll help you kill Cardassians all day long. What do you want me to do?"

"Open the door and leave it open," she answered. "When you hear me shout 'now,' eject the first pod in line through the docking nose. You'll need to use the manual override, but I think you know how to do that already."

"I do," promised Rizo. "Count on me."

He opened the door for her, and Dax entered the cavernous chamber. She was unable to suppress a horrible feeling of dread. The pods looked like what they suddenly were—enormous bombs. Conduits snaked across the ceiling like hungry vines, and robot arms dangled like the legs of giant spiders. Dax shook her head and tried to concentrate on her mission.

She was squeezing between pods on her way toward the freight turbolift when a noise sounded. She leaped back, startled, before she realized that it was just a nearby pod signaling the end of its diagnostic cycle. The Trill swallowed hard and scrambled toward the first pod in line.

She touched the panels to activate the pod's internal programming. After studying the readouts on its small screen, she was satisfied that she knew how to turn off its internal magnetic field at a given microsecond. Of course, nobody ever did that when the pod was full of antimatter, so she had to disable several safety features, too.

Finally, she touched her comm badge. "Odo, I'm ready."

"Good," he answered, "because the two Cardassian ships are at five hundred kilometers and closing fast."

"Are their shields down?"

"Still up," answered the security chief. "There is no point in firing at them. Shall I escape?"

"Do it," she ordered. She called to Rizo, "Ready yourself!"

"I'm always ready," he shouted back, "to kill Cardassians!"

The ship pitched slightly as Odo plunged them into impulse drive. Dax brought up the subsystem that regulated the magnetic field inside the pod, and she saw that the timer read IND for indefinite. She readied her fingers to change the setting. The Trill had already done a batch of calculations, and she had a set of rough equivalents in her mind. One second for every two thousand kilometers. Adjust for speed and add four seconds for the ejection process. This wasn't going to be very accurate, she knew, but an antimatter explosion didn't require great accuracy to do damage.

However, an explosion that happened too soon would catch the tanker as well. An explosion that happened too late would miss its target. Her fingers tensed in readiness.

She jumped when her communicator beeped. "Odo to Dax. They are demanding we stop, or they will open fire."

"Distance?" she asked.

"They fell back to eighteen thousand kilometers. Now seventeen. Bearing, sixty-three-mark-four. Full impulse. Now sixteen thousand."

Awfully damned close, she thought, and the longer they waited the closer they would come. Knowing that one second's mistake could cost them their lives, her fingers were a blur on the controls. Allowing for her own actions, she set the timer to shut off the pod in ten seconds. It was a nice round number.

"Now!" she screamed, leaping back.

The robotic arms lurched into action, lifting the pod as if it were a pillow and shoving it out the turbolift doors, which shut immediately behind the robot. She should run, thought Dax, somewhere! But she knew that there was no place to hide on a tanker full of antimatter.

She slapped her comm badge and announced. "Dax here. The pod is away!"

"Putting up shields!" barked Odo. Apparently not a second too soon, as the ship was jolted by a phaser blast.

"Was that *it*?" yelled Rizo from outside in the anteroom.

"No!" Dax shouted back. She was frozen while

mentally counting down the seconds. Four, three, two, one. . . .

Matter met antimatter and ripped the fabric of space open for a blistering moment. The light that burned was whiter than the newest star, but it was gone in seconds, leaving nothing in its wake.

Dax was knocked completely off her feet between two huge pods. The ship pitched again, and she could hear the groaning of the giant pods against their restraints. She feared she would be crushed! Suddenly strong arms were lifting her and dragging her into a clear area.

She looked up to see Rizo towering over her, panting and grinning. "Did we kill 'em?"

"I'll check," she breathed. She tapped her comm badge. "Odo, what about our pursuers?"

"Gone," answered Odo with satisfaction. "Not a trace."

Dax lay back on the cold floor and spread her arms in blessed relief. "Go to warp drive," she said. "I'll be right there. Out."

When she started to get up, Rizo stuck a beefy palm in her chest and pushed her back down.

"Sorry," he said, pulling a phaser from the back of his belt. "You're not going anywhere."

CHAPTER
15

Before Rizo could stun her, Dax whipped up her legs, curled her back, and gave him two heels in the stomach. The Bajoran staggered backward, gasping for breath but trying to aim his phaser. Dax rolled, and the brilliant beam flashed past her shoulder. Before Rizo could steady himself to aim again, she made a dash into the sea of pods and crouched behind them.

She yelled, "Don't shoot phasers in here! You idiot!"

Holding his stomach and gulping with anger, Rizo staggered along the row of antimatter pods. "I'm not the idiot!" he snarled. "You showed me how valuable this antimatter is—as a weapon! I can't let you take it back!"

"You *have* to," she insisted. "You have to end this way of life. What are you going to do with this ship and the antimatter? You've seen how it attracts nothing but trouble. Isn't that what you told me?"

Rizo looked away, anger being replaced by confusion and weariness. "What will you do with Petra?"

"I personally will try to help her," answered the Trill. She rose from her hiding place. "I can't speak for anyone else, but I'll do whatever I can. Listen, you cannot try to prove your points with death and destruction anymore. That time is past. Other Bajorans feel much like you, and they speak openly about it. The war for independence is over. You can see from what happened here that it's not the Federation who's in control. It's the Bajorans. They are in control of their own destiny."

Rizo muttered, "That ship they are building—it should be for Bajor."

"Perhaps the next one *will* be for Bajor," said Dax. "The shipyards are up and working. Perhaps the next shipment of antimatter will be for a Bajoran ship, the first one built in generations. Come back with us and see that happen."

Rizo scoffed, "I'll be in a cell."

"Voices from cells have been heard before," said the lieutenant. Her comm badge beeped, and she answered it. "Dax here."

"You said you were coming right up," Odo said with concern. "Is everything all right?"

Dax looked expectantly at Rizo, and he lowered the phaser. "Yes," she nodded, "I was just having a discussion with our prisoner. It will take me a minute to escort him back to the cargo bay. Is our course locked in for the wormhole?"

"Locked in," said Odo. "Estimated arrival at the wormhole in thirty-two minutes. We will probably overtake Commander Sisko before then."

"Give him a report," said Dax. She looked at Rizo. "And tell him our prisoner distinguished himself under fire."

"I'm glad I was wrong," admitted the shape-shifter. "Out."

She strode up to Rizo, and the hulking Bajoran let out a long sigh as he dropped the phaser into her hand.

"Have any more of these hidden around?" she asked.

"No," he murmured, "that was the only one." He gave her a wry smile. "Don't take this wrong, Lieutenant, but you're the first woman I've admired in a long time. Since Petra's mother."

Dax shook her head sadly. "I wish your lives had been different. As I said, I have no basis to imagine what you went through."

He shrugged his big shoulders. "It's over now. I knew this would be the end—one way or another."

Captain Jon Rachman lifted his glass of synthehol and said suavely, "I'm having a wonderful time."

Major Kira Nerys looked at a chronometer and grumbled, "I'm not."

"Relax," he told her. "They'll let you know if something happens. You're a minute away from the bridge, and I'm a minute away from my ship. If duty calls, we'll answer. Meanwhile, relax."

Kira tried to slump back in her chair and relax, but her shoulder blades refused to loosen up. She rubbed them against the back of the chair, trying to make them relax. She finally had to admit that she didn't want to sit back, so she sat forward and tried to relax.

"Couldn't you have picked some other time to ask me for a date?" she muttered. She glanced around Quark's Place with mild disgust.

"I'm sorry that your people are still missing," said Rachman soberly. "But after they come back, I'll be leaving. If not sooner. So you see, Major, this is the only time. There are a lot of poets who think the present should be lived as if it were the last moment of creation."

"Are there?" asked Kira mockingly. Grudgingly, she took a sip of her fruit punch. "I'm truly not averse to you as a person, Captain Rachman—"

"Jon, please." He smiled.

"But I can't think about, er, what you would like me to think about at the moment."

"What exactly would I like you to think about?" asked Jon Rachman, resting his chiseled chin in his hand and leaning forward.

Kira shifted in her chair and finally met his stare head-on. "You would love to seduce me."

Rachman looked thoughtful. "Actually I would prefer that *you* seduce *me*. But for the moment, I'm content to just get to know you. What do you want out of life?"

"Bajor," she answered immediately. "I want our homeworld to be free and secure and on her way to prosperity. Then maybe we can pay back the people who have helped us."

Rachman shook his head in amazement. "When I first read the report on *Deep Space Nine,* I couldn't understand what we were doing here."

Kira bristled, and her dark eyes flashed.

"Don't get me wrong," added the young captain, "I didn't object to being here. It's just unusual for the Federation to have coadministration of a space station with another party. Now that I've gotten to know you and your people, I can see how both sides needed this arrangement—to form a bond of mutual trust. I really admire what you're doing here. I mean that sincerely."

Kira took his hand and gave him a warm smile. Her shoulders suddenly felt very relaxed. "Thanks. I know how much the Federation has risked for us, and I'm grateful. I'm sure we can coexist."

Rachman laid his other hand on top of hers. "We can test that theory in a sort of microcosm. Just two people, say, on a long weekend down to Bajor—"

The major's comm badge beeped, and she shrugged an apology as she tapped it. "Kira."

O'Brien's voice had none of its usual playfulness. "Major, the neutrino level from the wormhole is very high. Something is coming through. Perhaps more than one ship."

She jumped up. "Any other unusual readings?"

"Other?" asked O'Brien. Then it dawned on him. "You don't think those Klingon ships went away?"

"They could be close enough to monitor the wormhole," answered Kira, already dashing toward the door. "Scan for all anomalies. I'm on my way!"

Captain Rachman rushed after her, but he turned the other way on the Promenade. "The *Regal* is ready," he assured her.

Kira paused on her way to the turbolift and gave the captain a glancing smile. "Maybe we'll have something to celebrate."

Quark ran after them both, shouting, "Who's going to pay this bill?"

When both the captain and the major ignored him and dashed out of sight, the Ferengi saloonkeeper stroked his earlobe and smiled. He could smell money changing hands, very soon now. Then he frowned.

Which way would the money be going?

"Please be alive, Commander Sisko," whispered Quark earnestly. "Please come back . . . alive."

Chief O'Brien frowned at the shifting readouts on the Ops table. Where was Dax? he wondered; she would be able to make sense of these mysterious fluctuations. Then he remembered where Dax was, and that he'd gone too many bloody hours without sleep.

He gazed up at the main viewer and the endless expanse of stars, expecting any moment for the wormhole to erupt in an orgasm of swirling colors. Suddenly it did, swirling outward like a giant rainbow turned inside out. He momentarily forgot about the unusual readings in the vicinity and stared at the screen, as did everyone else on the bridge. He heard the turbolift doors swish open as the first ship emerged from the wormhole.

"The tanker!" he shouted.

Kira rushed through Operations, pointing to the communications officer. "Hail them!" she ordered.

"There's a second ship!" shouted O'Brien. He pointed at the viewscreen, although it was hardly necessary. All eyes were riveted upon it. A smaller vessel was suddenly spit out, and the wormhole vanished.

"The runabout!" gasped Kira.

"Damn," muttered O'Brien, slamming his fist on the operations table. "Two Klingon Birds-of-Prey uncloaking at fifteen thousand kilometers!"

On the viewscreen, two vulturelike warships shimmered into view.

"The tanker does not respond," said the communications officer, "but the Klingons are hailing us."

"On screen," snapped Kira. "What business do you have here—" She started to say more, but she was stopped by the sight of a young Bajoran man smiling at her from the screen.

"Prepare to die," said the Bajoran. "We have had enough of Cardassian space stations and Federation meddling. With the help of our Klingon friends, we will put an end to all of it now. That includes the wormhole."

The screen went blank, and Kira and O'Brien stared at each other. The chief was almost afraid to look at his instruments, for fear of what he would find. When he did, his worst fears were realized.

"They're dropping their shields," he breathed. "Powering up phasers. The tanker is headed straight toward them!"

"Where's the runabout?" asked Kira.

"It's headed for the docking ring," reported O'Brien. "But if those crazy Klingons do what I think they're going to do, we'll *all* be chipped beef on toast!"

"They won't blow themselves up," said Kira hopefully.

"They're far enough away to avoid the worst of it," answered O'Brien. "But we're not."

"Hail them!" ordered Kira.

The communications officer shook his head. "They're not responding."

O'Brien took a gulp of air and changed the setting on the main viewer to show the Klingon warships. There were gasps all around as they unleashed a broad band of phaser fire. He changed the view to show the tanker, streaking to its doom in total oblivion.

"Brace yourselves!" yelled O'Brien.

An explosion ruptured the starscape, but it wasn't the cataclysmic end of the world that O'Brien expected. It was just your normal starship being blown to smithereens, a sight he had witnessed too many times in his long career with Starfleet. The station didn't even tremble.

"Where's the antimatter?" asked Kira in amazement.

O'Brien shrugged, but a smile began to creep across his ruddy face. "If it ain't there, it must be someplace else."

The communications panel beeped, and Kira answered, "Ops."

"Major, this is Ensign Pertwee at docking port three. I just want to report that the *Mekong* is docked and Commander Sisko, Lieutenant Dax, and Chief Odo are safe."

Kira looked at O'Brien and puffed up her chest, before expelling a long sigh.

Ensign Pertwee continued, "But the runabout is packed to the gills with antimatter pods, and we're not sure how to handle them. Could you spare us Chief O'Brien?"

"He's on his way," answered Kira. And he was, with a big grin on his face.

The major would have liked to savor the moment, but there were still two Klingon Birds-of-Prey within striking distance—and they had just been cheated out of their big kill.

She hit her comm badge. "Ops to Captain Rachman. There are two Klingon ships in the area. Be careful, but get rid of them."

"Aye, sir," the captain answered crisply. "Leaving spacedock."

Kira took over control of the Operations table, and she changed the angle on the main viewer to watch the *Regal* pull away from the station. The cruiser went quickly to full impulse and bore down on the Klingon warships. They hadn't come any closer, but they weren't backing off either. Kira widened the view to include all three ships, and she held her breath, knowing that Rachman had a skeleton crew and a dysfunctional ship. Yet he plowed straight toward them, as if he could wipe them out with a snap of his fingers.

She monitored communications frequencies, but there were no transmissions. The *Regal* was acting like the bouncer in an Orion nightclub, throwing out a couple of unruly bullies. It muscled closer and closer to them—five thousand kilometers, four, three . . .

Finally, the Klingon ships blinked. They made graceful pirouettes in space and were already going into warp drive when the *Regal* reached their former position and stopped.

With relief in his voice, the communications officer announced, "Captain Rachman reports that the area is secure. He requests permission to return to *Deep Space Nine*."

Kira finally took a breath and permitted herself a wide grin. "Yes," she agreed. "Let's get everybody home."

CHAPTER
16

"More wine?" asked Quark, brandishing a bottle under Commander Sisko's nose. "Trefethen from Napa Valley, California, 2361, which I understand is a very good year."

"Replicated?" asked Dr. Bashir.

Quark shot him a glare. "Of course not. I've been saving this for a special occasion."

Benjamin Sisko was beaming. "Absolutely. In fact, take it to your replicators and make a bunch of bottles. I want everybody to have a glass of wine for a toast."

Quark snapped his fingers and handed the bottle off to Rom. He had converted his largest holodeck suite into a palatial French dining hall modeled after one owned by some Terran geezer named Louis XVI.

Dr. Bashir leaned forward eagerly. "Commander, whatever gave you the idea to put the antimatter on the runabout?"

Sisko shook his head in amazement. "From the very beginning, that tanker was like a giant bull's-eye. We knew we couldn't protect it from another assault, especially with the condition of the runabout. So after we got away from the Cardassians and stopped on the other side of the wormhole, we decided to move the antimatter. We had a bit of luck in that the *Mekong* had an empty cargo module. Still, those nineteen pods were crammed in everywhere, even the cockpit. We had to turn off the artificial gravity to maneuver them around."

"Nineteen?" asked Bashir. "I thought there were twenty?"

Sisko grew somber. "We had to use one. Anyway, we didn't know what we would find in the Alpha Quadrant, so Dax plotted a course for the empty tanker and we beamed her off before it went through the wormhole."

Rom and several other waiters were suddenly at everyone's elbow, pouring white wine. Only Odo and young Jake Sisko declined, but they held up their glasses of water.

Quark bowed gracefully and gushed, "Your wine is served, Commander, and the appetizer is on its way."

Sisko looked puzzledly at the Ferengi. "I'm glad to see you too, Quark, but I must say I'm overwhelmed by this welcome. We were only gone a few days."

The Ferengi rubbed his hands together. "A few profitable days."

"I'm glad it was profitable for someone," said the commander. "I should tell you that Gimba and his Marauder will not be coming back."

Quark lowered his head. "Our esteemed colleague would be relieved to know that somebody profited by his death."

The commander nodded. Then he stood and lifted his wineglass. "I would like to propose a toast."

Everyone stood and lifted a glass. They were still laughing and chatting amiably until they saw the look on Commander Sisko's face. Quark was issuing orders to his waiters when he glanced at Sisko. He instantly drew himself to attention.

The commander held up his glass and said, "To the brave men and women of the *Phoenix*. They went down with their ship."

The glasses were hoisted and drained in silence.

"I'm sorry, Admiral Nicheyev," said Benjamin Sisko to the small viewscreen on his desk. "But you see, I'm alive. There's no need for a replacement."

The stiff-necked admiral bristled and cleared her throat. "Of course not, Commander. I didn't mean to say that we were *disappointed* you were still alive, only that your replacement will be disappointed. But we'll find another suitable post for Commander Shelby."

Sisko was in an unusually jovial mood, and not even an admiral could bring him down. "If she's a good officer, send her along! We can always use her."

"I'm afraid not," said the admiral. "Commander Shelby needs a command post to function at her best. Of course, you have recovered the antimatter as well, so we can recall the entire convoy, except for the escort ship which is carrying the parts for the cruisers."

"Whatever you wish," agreed Sisko.

Dax stopped in the doorway of his office and caught his eye. He motioned to her to stop. "It's been a pleasure, Admiral. I'm sorry we've caused you so much trouble, but I believe we can get the launch of the *Hannibal* back on schedule."

"Thank you, Commander. I look forward to seeing

what sounds like a most interesting report." The dour admiral signed off.

Sisko motioned Dax to come forward. "What happened at the hearing?"

Dax entered the room, looking a little embarrassed. "I made a strong plea for some sort of clemency, especially for Petra. She is being sent to a hospital for psychiatric evaluation, which is a good first step. There's no way to avoid punishment for Rizo, but he came up with his own unique sentence."

Sisko smiled. "Which is?"

"One of the old Cardassian prisons has several empty buildings, and he wants to turn them into a factory to make ship components. He's proposing that convicts of a free Bajor have to be given the right to work for Bajor, even if it's prison labor. The council may go along with him. At any rate, Rizo will be given a life sentence."

The commander stood at his desk and nodded thoughtfully. "We were lucky this time. Very lucky. We could have ended up like all the others, dead or trapped on Eco." He shuddered at the thought and began to rearrange objects on his desk. "Do you want to go with Major Kira and me to the launch? I hear it could be as early as tomorrow."

Dax shook her head slowly. "I don't think so. I believe I need to keep my own company for a few days."

"You earned a rest, old man. I'm glad you were there with me."

Dax nodded. "So am I."

Sisko chuckled but didn't look up. "I think I could even stand to see you in that dress again."

Dax smiled. "You should be so lucky."

* * *

The *Hannibal,* an Ambassador-class starship, remained imprisoned in a giant pit, where Commander Sisko had last seen it. But now the Lilliputians were on a far hill, watching the launch from bleachers, and only a few chosen VIPs were at ground level, staring into the pit. The commander and Major Kira were among them, along with dignitaries, such as Bajoran ministers and Federation envoys.

Unlike his earlier visit, no one was crawling over the gleaming hull of the ship, and no one was watching it from the six gigantic arches overhead. He looked down to see steam escaping from couplings surrounding the ship, and he knew that these couplings would soon let go and release the *Hannibal* from its earthy bonds.

The commander nodded and smiled at the dignitaries. He was in a magnanimous mood, having thought more than once that he would never live to see this day. Now, to have a starship named after Hannibal taking off from these historic shipyards, which had been in use since before airplanes flew on Earth—it was wonderful! Plus, he had the satisfaction of knowing that he had made his own small contribution to the proceedings. Other antimatter could have powered the *Hannibal* on its maiden voyages, but it was the antimatter they had rescued that would be doing the job.

Despite Sisko's delight in the proceedings, he couldn't help but notice that Major Kira looked pensive and suspicious. The way she studied some of her own government officials, such as Minister Roser, made him wonder if they might be wanted criminals. He wondered how to broach the subject, and he decided to come around to it slowly.

"Major," he said, "I wondered why you didn't

request to be assigned to the shakedown crew. They would have welcomed you, even as an observer, and I would have agreed."

"I didn't want to be gone for so long," answered Kira. She shrugged, trying to make light of her lame excuse. "After everything that's happened, I didn't think it was appropriate."

"Yes," said Sisko, lowering his voice. "I forget what it must have been like here. These people put you through a lot, did they?"

"Some," answered Kira. She lowered her own voice to say, "Actually, Commander, I can explain it all much better after the launch, when we go to see Director Amkot."

"Director Amkot," echoed Sisko. "I wonder why he isn't here?"

"Probably in the control room," she answered. As Sisko had hoped, conversation was beginning to relax Major Kira, and she gave him a smile. "I have to tell you, Commander, I've been reading up on Terran history. You know, when Hannibal led those fantastic creatures—the elephants—over the Alp Mountains to attack Rome, he was defeated."

"After taking two-thirds of the country," said Sisko, "and only after Rome mustered every able-bodied soldier she had."

"But they were defeated," Kira mused with pleasure. "It makes me think fondly of your culture that you would memorialize a general who was defeated, even though he was courageous and visionary. It gives me hope that our people can make mistakes and learn to appreciate them."

"Oh, we've made lots of mistakes," said Sisko with a chuckle. "You've got to learn from them, or keep making them."

Kira shook her head. "I know revenge is a powerful emotion and victory is an aphrodisiac, but we have to stop fighting, every one of us. After the Cardassians conquered us, we learned to be warriors. But how do you learn peace?"

"Practice," answered Sisko. "We had a captain in Starfleet who used to say that being civilized doesn't mean you'll never fight, only that you're not going to fight today."

"Not today," said Kira thoughtfully. "Do you mind if I pass that saying on? I don't think we can ever go back to being pacifists—not in my lifetime—but we have to know that peace is an option. It's the preferable option."

Before Sisko could give his heartfelt approval, there was a buzz of conversation, and they looked up to see the arches overhead starting to glow with a greenish light. A weird humming sound pierced the air, and people began to step back from the giant pit. Not Commander Sisko. A full-sized starship taking off from a planet was a sight that hadn't been seen on Earth in hundreds of years. He didn't want to miss this launching.

Kira stood at his side, and he could see the concern on her face dissolving into pride. This starship had been built on Bajor, and wherever it went, it would serve as a monument to their recovery.

The tractor beams on the arches locked on, and the mammoth ship gave a palpable shudder. The steam stopped shooting from the couplers, and their hydraulics yanked back to release the twin nacelles, the cylindrical hull, and the gleaming saucer section. The *Hannibal* rose gracefully into the clear desert air, and Sisko felt his feelings soaring with each meter it rose.

The hole in the ground was no longer a mysterious ruin but a mother giving birth, and the arches were the calm midwife.

The *Hannibal* was securely cradled inside the massive archways before the crew took over. Shuttlecraft hovered nearby like anxious pilot fish, but the *Hannibal* was going to leave the forcefields under her own power. Sisko could see the lights ripple on along the length of her hull, and they were brilliant even in the bright sunlight of the Okana Desert. He could hear the oohs and ahs, and knew he was saying them, too. So enraptured was he by the magnificent sight that Sisko lost track of time—he had no idea how long the starship remained tethered inside its metallic cocoon. When its thrusters finally came on, it shot off like a butterfly bursting free. He was amazed that such an enormous object could grow so small so fast, because it was soon the merest blip in the sky to the naked eye.

Beside him, Kira nodded with satisfaction. "This is a good day, a very good day."

"Yes," said Sisko with a smile. "I can hear the admirals calling up now, placing more orders."

Kira tapped her comm badge. "Major Kira to Director Amkot."

There was no response, and she frowned puzzledly. "Major Kira to Director Amkot."

Again the response was nil. She tapped her badge and requested instead, "Major Kira to the control room."

"Chief Engineer Daken here. What can I do for you, Major?"

"I was looking for Director Amkot, but he doesn't respond. Is he with you?"

"He was here until the launch started," answered

the engineer. "Then he said he wanted to watch the rest of it in his private office. Do you know where that is?"

"Yes," answered Kira. "But why doesn't he respond to his communicator?"

"I don't know. We leave him alone when he goes there."

"Thank you." Kira turned to Sisko and said with alarm, "Let's go find him."

The door to his office was closed, and a middle-aged Bajoran in coveralls was trying to override the circuits to gain entry.

"Hello," he said, slightly out of breath. "You must be Major Kira. I'm Chief Daken. We spoke a moment ago."

"Yes," said Kira. "What's the matter?"

"Right after I talked to you, I tried to contact the director, and he didn't respond. The computer says he's in here, but he doesn't answer even when I bang on the door!"

Sisko stepped forward. "What about transporters? Can we beam inside?"

Chief Daken shook his head. "No, all transporters are on emergency standby in case there's some malfunction with the *Hannibal*. That doesn't seem likely, but we can't use them until the *Hannibal* establishes orbit."

Kira drew a small phaser from her pocket. "With your permission?"

"Yes, yes!" agreed Daken.

"Major," asked Sisko with disapproval, "do you always arm yourself when you come to Bajor?"

"Lately, yes." Kira took aim at the controls of the door and fried the instruments with a pinpoint blast.

The door slid halfway open, and she was the first one through.

She froze in shock, as did Sisko and the engineer a few steps behind her. Slumped over his expensive but chipped and weathered desk was the director of the Okana Shipyards. Under a thatch of thick white hair, just above his right temple, was a small blackened hole. A phaser was lying close to his curled fingers, where he had dropped it. There was no way in or out except for the door that had been locked.

Chief Daken pounded on his communicator and shouted for help, while Sisko strode to the desk and lifted the man's wrist. He could feel no pulse—the man was dead. He touched Amkot Groell's neck and reached the same conclusion.

"It's too late," said the commander, shaking his head in astonishment. "Why the hell would he kill himself? On the day of his biggest triumph."

Kira looked dazed. "Guilt," she muttered. "Or maybe just weariness. I was going to tell you, Commander—the last time we came here, he set us up to be killed."

"Why?"

Her voice was hoarse as she answered, "Because he had to make unholy alliances to keep the shipyards open. Because he had to sell his soul over and over again to build that ship. His silent partners never let go of their hold on him."

"The Circle?" asked Sisko.

Kira shrugged. "What does it matter? He's free of them now."

The commander glanced around the room, and his eyes came to rest on the empty spaces on the wall, where commendations from the Cardassians had once hung. Sisko had suffered his share of tragedy and sacrifice, but they paled beside what the majority of Bajorans had gone through. He turned to ask what Engineer Daken thought, but the middle-aged Bajoran had retreated to the corridor. Sisko couldn't blame him.

He put his hand on Kira's shoulder. "Someday the casualties will stop. There will be whole generations to whom the Cardassians are nothing but ancient history."

The Bajoran stared down at the lifeless body, and he could tell she was fighting back tears. "As long as we keep building—like he did—we'll make progress." Her jaw tightened with resolve. "We have to break this news to many people, but let's remember that this is a victorious day, especially for Amkot Groell."

"I agree," said Sisko, and they walked out together.

**AN IN-DEPTH LOOK BEHIND THE
SCENES OF THE SMASH-HIT
TELEVISION SERIES**

THE MAKING OF
STAR TREK
DEEP SPACE NINE®

by
**JUDITH & GARFIELD
REEVES-STEVENS**

**Available mid-November 1994
from**

POCKET
BOOKS

1020